HERO

MARRY THE SCOT, #3

JOLIE VINES

WWW.JOLIEVINES.COM/NEWSLETTER

PRAISE FOR THE MARRY THE SCOT SERIES

Paula - "I loved this book! It had all that I would expect with **hot Scots and rambling castles.** I had to giggle when I discovered that I was reading this book with my own manufactured Scottish brogue! Can't wait for more."

J. Saman, Bestselling author - "Jolie Vines has fast become a **one-click author** for me!"

Zoe Ashwood, author - "I'm impatiently waiting for the next book - I just know it'll be **another sizzling story** from Jolie Vines."

Viper Spaulding - "(Hero) is an amazing work of art, highly recommended for anyone looking for a **modern-day Highlander to swoon over.**"

Chikapo9 - "I swear, every time I pick up a Jolie Vines book I think: this is him, **my favorite hero,** no one will be able to top him. And then I read the next book and the process begins again."

Pam Graber - "If you haven't read the other books in the series Marry the Scot, you should really start with Storm the Castle, then move on to Love Most, Say Least before diving into Hero. **I cannot wait to see what Ally and Wasp get up** to **in their stories!** I've enjoyed the first three books immensely!"

Carmen Davis - "Jolie Vines is an amazingly talented writer. I am so **completely obsessed with this series** and so madly in love with the characters. Each book gets better than the last and when you start off with a 5 star? There just aren't enough stars. I can't wait for the next book in this series and anything else Jolie Vines writes."

Editing by Emmy at Studio ENP

Proofreading by Zoe Ashwood

Interior formatting by Images for Authors
www.facebook.com/imagesforauthors

Cover design by Natasha Snow www.natashasnowdesigns.com

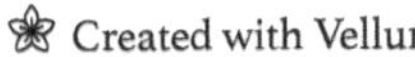 Created with Vellum

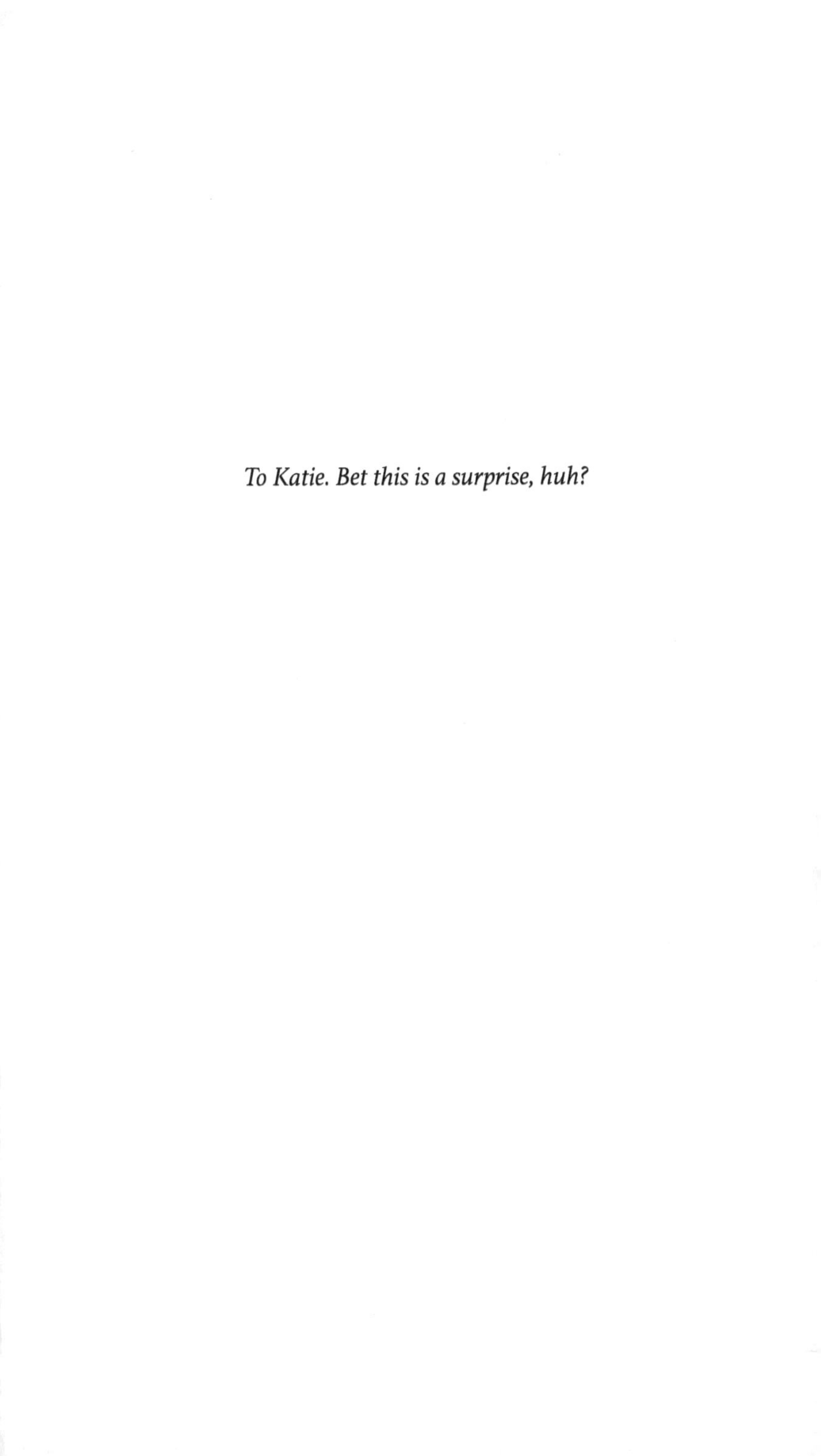

To Katie. Bet this is a surprise, huh?

BLURB

Hero (Marry the Scot, #3)

Her life was just getting started, while his was falling apart.

Ella has finally broken out of her gilded cage, but with her limited life experience, she doesn't trust her instincts. Especially when it comes to the handsome Scottish pilot who plucked her from the jaws of danger. No way is she going to stumble upon Mr Perfect right away.

Gordain's military career is in freefall after a night he doesn't remember. His burning need for his best friend's younger sister is surely a knee-jerk reaction to his problems. He should walk away, yet he cannot say no to the lass.

When her evil uncle seeks to destroy Ella's happiness, a wedding is the only way to save her inheritance. Gordain is the only man she'd consider asking. But can he fake-marry someone he truly loves?

PROLOGUE
I'M COMING FOR YE

E^{lla}
From the cover of my hiding place, I silenced
my phone and tapped out a message to my brother, my
hands shaking. *I need to get out of here. Where are you?*

"Elinor! Come here, you stupid little bitch." Richard's
voice reverberated through the halls, and an almighty crash
followed—a table thrown over, or a bookcase, perhaps.

On cramped limbs, I shrank back in the musty
cupboard, the strip of daylight under the door slicing over
my ballet flats. Coming home had been a huge mistake. If
he found me, my bid for freedom was over.

My phone lit with an incoming message. Not from James
—the number was unknown.

*Ella, I'm Gordain. Your brother sent me. I'm coming for ye by
helicopter. Keep out of your uncle's sight. I'll be landing soon.*

Gordain? I knew the name, though I'd never met the
man. He was James's closest friend and a pilot in the Royal
Air Force. Relief washed over me. The military ate rescues
for breakfast, right? I might make it out of here in one piece.

I replied, all the while listening for any sounds of

Richard closing in. His unhinged voice had come from the mansion's central entrance hall, the echoes from the marble floors and high ceiling giving him away. He was close. Far too close for comfort.

I'm hiding in the ballroom. He's hunting me.

Gordain's reply arrived instantly, and I pictured him chopping up the air, joystick down, zooming to my side. *Sit tight, lass. I'll find ye.*

Thank God, I didn't know how much longer I could hide. Or what Richard would do if he found me. I'd never been good at following orders, but on this occasion, I'd listen.

I waited, arms wrapped around my knees, my pulse an accelerated thrum in my ears. Outside, the commotion had stopped. No smashing or crashing came from the depths of the vast Fitzroy mansion.

But I wasn't dumb. I knew my uncle.

Earlier this afternoon, after he'd arrived, he'd hit the bottle. I'd kept out of his way, hell-bent on a personal mission of my own, taking a little piece of revenge before I left. I should have escaped when I had the chance. Richard wouldn't give up easily on trying to find me. Not if he spotted what I'd done.

A dull *clunk* came, maybe from a glass being placed on a wooden floor. Suspiciously near. Was he in the ballroom? I twisted to peer through the gap under the cupboard door. A shadow moved by the windows.

Oh shit.

Landed. I'm closing in on the house. Where's Richard?

I typed back, careful to move the minimum possible for fear of him hearing. *Right outside my hiding place. I'm stuck. If I leave, he'll find me.*

Don't move. I've got this.

I held my breath. Gordain couldn't just walk in here and grab me. Richard wouldn't allow it. Then a memory hit me, and my heart gave an almighty thump.

Richard had a gun. A rifle. I'd seen it when I'd visited one summer holiday.

He might be armed, I typed fast.

A dragging noise sounded nearby. "Elinor!" Richard blared.

Oh God, oh God. I froze, digging my nails into my legs, clamping my lips shut.

A smash broke the silence. Then another. But it wasn't my uncle; it came from a distance, like a window had been broken at the front of the house.

"What the fucking hell was that? She's not getting away that easily," Richard slurred, so near I could almost smell the alcohol fumes on his breath. After a beat, his footsteps moved away, then the ballroom's double doors swung out with an unmistakable thud.

Had he gone?

My phone lit up. *Come out. Stay low and quiet.*

God! It had been Gordain, creating a distraction. In a cautious crouch, I pushed the door ajar and peeked outside. Nothing moved in the opulent room.

I twisted back, grabbing the handle of the bag stashed alongside me. Metal clanked as the loot shifted. I stopped, wincing.

Then a figure loomed large at the window.

I suppressed a shriek, shooting my hand up to cover my mouth.

At pace, the shadow forced open the ballroom's French doors and crossed the room on silent feet. I sucked in a breath and drew myself upright.

Gordain McRae, RAF pilot, Highlander, and my brother's closest friend, stopped dead in front of me.

Holy macaroni. My heart skipped a beat.

With practiced motions, he grasped my waist and pulled me close, his gaze taking in the space and the pair of open doors leading to the hall. Neat, efficient actions. In total command.

I couldn't remember the image I used to have for this guy, but it was nothing like the man holding me. Big. Muscles rippling under his tight t-shirt, the name of a band scrawled across his broad chest.

"Listen. Here's what we're going to do." He ran his free hand over his shorn fair hair, then his fierce gaze finally fell on mine.

And stuck.

For a second, neither of us said anything. Or moved.

My experience of men, real men, was beyond limited. The boarding school I'd recently left had been a ladies-only college, and it had been a trek to the nearest village. I'd certainly never been close to a hard-bodied, hard-breathing, rugged example of the gender like Gordain.

That was my excuse for freezing up. For staring at the line of his jaw and having the most compelling urge to touch his light scruff.

But what was his?

He blinked and broke the spell. "I... Right. Ella. We need to get out of here. Richard's on the second floor. I tossed a rock through a window. He staggered up the stairs."

A howl came from a distance. "Elinor!" my uncle bellowed again. "You smashed my fucking window. You will pay for that."

Gordain stiffened. With urgency, he ushered me towards the door. "Let's get going. We'll get to the heli and be away before the arsehole even registers you're gone."

That was the plan, but I had another priority. I stooped and grabbed my bag. "Wait, I'm almost done."

Gordain paused, his eyebrows drawing in. "We need to leave. Now."

"I have one more thing to get."

"Are ye kidding? We have maybe a minute until he's back."

"Help me, then! I'm not leaving without it."

Gordain stared, his disbelief melting at whatever he saw in my eyes. Steely determination, I hoped.

Interest crept into his serious expression. "What do ye need to grab?"

I expected him to demand that I leave it—if he wanted to pick me up and throw me over his shoulder, I wouldn't stand a chance. But he didn't. My energy came back in a rush.

"My violin. I've already got the contents of my parents' safe. All the paperwork on my and James's inheritance. A few priceless antiquities." Excitement rippled over me, and I leaned in. "Richard will notice. He knows every piece of art, every vase. Our heritage is his world, and knowing I stole it is going to drive him nuts."

Gordain's gaze slid to a darker mien. He took my arm, his fingers warm. "How about a compromise. Tell me where the violin is, and I'll be the thief. You get out of here."

Good enough. "It's in the entrance hall on a table."

It had been my mother's, and even though it wasn't particularly valuable, I'd kept it with me through the long years following the destruction of my family. I'd held on to it as a grieving child, bested it as a rebellious fourteen-year-old, and played the heck out of it as a young woman.

If my life had a symbol, it was that instrument.

"That's the direction your uncle's in." Gordain shook his head. "Not worth the risk."

He didn't know. I hadn't explained. "No," I said, placing my hand on his. "It was Mum's—"

Crash.

The unmistakable rattle and yowl came of a stringed instrument being smashed. Horror struck me.

Oh God, no.

The sound reverberated through the ballroom. I leapt towards the inner doors and instantly fell back again. Dragged by Gordain. He held me against his broad chest.

"Don't," he urged.

"Elinor!" Richard called, his voice closer, as if he was coming down the stairs. "You can't hide forever."

Smash. The tinkle came of small pieces of wood landing on the marble floor.

I sobbed, unable to help the upset wrenching from my throat.

"Shite. I'm so sorry. But we have to go." Gordain took my face in his hands and made me stare at him. Another crash came from the hall.

"I want to kill him," I uttered, but my rescuer said nothing. The look in his eyes told me he understood, except how could he? Richard had broken my violin. In a house full of antiquities and relics, it was the one thing I valued.

Gordain grabbed my hand and slung the heavy bag over his shoulder like it was weightless. He kept me at his side, half dragging me out of the French doors.

Then I got with the programme and found my feet.

We sprinted along the side of the house. Around the corner, we emerged into the car park. Richard's green Jaguar sat on the gravel.

My anger spiked.

I dropped Gordain's hand and darted to the flower bed, picking up a rock. My chest heaved, and tears spilled down my cheeks.

"Ella!" Gordain growled.

I raised both hands above my head and ran at the car. The rock left my fingers.

It bounced off the windscreen.

"No!" I exclaimed, hoarse. Dismay flattened me as the rock rolled harmlessly away. That wasn't supposed to happen.

Gordain jerked to a halt at my side. He crouched, and when he straightened, two enormous edging stones left his grip and took out the Jaguar's windscreen with an almighty *crack*.

Glass exploded in a savage-edged shower, raining onto the gravel at our feet.

I stared, agog, then switched my astonished gaze to Gordain. His muscles rippled where he lowered his arms. He... He'd...

The alarm blared.

"Fuck!" we both yelled in unison.

Gordain whooped then snatched up my hand again, pulling me with him as he retrieved the bag. "Aye, fuck! Now run!"

* * *

We fled the estate's formal gardens and entered the parkland—still owned by my family but borderless and wild. Better suited for hiking than running. Gordain set a fast pace, and I did my best to keep up, glad for the early morning jogging routine I'd gotten into.

On a patch of flat ground behind the first rocky ridge,

the helicopter waited, the last of the evening light reflecting off the glass cockpit. Gordain boosted me inside then climbed into the pilot's seat. He stretched over to strap me in, then began a process of flipping switches and pressing buttons.

Ridiculous maybe, but only now, with my sweat cooling and adrenaline churning in my stomach, did I realise I was about to fly. The blades above our heads rotated, speeding up. The sound levels escalated to deafening proportions.

"Holy shit," I whispered.

Gordain swung a look at me, somehow hearing me over the racket. He handed across a wireless headset.

"At last, I get to take a Fitzroy up in the air," he said, his voice clear as day through the headphones. Then he grinned, the effect dazzling. "Are ye ready?"

"I have no idea." Despite everything—the rush in which I was leaving the estate, the rage my uncle had flown into, the million and one other things that had gone wrong, and my poor, poor, violin—a rush of excitement ignited my blood.

The sheer delight dancing in Gordain's eyes told me he felt the same. With a last glance around us, he moved the controls, and the helicopter took to the skies.

* * *

We rose, speeding over the ground. Up, we soared, skirting the craggy edges of the national park, dizzying in the rate the aircraft moved. Soon, the Belvedere house and estate was a speck in the distance far behind us.

In the air, no one could chase us. I was safe.

I switched my gaze to my hands. The tremor remained,

and I hated it, the fear that man had instilled in me. The panic even his name brought. For a moment this afternoon, I'd truly believed Richard would hurt me. He had been backed into a corner. He'd lost everything. What did it matter if he took out that loss on me?

"Your brother called me from the road, but I'm behind in how all this went down. Tell me, what happened?"

Gordain's voice brought me out of my funk.

I inclined my head. *Safe, Ella. Saved.* "First of all, thank you. I didn't say that yet. You don't even know me and you came all this way—"

I stopped as Gordain's hand found mine. Reaching the short distance between our seats, he gave my fingers a squeeze, and it should have felt reassuring, it had certainly been intended as friendly, yet heat painted my cheeks.

Whew. His touch sent ripples of an unknown sensation through my veins. Nice, the feeling. Warm and vital.

"It was nae trouble, and my pleasure," Gordain's voice dipped low. He released my fingers and cleared his throat. "I know about your brother, but what about you? Why was your uncle after your hide?"

I raised a shoulder. "Control. He's still my legal guardian, until we can get the lawyers to change it. I'm supposed to be locked away in boarding school, but I'm never going back."

"We'll be prepared if he comes after ye."

If Richard showed up at the McRaes' castle home—the location Gordain was flying me to—could he demand to take me away? It was unlikely; I was hardly a child. What I did know for sure was Richard would use me in any way possible to get to my brother.

"His priority is James. It always has been. He'd only want to use me as a pawn."

That, in a nutshell, summed up the relationship I had

with my only living relative, aside from my brother. Even with James, I barely had a connection. We'd been raised separately after our parents died.

For ten years, I'd hardly had anyone. A fresh new world lay ahead of me.

"James is waiting for you with his lady. And ye have us now." Gordain answered my sad little thoughts. "You're not alone."

My shuddering breath took me by surprise.

He glanced over. "Are ye okay?"

"One day, I'll kill that asshole for everything he did to my family."

A low chuckle came from my rescuer. "You're nae similar to your brother at all."

If that was a compliment, I had no idea. But the spark in his eye stirred something deep in my belly. Gordain's gaze dipped to my lips, and the same thing happened as in the ballroom. His focus found my eyes and we both stopped moving, staring for a long moment that gave me a rush of chemicals, fizzing and wild.

Then he huffed a laugh and gave his full attention back to the helicopter's controls.

I linked my hands in my lap and summoned my strength.

Of two things, I was sure. One, now I was almost eighteen years of age, my life started here. I'd leave behind the awful existence my uncle had abandoned me to and never look back. Richard Fitzroy would pay for what he did to us, one way or another.

And two, I was a mess, my emotions spiralling. In under an hour, I'd rocked from despair to elation, and right now, I was in danger of developing a hefty crush on my brother's best friend. That had to stop.

1
———

NEEDY

*E**lla*

Two months on from the drama that marked my flight from Belvedere, I lay in my bed, pondering my rescue from this very house. How things had changed. After weeks regrouping at Castle McRae in the Scottish Highlands, James, Beth, his new wife, and I had come home to claim the place in my brother's name. Belvedere was his, now.

Richard had shown up at my brother's inheritance meeting and, in the presence of witnesses including the police, bled fury from every pore. My brother threw him out and we hadn't seen anything of him since. We'd won.

It wasn't my family's issues that had frustration overtaking me.

"Oh, for the love of God!" I flung back my covers and jolted up in my bed, my room swimming into focus in the pale morning light. For half an hour, I'd lain awake, hot and bothered from my dreams about a certain handsome pilot.

Dreams that left me needy and breathless.

They happened almost every night and never

concluded...satisfactorily. Just like my little crush hadn't gone away. My attempts to relieve myself of the tension had been unsuccessful. In fact, I hadn't been able to get myself *there* for months, and my body was strung tighter than the strings on my replacement violin.

My new life had some excellent aspects to it, but this particular problem was a side effect I had no clue how to fix.

Thinking about anything Gordain-related brought on an ache in my chest.

Coffee! my brain suggested. Hmm. Plan. And something sugary for breakfast. Springing up, I crossed the polished wood floor and entered my bathroom, switching on the shower. Then I got under the hot water and scrubbed myself until some of the need ebbed.

Maybe my overreaction was due to the stream of text messages I'd received last night. All from Taylor, my ex best friend from school.

My only friend, really.

One who'd happily betrayed me all the same.

I rinsed the conditioner from my hair and switched off the shower, trying to shut down my ricocheting thoughts. In a few weeks, I was going to university. The new start had to help. New digs, new people. No crush on a man who I hadn't had the nerve to ask out. Not that he'd given me any sign he wanted that. After the boom of chemistry between us on the helicopter flight, he'd been nothing but polite. Cool, even. Maybe I'd imagined the reflected spark in his eyes.

After dressing myself then drying my hair, I opened the big white-and-gold door that led to the private corridor. My brother and his wife had a separate apartment in the mansion, just along the hall, so I made my way along and knocked.

Beth, my sister-in-law, answered. She had her hand to

her belly, and a wide smile. "Ella! I was just coming to find you. There's something we need to talk to you about. Come in. Breakfast's waiting."

Beth and James had turned one of the rooms in their apartment into a large kitchen. With a baby on the way, it would be easier for them than traipsing down the long halls to the mansion's vast kitchens one floor down. I either ate with them, or with the Hinchcliffes, our housekeepers/adopted grandparents, in their cottage.

"James and I need to take a trip," she said, ushering me to the breakfast table in their sunny parlour. A platter of pancakes waited with a steaming pot of coffee to the side.

My mouth watered, and I grabbed a plate. "Like a honeymoon? You didn't take one yet." Their wedding had been weeks ago, but all the drama had left little space for fun.

"Not exactly." Beth gazed at the food then swallowed. Her morning sickness had worsened these past couple of weeks.

My brother joined us, offering a brief smile for me, but his attention was squarely on his wife.

"I said I'd go. You need your rest," he murmured.

"Ella was right outside the door. I didn't even leave the apartment. If you wrap me in cotton wool, I'll wind up so lazy you'll be waiting on me hand and foot throughout this whole pregnancy." She slipped her arms around him and pressed up on her toes to kiss his cheek.

"I don't mind that." James pulled his wife closer, his gaze soft.

So cosy.

I loved it—my brother being happy. He deserved it after the long years of abuse given to him by Richard. Where I'd been banished to a boarding school, Richard had kept James, the heir, close.

That didn't change the fact it was oh-so awkward being around such a loved-up couple. Beth and James radiated happiness. They always made space for me, but at every meal, or every trip out, I intruded in their intimacy.

Taking up a forkful of lemony pancake, I ate. "Where are you headed?"

James's gentle expression evaporated. He moved a chair for Beth then took a seat next to her at the table. "We've been looking into the money Richard spent prior to us cutting him off. The lawyers have proof he ran his businesses by siphoning cash from both me and you."

I nodded, continuing my attack on the pancakes. This wasn't news. We knew Richard had leeched off the Fitzroy fortune for years. He'd been both my and James's guardian for a decade, and he'd abused the role in every way possible.

James continued, "If those businesses have any value, we could sue him for ownership. But he registered them from his apartment in Manhattan. So in a couple of days, Beth and I fly to New York to meet with a legal team there to see what can be done."

Cold trickled down my spine. For all my yelled statements about Richard, I never wanted to see his face again. "Are you going to try to see him?"

In unison, they both shuddered.

"God, no," Beth said. "This is just about progressing the legal stuff. Do you want to come?" She picked up the coffee pot and poured me and James a cup. "There will be time for sightseeing as well as the dull stuff."

Strange, the instant response my mind had to a trip—a clear and vibrant *no*. I'd been to New York City many times with my school, so there was no novelty, but it was also the city where Richard owned a home. I wasn't ready to be anywhere near him. Not yet. His presence had haunted my childhood, and now, I had an aversion to even being in the same time zone as him.

The lawyers were working on undoing the guardianship order he held over me. But no one could take back all the years he'd separated me from my brother, the times he'd ignored my messages, his refusal to acknowledge me.

In time, I'd come into my own, and I'd take him on. But not now.

Which meant staying alone here. Belvedere would be empty—Mr and Mrs Hinchcliffe were away. Lonely me would be on my lonesome, rattling around this empty place. Beth and James waited on my answer.

I blew out a breath. "I'd rather you two had the time together. My school arranged trips to New York a few times, so I've seen every art gallery. Museums. Ballet at the Met."

Beth stared. "You did that on school trips? That place was bizarre."

I snorted in agreement. Neglected I might have been, but my uncle had placed me in one of the top ladies' colleges in the country. It produced refined young women, well versed in culture and exquisitely mannered.

Ack.

Whatever plans he'd had for me, he'd expected me to be dutiful. I think I broke their mould.

"There is another option," Beth added. "I talked to Mattie. She said you could stay at Castle McRae, if you wanted. She told me to say you'd be more than welcome."

Mathilda was Callum's wife and Beth's best friend. Lady McRae now.

My mind drifted to the castle and the time I'd spent there. To the McRae brothers and the kindness they'd shown us. Ally and Wasp, the twins, were boisterous and always in trouble of some kind. The oldest brother, the laird, Callum, was kind but stern and a little intimidating.

Then, of course, my mind summoned Gordain in all his tall and handsome glory.

Nng.

"Who'll be there?" I asked, my words coming out fast. I liked Mathilda. She had a cool head and gorgeous dress sense. But staying at the castle meant perhaps seeing Gordain. Not ideal for getting over a crush.

However, there would be the added bonus that I could avoid Taylor. In her last message, she threatened to doorstep me if I didn't reply.

"Just Callum, Mattie, and the twins. Why?" Beth cocked her head.

No brooding pilot, then.

"No reason." I finished my plate and took a long drink of coffee. "If they are happy to have me again, then sign me up."

Suddenly, things looked brighter.

"Deal," my sister-in-law said with a grin. "Then tonight, pack a bag. We'll drive up in the morning."

* * *

After dinner, I holed up in my room, the glow of my laptop screen the only light.

Beth and I had made plans to drive to Scotland. She would accompany me, giving me some much-needed hours behind the wheel before I took my driving test, visit with her friend, then fly home. James had contractors to deal with, so he reluctantly had to stay. I didn't mind—Beth was easier to talk to than my brother. He and I had a long way to go before we got back the close relationship we had as kids.

If we ever could.

One thing was for sure, I didn't want him to feel he had to support me while the lawyers worked on making me independent. Luckily, I had a little money of my own stashed away.

With a few taps on my keyboard, I logged on to Music-Linkt, the site where I'd been selling pieces of composition for the past two years. I found my profile—I sold under the name of Melody Fitzroy—and checked my sales. Last year, I'd put forward a new piece every month or two. Short, buzzy recordings, intended for use by advertisers or for radio or TV infill. I'd made a little over three thousand pounds in licencing. My own money that my uncle didn't know about and couldn't touch.

A glance at the sales categories quickened my pulse. Maybe in a year or two, I'd target the areas I was truly interested in. When I was better at my craft and knew what I was doing.

I bit my lip and closed down the site, the sheer distance of my dream daunting.

I had a long way to go before I was good enough, but that was the point of going to university—to have them fill in the gaps and tell me all the things I didn't know.

Which reminded me... I took Suki, my new violin, from its case. I'd been working on a piece and needed to hack out the middle. With any luck, I could record it and package it up for sale ahead of term beginning.

My side hustle might have to become my main source of income, depending on what my brother found out about Richard's spending.

I plucked the strings to test the tuning then drew my

bow with a hiss. The benefit of living in a big house meant I could play uninterrupted for hours, so I set about my task and let my warm-up routine settle my overactive brain.

It stopped me thinking about all I'd lost.

At least I still had this. A place to live in my brother's house, the start of a family, even if I was on the outside. If I didn't think too much, I could pretend everything was just A-Okay.

2

———

GROUNDED

*G*ordain

The door to the office closed behind me with a click, and I marched into the grey corridor, my movements automatic, carrying me outside. My breath came unsteady, and I blinked at the bright sunlight, its cheerfulness at odds with the news I'd just been given.

Grounded, again.

This morning had been an official meeting with a senior officer at my RAF base. No conclusion had been reached on my case, but the message had been apparent all the same.

'You are to remain on hold, Lieutenant McRae. Expect to receive formal notification within the next few days, at the wing commander's leisure. I suggest you take a week of leave. Off the base.' Not an order, but the instruction had been clear. They wanted me gone.

I'd really fucked up.

Across from the low-rise office block, the airfield lay. A Sea King started up, the rotors chopping up the brisk breeze coming off the freezing North Sea. By rights, I should be flying one of those helicopters by now. Only a few months ago, I'd been awarded a prestigious search and rescue training course. At twenty-two, I was one of the youngest airmen ever to do so. My strength and leadership qualities had been commended. It had been an enormous privilege.

Then one evening of celebrating with my fellow officers, and everything had gone wrong.

"Gordain," a voice hailed me. Jordie, another pilot who'd been on the same elementary flying training as me, jogged over the yard, his expression already set to deliver sympathy. Few people on the base knew what had happened, and no one outside, but Jordie had been there. He knew the truth.

Well, about as much of it as I did.

Countless times, I'd been over and over what had happened. The strenuous practice mission we'd returned from, brains frazzled from flying low over the sea, the heli's cabin an oven, heated by the sun. Then the single pint of beer I'd drank at the bar that evening. I remembered Autumn, the wing commander's daughter, talking with me, and the headache that had me politely excusing myself. I'd stumbled through a closed door into a dark room, then my memory blacked out.

Next thing I knew, the lights came on and I opened my eyes. To the half-naked woman straddling me. To the shocked then angry face of Wing Commander Phillips, Jordie behind him.

What a mess.

"News?" Jordie asked.

"No. Another week." I dropped down the last step from the office and crossed to meet my friend.

He slung an arm over my shoulder and gave me a conciliatory hug before slapping me upside the head for good measure. "Sorry, bud. What are you going to do?"

What indeed? I shrugged. "Take off my uniform and go home, I guess."

Though home meant facing my brother. Callum knew I was in trouble. As the head of our family, he'd been my greatest supporter, encouraging me to join the RAF as a troubled sixteen-year-old. Now, six years later, it looked like my career was over.

His disappointment was going to kill me.

My stomach dropped, realisation sinking in that this problem wasn't going away.

"I'm on leave this weekend," Jordie said. "My wife's birthday. We're throwing a party. Barbecue food, music. Why don't you drive over tomorrow? Stay a few days. Get wrecked." He nudged me, a twinkle in his eye. "Annie's invited her college friends. Not a ring among them, and they party hard. Every time those women go out as a group, it's carnage. Annie has a hangover for days."

I forced a smile. My friend had married young, and his wife had only just graduated with her degree. I'd liked her, the few times I'd met her, but screwing around with her friends was not the solution to my problems, though the oblivion that would come from getting drunk and laid had a certain appeal. "Sounds dangerous. In a good way. Can I let ye know?"

"You've got my number." He gave me a shove and pivoted away, heading in the direction of the airfield. "We're a family here, don't forget it."

Then why did it feel like my military family had turned its back on me?

* * *

With my motorbike purring, I left the base, accelerating too fast on the wet roads leading out of the tiny town of Lossiemouth. I took the route south into the vast, empty Highlands.

Heading home.

However shite I felt, I loved this journey, the bleak beauty of the Scottish countryside. The remoteness of the mountains and glens. There were few cars on the road and even fewer people idiotic enough to make two fast wheels their transport of choice.

But fuck it, this Highlander got a buzz out of taking the bends with a knee almost to the tarmac. It was almost as good as lifting off in a heli, an urgent mission underway.

An experience I might not have again.

The last time I'd flown was in a hired helicopter to collect Ella Fitzroy from Belvedere.

Ella...

Instantly, I stomped down on all thoughts about the lass. *For Christ's sake.* If I was lusting after her again, it was only because my life was taking a nosedive. My glum feeling expanded, and I gripped the handlebars like I was strangling them.

A typical out-of-nowhere squall turned the sky grey, coming off the coast where my base was situated. Now, the weather matched my mood. Drizzle soaked me through my leathers. A cold shower if ever I needed one.

I tucked my head down and sped on.

An hour later, and I'd rounded the mountain that stood in the centre of clan McRae land, and skirted the loch. Castle McRae rose ahead of the foothills. Solid and timeless. I halted the bike in the car park, killed the engine, and dragged off my helmet, taking my first lungful of fresh mountain air.

No matter the state I was in, I loved coming home.

A stranger's car sat beside the trio of Land Rovers my brothers used. A top-of-the-range 4x4—a dark silver Audi Q8. Brand-new, by the look of it. My mind instantly jumped to James, my closest friend. He'd recently inherited a shite-load of money and could easily afford a car like that.

I was no stranger to old names and old houses, having been raised in a castle, but we worked hard for every penny we earned. Da's debts left us, after he died, fighting to keep our home. Half my salary had gone on keeping the castle going, until recently when Callum had married and his wife started a business here. Mathilda's investment couldn't have come at a better time. If things went the way I expected, I'd lose my income soon. At least it would only be me impacted. Letting my family down might well be the last straw.

Movement at the car caught my eye.

Mathilda, my sister-in-law, straightened from talking to someone in the driver's side. Then Beth, James's wife, hopped out of the passenger seat.

A ready grin broached my lips, and I took a breath to holler a greeting to the women, both good friends of mine.

Then my smile died. Because the driver's door opened, and another figure emerged. A slender, graceful lass. Night-dark hair fell in long waves. She had the face of angel, yet when she raised a sardonic eyebrow you could see the devil in her.

My heart gave an almighty thud.

Ella Fitzroy was here.

Which meant that I one hundred percent needed to go.

* * *

*I*nside the garage, I grabbed a cloth and swiped the worst of the rain off the bike. Delaying. Or hiding. Forcing my reaction under control.

I scrubbed the bike harder.

The same longing overwhelmed me. It had begun the first second I'd seen Ella—a startling bolt of lust that left my head spinning. I knew that was all it was—lust. Fast, hot, and inappropriate. She'd been seventeen then. Eighteen now, but still so young, hurt by years of neglect, and in need of care.

Also, utterly beautiful.

Ella shone bright. I was an arsehole for even looking at her in the way I had. I thought I'd got it under wraps. But no.

The reaction my body had a few minutes ago was twice as strong.

Confusion had me throwing the drying rag across the garage. Everything going wrong on the base had my mind fixating on her once more, that was all. A lass in need of aid. A dangerous combination for a man seeking solace.

I'd keep my distance.

I shook my head and rested a hip against the workbench cluttered with tools. Then I pulled out my phone and dropped a text to Jordie.

I'll take you up on that offer. See you tomorrow.

His reply almost made me smile. *Got a beer in the cooler with your name on it, McRae.*

For tonight, I could pretend—or just avoid her, but then I'd be gone.

* * *

I stomped my way into the kitchens and my brother lifted his chin in greeting, paperwork covering the island in front of him. I'd looked up to Callum my whole life. Not only because he was unreasonably tall—I was six-three and he towered over me. He'd been my defender, my ally, and now he was a husband and waiting to be a da.

We'd raised ourselves to be honest men, but he deserved happiness, not to be burdened with my troubles.

"Good to see ye home." Callum reached for a coffee mug then held it up in offer. It was new and had flowers on it. Not one of our old, chipped numbers. "Ye ken Beth and Ella are on their way?"

I declined the drink with a hand gesture. "They've just arrived. I'll go and say hello but I'm not staying."

My brother's gaze took me to pieces. He replaced the mug on the shelf then cleared his throat. "This to do with work? Want to talk about it?"

"Not yet."

He grumbled, picking up a heap of letters then stacking them into an unnecessarily neat pile. "So you came home so we could all see ye being miserable? Where are ye going?"

"A friend's house to drink myself into a stupor."

Callum snorted. "And then?"

With my mouth in a grim line, I tapped the counter. "Ask me again in a week when it's all decided."

A final look, with deep lines furrowing his brow, showed me he understood, but I didn't stick around to explain more. I had a game face to put on and a lass to resist.

TWO OF THE BEST MCRAES

Ella

I glanced again at the corner of the castle. What on earth was that all about? Gordain had stood there, grinning, and poised to say something to Beth and Mattie, then I'd got out of the car and the happiness had melted from his face. He'd raised his motorcycle helmet in a salute instead then wheeled his bike in the opposite direction.

He'd avoided me, that much was certain. True—at the end of my last stay in the Highlands, I'd taken to avoiding him—but that had been self-preservation. My crush had steadily escalated, but I was sure I'd kept it under wraps.

Hadn't I?

I couldn't help my body's reaction to him. Whenever he'd touched me, with a friendly hand to direct me or to gain my attention, I'd shiver. On the occasions he'd look me in the eye or give me one of his confident smirks, I'd melt, and it took a concerted effort to keep my cool.

His leaving for the airbase had been a relief.

But his reaction a moment ago... Perhaps I hadn't done such a good job of hiding my regard after all.

Beside me, Beth and Mattie chatted on, clearly oblivious to what had happened. Both women were newlyweds, both expecting babies early next year. Mattie's wedding planning business had started with a bang, and she talked excitedly to Beth about her bookings and how she was realising her dream career. I should have been taking notes—eventually I wanted to run my own business, too. But my attention had gone with a certain broody pilot.

The sight of him standing there, leather jacket, shorn hair, that dark look descending, where before he'd been sunny, or cocky, even...

I'd done that. I'd wiped the smile from his face.

"Ella, I knew there was something I needed to remind you about. While you're here, book in your driving test in Inverness. You're running out of time." Beth's voice brought me back to the myself.

Driving? Oh, right.

"That's not a bad idea." I wanted my licence before I started my degree. Needed it, actually. The journey to my university in Manchester took an hour minimum. I was staying in digs for the first year, to see how I liked living in the city, but I'd still want to go home on weekends. Particularly after the baby was born.

Glad for the distraction, I searched on my phone, explaining to Mattie as I navigated to the right page. "The test centre near home is booked for the next two months. Uni starts in a couple of weeks, so I want to get this out of the way." I found the Inverness centre and scrolled through the dates. "They have space. I can do it this week."

"Book it!" Mattie inclined her head, her golden ringlets bobbing. "There are enough drivers here to make sure you get plenty of practice."

I chose a date a few days ahead and made the payment. "Done."

"Ella!" A shout reached me from the other side of the car park.

"Lady Elinor Fitzroy, get your arse over here!" Two shouts. The twins approached.

"What did I tell you about using the title?" I stuck my hands on my hips and gave them a hard stare.

Neither were daunted. Ally grabbed me by the waist, whooping as he hugged me, then released me for his brother to take a turn. I giggled, hugging them back.

"How long are you staying?" Wasp asked. He'd cut his dark-blond hair short.

Ally still wore his long enough to fall in his eyes. "Wait, is this your car?" Ally's jaw dropped, and he took me by the shoulders and turned me around. Then he patted my jacket pockets. "Where are the keys? Take me out, baby. Better still, I'm going alone. See ye later."

"Get off, you pest." I gave him a shove. I'd texted them last night, giving our arrival time.

The two of them were like playful pups, or annoying little brothers, though both were six foot and constantly working on their muscles.

"To answer your questions, I'm staying maybe a week, and yep, that's my baby. Oh, and no way are you getting behind the wheel." I grinned broadly at them.

They'd both been driving for years—a necessary skill in the remote Highlands, but that didn't mean I'd trust Ally in my car.

Ally swung around and tucked me under his arm. Wasp took my other side, and we walked into the castle together, the two of them talking nonstop. This visit was going to be fine. I'd spend time with Mattie and the twins and have a blast. Gordain was probably only here for the afternoon. I'd get over pining for him. Just as soon as he left.

* * *

ou were tagged in a post so I know you're in Scotland. Please, Ella, talk to me. If you don't, I'm coming there. I swear to God I have a good reason for what I did. Love you – T

My eyes stung as I read Taylor's latest message, and I shuffled back in the heavy wooden chair, the last person left in the dining room, long after supper had ended.

In all the drama that had come over the past couple of months, my best-friend's betrayal had been the bitterest pill to swallow.

Taylor took highly personal information that I'd shared with her and turned it to her own advantage. She knew James had to be married. She knew my family was in pieces. At the time my brother had been poised to overthrow Richard, Taylor had shown up at Belvedere.

I'd assumed she'd wanted to see me.

But no. She'd come as a bride to my brother in a deal she'd negotiated.

Now, she sent incessant messages, using words like *love*. She was the only person to tell me they loved me in a decade.

A fresh wave of hurt washed through my veins. Maybe she had a great reason for what she'd done, like someone held a gun to her head or kidnapped her mother.

Not that I could imagine her giving a damn about her parents. Their savage divorce was the reason she'd been sent to the same boarding school as me.

Our beds had been side by side in the dorm. We used to

stay up late and conspire in our small ways to disobey the strict rules. I made a name for myself as a troublemaker, and it left me isolated. The other girls were dutiful and hard-working. Glad to be in a school that trained girls to be excellent wives. Princesses from the Middle East, old families from Europe. I was the daughter of an earl, nothing special on their pecking order.

Tay made everything better. She was all I'd had for a long time. She knew everything about me.

A tear escaped my eye, and I allowed it to roll down my cheek. This mess deserved crying. If anything, to prove I could feel.

Why, Tay? Why not just tell me? I wrote the message, and another tear fell. I didn't hit send.

Another message arrived from her in a flash. *I can see you typing. Press send. Talk to me!*

Footsteps sounded behind me, and someone entered the dining room. "Fuck! I didn't realise anyone was still here."

I jerked at the voice then slid the side of my hand over my cheeks, erasing the tear lines. Gordain appeared at the end of the heavy oak table, a beer bottle in his hand. He stopped, taking hold of the back of a chair.

"Ella? What's wrong?"

I hadn't seen him all afternoon, but he'd come in for dinner and given me a polite greeting. It lacked the warmth I'd briefly known, and I wasn't exactly happy for him to find me upset.

"Nothing. I'm good." I pocketed my phone and stood, my chair grating on the flagstone floor. I forced a smile and raised my gaze, looking at Gordain's shoulder rather than his eyes. "I didn't expect to see you here."

"Same."

Right. We stood for a moment in an uncomfortable silence.

"Any idea where Beth is?" I asked.

"With Mathilda in the den. They're making plans for New York. A shortlist of places they want to see," he replied.

I drew my eyebrows in. "Mathilda's going?"

"Aye, from what I heard. Callum doesnae want her to miss out. They're both going. Maybe Wasp, too." He hesitated. "You didn't know?"

I opened and closed my mouth. There ended my stay at the castle. If Mathilda was going, too, then I'd go home to Belvedere.

"You'll all have a great time," Gordain said.

He didn't know I was meant to be staying. Well, I wasn't about to sit around and make this worse. "Sure. Thanks for telling me."

Without looking at him again, I raised a hand in farewell then left the room, crossing the great hall to get to the den. Inside, the rest of the family plus Beth sat on the green couches. I paused at the door, sensing Gordain at my back. He'd followed me over.

"Ella." My sister-in-law grinned at me. "There's been a change in plans. We're throwing the invitation out. Callum and Mathilda are considering coming with us now. The twins, too."

I summoned a smile. "What a fun idea."

Mattie's eyes sparkled with eagerness. "Oh Beth! I'm going to take you into the shops on Fifth Avenue. We can buy baby clothes! Just don't check the prices."

"I'll try cityscape photography." Wasp propped his feet on the coffee table. "Expect to see me at meal times only."

"Not me." Ally folded his arms. "You won't get me into a

plane. Els." He looked my way. "You're still staying, right? I won't be here on my own?"

"You weren't going?" Gordain's low tones sounded over my shoulder.

I twisted around. He positioned himself on the other side of the doorframe. We watched each other.

"No. I have things I need to do on home turf."

"But you were going to do them here?" he persisted.

I gave him a look. Why so interested now?

"Ella? Gordain?" Mattie called our attention back. "Want in?"

Gordain gave a ghost of a smile. "No. Thanks, but I have somewhere I need to be."

I waved her off, far too aware of the man opposite me. "I'll go home."

Mattie sat back on the green sofa and shook her head. "Wait, we're messing up your plans. What about driving? Can it wait a few days until we're back?"

Yeah, that did cause a problem. Suddenly, all eyes were on me. "Don't worry, I'm sure I can rearrange."

"What's this?" Gordain asked.

"Ella's booked to take her driving test here in a couple of days. There's no availability at home, and she needs the car for university," Beth said.

Ally hopped up and joined me and Gordain at the door. He stood shoulder to shoulder with his brother, not matching Gordain's height but still half a head taller than me. "Stay, Els. The three of us will have a blast, aye? Gordain will take you out in the car. G, you will, right?"

Awkward city. There was no way Gordain wanted to—

"Sure," Gordain replied. "I'll stay."

I narrowed my eyes at him. "You have plans. You said so yourself."

He shrugged.

"Perfect!" Mattie said. "Everyone's happy."

The conversation continued behind me, holiday fever growing.

The two brothers regarded me. Gordain's features were unreadable, Ally's the opposite.

"Why the long face?" Ally reached out and patted my cheek. He pushed his way past into the great hall. "You love it here, and you've got two of the best McRaes to take care of ye."

Yeah, but one was only here because he felt obligated. Well, fine. I'd just have to find a way to make friends with him again. Whatever his problem was, I'd work it out.

"It'll be great." I lifted my chin, my smile directed at Ally but my attitude all for his brother.

* * *

The next day, Callum, Mathilda, and Beth left for Belvedere. Wasp stayed at the castle, planning to catch an early flight from Inverness to meet them at Heathrow in the morning.

Weird, though it was only a week, I had a small sense of abandonment that took a little while to shake. But I had plans, and they didn't involve sitting around a mostly empty castle feeling sorry for myself.

I needed to make things normal with Gordain again.

During the night, I'd lain awake and tried to work out the point I'd been weird around him. Because if I could find it, then I could fix it.

But it was no good. No single event stood out, and the conclusion I'd reached was I just needed to talk to him. He was staying, I was staying. We'd be spending a whole lot of time together. I didn't want a cloud hanging over us.

With my resolve in mind, I set out to find him. He wasn't in any of the main rooms, so I stepped out of the front door into the mild Highlands afternoon. The loch glinted, reflecting back bright sunlight, so I raised my hand to shield my eyes. My ears served me better, picking up a *thud-thud* of someone chopping wood.

I followed the sound. The McRae brothers had a thing about never letting the fire in the great hall go out. With the twins being night owls and their older brothers always up and out early, someone was generally around to throw an armful of logs into the flames. I'd taken to doing it myself, last time I was here.

An ever-burning fire meant a constant supply of wood. I took the corner to where the garages and the woodshed lay and spotted movement. Bingo.

Gordain swung the axe in a precise arc, cleaving a log in two. Then he repositioned the stump and swung again, cutting the pieces into chunks.

I'd like to say his proficiency with the weapon was what stopped my mouth, but no. Gordain's half-naked body won that award. His bare torso was on display, his t-shirt discarded. Dressed in just a pair of jeans, he worked his bulky shoulder muscles, bringing the axe down, twisting his neat waist.

With his back to me, I had an excellent opportunity to stare.

And so I did.

My mouth dried. I knew he was tattooed. I'd seen them peeking out under the sleeves of his t-shirts. But I'd never seen the detail. Across his back were three bold lines, black and blue slashes. Over his biceps were patterns and, as he turned, a few bled onto one side of his chest.

In all my eighteen years, I'd never seen anything as hot as Gordain McRae in a sweat.

My sexual frustration hit the roof.

"Ella?" His voice roused me from my gaping.

I blinked. "Oh! God, I'm sorry. I didn't mean to stare." I snapped my hands to cover my eyes. "I can come back when you're, you know…"

"Don't go. Let me put my shirt on."

I peeked between my fingers to see him grab his black t-shirt from on top the pile of logs. He wiped his brow with his forearm then dragged the shirt over his head.

Pity. I missed the view already.

His gaze met mine again, and humour danced in his grey eyes. His lips tweaked with amusement. I dropped my hands and blew out a breath, relieved he could still smile at me.

"It's safe to look," he teased. "What do ye need?"

"A minute of your time?" I asked, not sure why I'd made it into a question. Advancing, I mustered my courage. "With us being here together for the week, I wanted to clear the air." His brow furrowed, but I rushed on, my cheeks already warm. "I think I annoyed you when I was here before. I want us to be friends again. Whatever it was I did, I'm sorry."

"What? Wait." Gordain reared back.

"No, it's okay." I cast around for the words to explain myself. "It was a difficult time, and I was reeling from one disaster to another. You're my brother's best friend. Even if you don't like me, I still like you. Can we start over?"

Gordain groaned and smacked his face. "No, Ella. Just no."

I paused, my mouth open. "No?"

"No to us not being friends. No to you pissing me off."

He moved closer, and I tilted my head to gaze up at him. Heat radiated from the man. Tendrils of it touched me, and I couldn't help leaning in.

Goosebumps raised on my arms.

Confusion marred his handsome face. He heaved a sigh. "You've got it wrong. Before, I was—"

"Ella? Ella! I know you're here!" A voice halted us both, the sound coming from the front of the castle.

A voice that shouldn't be within five hundred miles of this place.

"Taylor?" I whispered and spun around.

At the corner of the castle, my former friend stood, Wasp by her side.

My calm emotions—though heated from the sight of a half-naked Gordain—vanished.

"What are you doing here?" I stared her down. My tone came out flat, but under my skin my blood slowly boiled.

Taylor stepped forward on expensive shoes until she was a few meters away, Wasp trailing behind her. He exchanged an oh-fuck glance with Gordain, but I barely cared that we had an audience.

"You wouldn't answer my messages," Taylor replied. Her iron-flat blonde hair fell in a shimmering sheet, and she had on one of her power outfits—a ruffled purple blouse and a pin-striped skirt, like she was going to a business meeting, not seeing a friend.

A former friend.

"And why was that?"

She opened then closed her mouth. "I know. Okay? I know it sounds bad. But if you'd been in my shoes—"

"Huh." I folded my arms. "Would that be when you walked the information I gave you right up to my brother's house? Or when you used it to tried to sell yourself to him?"

Taylor recoiled as if I'd slapped her. "It wasn't like that!"

"It was exactly like that. You'd never met him before, but you knew..." I paused and changed tack before I said too much. Gordain was close to my brother. I didn't want to spill all my worry and confusion about ever having a happy relationship with James. All the fears I'd confided to Taylor.

"You were one of the only people I trusted. In the whole world. At the house, I saw you there and I thought you had come to see me." I shook my head. "Why am I explaining? There's nothing more to say."

"Can we talk in private?"

"No."

Taylor gave an exasperated squeak. "I got on a plane from London to see you. Tomorrow, I fly back to the States and I don't know when I'll be here again. I want this over with. I want my friend back. I don't have anyone else in my life as close to me as you are."

"Neither do I. But the difference is, I would never have done what you did."

"So what, I just go?"

"Sounds like a plan." I shrugged, hating every second of this.

"No! I'm not going to leave. I'm willing to wait it out."

She raised both eyebrows like I was being unreasonable. Which I probably was, though I couldn't see my way through it.

At school, I'd seen her do this—mask her emotions with a steely resolve. Taylor could play the ice queen when needed. In doing it now, she was showing me she meant business. Her stubborn streak was even wider than mine.

"Do you want her here?" Gordain's words, meant just for

me, had me swinging around.

"Do I?" I repeated. Then I registered the look on his face. Pity.

Oh hell. This was a disaster.

"Hold up," Wasp said.

Suddenly, I was glad for the two men being here, interrupting before I told Taylor to get the hell out of here. This wasn't my home, I couldn't kick her out. It wasn't my right.

"Let's all cool off a minute," Wasp continued. "Taylor, come inside, and I'll get you a drink. You've travelled a long way."

Taylor gave him an ultra-polite smile. "You're so kind. Is it Alasdair or William?"

"William. Everyone calls me Wasp."

She tilted her head, taking him in. "What should I call you?"

"Whatever you like," he replied, blindsided. Men usually were.

She threw a glance my way, but her gaze settled on Gordain. "And the big guy is Gordain. Ella's hero, right?"

"Taylor!" I spluttered. I'd met Gordain after she'd blown up our friendship, but for the two years previous, I'd had this little fantasy about the guy who had befriended my brother. Who'd given James a path to freedom and had inadvertently turned my family around. Taylor knew all about that.

Taylor stared at me for a moment, then she turned a cool shoulder and strode away. Wasp gave me a questioning look, like I should stop him if I didn't want this.

I had no idea what I wanted right now, apart from to bury my hot head so nobody could see me.

They vanished, leaving me with Gordain.

I swivelled on my heel and walked the other way.

4

——————

DISRUPTION

*G*ordain

Ella hit the path that led to the loch edge. I paced alongside. She gave me a fake smile, but her face was glum, and it stung me.

"I know I'm being a bitch. You don't need to tell me." She tucked her hands under her armpits. Pink stained her cheeks, and her eyes shone with tears.

"Why do ye think I'd say that?"

"Because any reasonable person would hear her out and judge it rationally." She stopped and fixed her gaze on a boat bobbing on the calm waters. "I can't do that."

"You don't have to. What she did was shite." I scrubbed a hand over my hair because I had no idea what to say. Not a clue. And I was the last person who should be doling out advice. My instincts ordered me to reach out and give her a hug, but that was wrong, too. *Fuck.* "Can I do anything?"

Ella gave a short laugh, already leaving. "No, but thanks for the offer. I'm going to take a walk."

"I'll make dinner in an hour, aye?"

Because that was going to help.

By way of an answer, I got a wave. But Ella's attention had already gone.

* * *

*B*y sunset, Ella had returned, but she'd gone straight to her room. I sent Ally up, but he came back down saying she was about to take a shower and had told him through the door to go away.

Her friend, Taylor, waited it out. She ate at our table, the twins keeping her company. I had no appetite. Instead, I sat at my laptop by the great hall's fire and stared into the flames. Before Callum had left, he'd taken me to one side and gave me a list of things to keep an eye on while he was gone. Contractors laying a cable up to two cottages he was converting. A new tenant who would be calling at the castle to collect their keys.

He'd then asked if I was sure about staying. I'd given him a look because, as much as we both loved Ally, there was no guarantee the centuries-old castle would still be standing if he was left in charge.

But that wasn't my main reason.

I dropped a line to Jordie. *Change of plan. Can't make it tomorrow.*

Shame. Got a better offer? he replied.

Something like that. I typed back, though that wasn't true. Not in the way he meant.

Finally, Ella appeared on the stairs, her freshly washed hair still damp and tied back, and her long sweater loose over snug leggings.

I sat forward, but her gaze didn't come my way.

"Taylor?" she said.

"Funny story," her friend said, crossing to the centre of

the great hall. "Wasp's on the same flight to the US as me. I'm flying out with him in the morning. Catching the same transfer. So, you know, I hung around."

Ella gave a wan smile, appearing far more composed than before. "I should've guessed you wouldn't take no for an answer."

Taylor flapped her arms. "Like I said, you know me."

"Fine. We'll talk." Ella swung her gaze around the hall.

I leapt from my seat. "Talk here. We'll go into the den."

Later, I'd grab time alone with her. I'd acted badly when she'd arrived here, and that I could rectify, along with all those wrong ideas she had in her head.

First, she had Taylor to deal with, and there was nothing I could do to help with that.

Ella gave me a small chin lift and descended the stairs. Taylor passed me, her confident smiles gone now.

I gave them their privacy and ushered the twins into the den. Ally dropped into an untidy sprawl on the couch, lost in his phone for a few minutes. Wasp fidgeted, glancing between the door, us, and his screen, an expression on his face I'd never seen on him before. Some mixture of excitement and nerves.

Finally, he decided to share his thoughts. "How pissed off do ye think Ella will be if I sleep with her friend?"

My mouth dropped open.

"Fuck! Are you serious?" Ally's eyes bugged out. "No, ye can't. She'll be cut up."

"Or she won't care." Wasp pulled at his collar. "Either way, I don't think I have a choice. The lass practically pinned me to the wall earlier."

Ally turned his gaze on me. "Why are you glaring at Wasp like that? Like you carefully choose who you sleep with. You're our idol. He's just copying what you do."

"No. God." I scrubbed a hand over my head. Callum and I had talked to the twins about sex, their mother happy to hand the job over to us since she'd moved in with her new husband and had another baby. We'd told the boys to wait and find someone they cared about, and counted ourselves successful as, unless something had changed recently, neither boy had gone...there.

The same rule hadn't applied to me. Wasp wasn't wrong. I went there whenever I had an itch that needed scratching. I'd never needed a girlfriend. Sex was a pastime like running or climbing, and finding a willing partner was easy.

"I can't believe you're going to lose your virginity before me." Ally picked up a cushion and flung it at his brother. Then he grabbed his phone from the coffee table. "Fine. The race is on."

"What are you doing?" Wasp squinted at his twin.

"Finding a lass to come screw me tonight."

"Christ! Stop it, the pair of ye." I knocked the phone out of Ally's hand, wishing Callum was here to manage them. He would yell orders, and eventually they'd listen. I was so far away in my own problems and worrying about Ella that being a good role model wasn't coming naturally. I had to force my brain back into the room.

"First," I looked at Wasp, "aye, Ella might be upset if you sleep with her friend. She's family and deserves our loyalty. Think about that before you get too far to think straight. And you," I turned my attention on his twin, the lad busy retrieving his phone from the rug, "what I get up to is none of your business. It's definitely not an example to follow. Go on dates and find a girlfriend. Having someone you care about is better than screwing a stranger."

The twins looked at me with identically baffled expressions.

"Didn't you sleep with the bartender at Lachlan's party a wee while ago?" Ally peered at me. "Are you in love with her and planning on proposing?"

How the fuck did he know about that? It was true, but I'd been drunk and upset. Lachlan, our relative, had made a deal to sell his home and land to property developers. The place I'd dreamed about owning since I was a boy. Not that I had a hope in hell of affording it.

"Who's proposing?"

In unison, we swung our heads to the door. Ella waited in the frame. Alone.

"Gordain. To a barmaid he's in love with," Ally helpfully filled in.

Oh, for fuck's sake.

I leapt to my feet and closed in on her, examining Ella's face for signs of tears or upset. "He's talking a load of balls. Ignore him."

She wore an inscrutable expression. "I'm going to bed. Wasp, Taylor said you offered her a room for the night?"

Ally choked on a laugh then coughed to cover it up.

"Aye. I made up a spare room. We're on the same flight from Inverness, so I'll see her away safely," Wasp replied.

"Bet you will," his twin said under his breath.

"Great. Thanks for taking care of her. I appreciate it. Sorry for the disruption." She gestured, encompassing us all in her apology.

I gave a long look at Wasp then followed Ella out of the room. Her friend sat on her own across the hall. Whatever they'd said or agreed, it wasn't apparent in either of their faces.

At the stairs, Ella didn't stop, and I kept up with her, not sure what I was doing. Then at the door to her room, Ella halted.

"You walking me to my door, G?"

G. She'd called me that before. The nickname the twins used for me. "I am. Are ye upset?"

Ella rolled her shoulders. "No. So when's the wedding?"

"The what?"

"You and the bartender?" A smile tweaked the corner of her lips, but it appeared forced.

My bloody brother. "Listen, what you said before, about me not liking you because you'd been emotional..." My chest ached, and I rubbed my knuckles over the pain. "That isn't true. I have a world of problems—"

"With your job. I know."

But she didn't. Nobody did.

"Want to talk about it?" she added.

"No. Want to talk about your friend?"

She held my gaze, her silence telling me everything I needed to know. Stalemate.

"What I mean is that my mood was nothing to do with you. I was caught up in my own head."

"Uh-huh." Ella's gaze dropped.

"I like you just fine. We're friends, aye?"

"Great." She drew a heavy breath, still not making eye contact, then bobbed her head and disappeared into her room.

While I considered all the ways I could smack sense into my own head and make Ella smile again.

* * *

*I*n the early hours of the next morning, I drove Wasp and Taylor to the airport. No one chatted through the dark drive, and the two of them seemed exhausted.

I didn't want to know why.

At the drop-off point, Wasp bear-hugged me goodbye and wrangled the luggage from the car. Taylor stopped in front of me, her arms crossed over her body against the chilly predawn air. In my t-shirt, I wasn't cold but I was made from hardier stuff than most.

"You're a pilot, right? Did you know Ella had a fantasy about you flying to our school and taking her away?"

I blinked at her. "What?"

"Before she even knew you, when you were just a guy her brother told her about. You became her symbol of hope."

"Why are you telling me this?" I had a feeling Ella wouldn't want this shared. Even so, my pride sat up and paid attention.

"Because you kept her going. That boarding school was a shitty place to grow up, and we clung on to our little daydreams. But when I asked her about you last night, she just looked sad. How can that be? You're her hero."

Taylor lifted her pert chin. "I fucked up my friendship with her but I will get it back again. If you screwed her over, undo it. She can count on one hand the people who truly care about her. And there's even fewer who she's sure would step up for her."

"Is that what you're doing?" The lass was starting to piss me off but only because the truth hurt. I had messed things up with Ella and the guilt cut me to pieces.

Wasp joined us and glanced between our faces. "Our flight's boarding. We better run."

"Safe journey," I forced out.

"See you again, Gordain. Hopefully under better circumstances." Taylor turned her shoulder and walked away.

My brother blew out a breath, made a poor attempt at a salute, and fell in at her side.

* * *

I drove home with my mind churning over everything I'd done and said. It wasn't like Ella and I had ever been friends, not really. Desiring her had put paid to that. But I had that under wraps now. She was too young, as well as my best friend's little sister.

There was a line to walk, and I'd find it. She needed a friend far more than I needed to kiss her.

Dawn broke as I parked up outside the castle, a pale light straining through a fog that had descended, obscuring the mountain. I'd planned to go for a run—sleep impossible now—but maybe I'd stick to the gym situated on the floor beneath my rooms in the tower.

The gravel crunched under my boots, and I stuck my hands in my pockets, striding over to the oak door.

It swung open ahead of me.

Ella appeared in the gap, adjusting a headphone in her ear, her other hand holding the heavy door. At first, she didn't notice me.

But fuck, did I notice her.

Her tight shorts and cropped sports bra which left her belly bare. Her arms. Her lower legs. The kit showed off her curves and left little to my imagination.

Ella didn't usually wear revealing clothes.

All plans I had to stop thinking of her in a sexual way flew out of the window. Every male instinct surged.

"Gordain?"

"What?"

"Why are you staring?"

"What?"

She chuckled. A beautiful sound. The first genuine laugh since she'd arrived.

"I'm not— Fuck, I was. Sorry." I scrubbed my hand over my eyes, stumbling over my words. "Where are you going?"

"For a run. I couldn't sleep." She pulled on a long-sleeved top and zipped it up halfway.

"Wait a minute? I'll come with you."

I finally met her eyes, and Ella was giving me a curious once-over. "I'll start slow. Catch me up."

I'd never ran so fast in my life. Across the great hall in seconds, I belted into the corridor that led to my tower, taking the spiral stairs two at a time. I half fell through the door into the hall, dragging off my t-shirt and kicking off my shoes as I went. In my bedroom, I dropped onto my bed and shucked off my jeans and boxers, then grabbed my Under Armour kit and pulled it on.

Usually, I'd wear a loose military-issue PT kit, but the Under Armour was tight. Form-fitting over my muscles. It showed off my body to best effect.

I had a moment at the door, pushing my feet into my running shoes, where I wondered what the hell I was doing, what message I was trying to give. *Look at me, all big and strong.*

But I wasn't about to stop, and I descended the stairs with a grin lighting my face.

5

CAMHANAICH

$\mathcal{E}$*lla*

There was a peace to the morning, helped by the thick fog that cloaked the castle and grounds. It muffled my footfalls, enclosing me in a fluffy, if cold, cloud hug.

Seeing Taylor last night had lifted some of the pressure off me. She'd felt desperate and reached for a desperate measure. In many ways, I understood. The situation she was in with her father—a big deal in the US government—was yet another trap when we'd only just been sprung from the prison that had been our school. She saw the marriage to my brother as a path to permanent freedom.

It didn't mean I could trust her again, but we'd parted ways in a more civil fashion than when she'd arrived.

That wasn't the only reason for my change in mood. Gordain had made a point of telling me he liked me. Then, a few minutes ago, he'd stared at my body like he'd never seen a woman before. Good to know I wasn't the only one of us checking out the other.

Swear to God he'd blushed after I'd called him on it.

I chuckled to myself and picked up the pace, knowing

he'd be hard on my heels. Sucking in a lungful of damp air, I crossed the bridge over the river that fed the loch—invisible, thanks to the fog—and put my head down, flying along the road. After a couple of minutes, two shapes loomed out of the murk—the huge, stone gateposts that marked the entrance to the McRae estate.

I slowed, debating which direction to take. The left-hand road went back along the loch to the village. Right went…I had no idea. I'd never taken it. Through a forest, that was all I could tell. Either way, I'd wait—

"Hey." A warm hand took my waist and spun me around. Gordain grinned down at me.

I pressed a hand to my thudding heart, a thrill in my veins from his touch. "You made me jump."

"You didn't go slow."

"I knew you'd find me."

We eyed one another, and he stepped back. It was all I could do not to glance down at his body.

"I was trying to decide which way to go. And not get lost." I tipped my head at the monoliths, not taking my gaze off Gordain.

"Let me choose? I've been running the same route since I was a lad."

"You went jogging as a kid?"

"Something like that." There was a little pause before he spoke, and it snagged my attention. It felt loaded. If he wasn't jogging, then he was…fleeing? *God, Ella!* I almost laughed out loud at myself, at the drama I sought in everyone else's lives. What would Gordain be running from? I shook off the strange idea and scanned the invisible surroundings.

"It's eerie, this light." The sun tried to force its way through the mist. Not successfully.

"There's a Scottish word for the morning twilight. Camhanaich."

"Camhanaich," I repeated the word back. *Cav-an-ach.*

He raised an eyebrow. "You're half Scottish. Where's that in your accent? James sounds Scottish every now and again. You don't."

"Beaten out of me at school." It was a joke, but Gordain's face lost its humour.

"Not literally," I added then blew out a breath because I didn't want to go there now. Not in this lovely moment. "I'll work on getting it back just for you. Now, Highlander, choose our path. Lead the way."

Gordain took the right, leading me along a track away from the road and into the thick pine forest. A dense canopy of trees hung overhead. We crushed pine needles under our heels as we ran, the smell heady. A hundred yards in, Gordain stalled to let me pass him so I took the lead. Setting the pace.

We didn't speak, which suited me—the uphill gradient had my breathing laboured in no time. After the terrain levelled out, I took more notice of my surroundings. The sturdy trees. The occasional glimpse of an animal. Amazing I could notice anything, seeing as my awareness of Gordain swamped my senses.

Then the forest thinned, ending.

"Where are we?" Breathing hard, I stopped at the edge of a well-managed garden—it could only be someone's property, though I couldn't pick out a building through the thick mist.

Gordain halted beside me, no sign that he was at all tired by the run. He placed a hand on his chest and rubbed, his gaze on the distance. "My destination, as a lad."

"Is it a house?"

"Better. Want to see?"

I paused, glancing from him to the empty space. Excitement resonated in Gordain's tone, just a trace, but I paid attention. Whatever this place was, it held importance to him. "Won't the homeowner mind?"

Gordain shook his head and touched his fingertips lightly to my shoulder to propel me on. We walked over the grass. Somewhere far to my left came the sound of rushing water, likely the river that came out at the loch. Then the mist cleared, and the edges of a building appeared.

"It's another castle," I said, gazing up as two towers came into view, making up the corners of a hefty stone frontage. Symmetrical, with an impressive entranceway, it was a handsome place, much prettier than Castle McRae, though I didn't like to say.

"It's called Braithar," Gordain replied. His hand still rested on my shoulder, heavier now, and his palm warm.

I leaned into the touch. "It's beautiful. Who owns it?"

"Gordain! What are you doing here, lad?" boomed a voice from the entranceway. A man strode out, a huge giant of a Scot, of Gordain's build but much older. "If you've come for a visit, your timing's off. I'm heading out to help Marianne with the cattle down at the farm."

"Nah, just out for a run."

The man eyed me. "Who's your friend?"

"Lachlan. This is Ella Fitzroy. Ella, Lachlan McRae. Cousin to my da."

I shook the man's hand. He beamed wider, his expression kindly. "Fitzroy, aye? As in James?"

"My brother. You know him?"

"I do. You've the look of him." Lachlan clinked a set of keys in his hand. "I was glad to hear about his wedding and the bairn on the way. You must be over the moon."

"So much. They'll make great parents." Some people were automatically ready for the role. I had no intention of having kids until I was at least thirty. Being an auntie, on the other hand, meant I'd get to spoil the baby.

How different that child's life would be compared to ours. James and I had had the best start with wonderful parents, but it had all gone to hell after their death, with us being placed in the clutches of Richard.

I took a vow, there and then, to protect that baby at all costs. He or she would be loved and supported through thick and thin. Richard would never wield his brand of evil again.

As I'd become lost in the thought, Lachlan said something to Gordain about becoming an uncle, too—of course, with Callum and Mathilda due to be parents as well, he and I were in the same boat.

Then the older man took a step back. "Tell ye what, why don't the two of you come for lunch tomorrow. We'll be glad to know you better, Ella. That suit ye?"

Gordain and I exchanged a glance.

"I'd like that," I answered for both of us.

Lachlan tipped an imaginary hat to Gordain. "Twelve hundred hours, airman."

"Understood." Gordain snapped a smart salute, and Lachlan walked away.

"Is Lachlan military?" I asked.

We turned, heading back towards the forest.

"No. But he's close friends with someone who is. The man who runs the helicopter training school out at Inverness airport. He and Lachlan took me up the first time in a heli. Before I decided to join the RAF." Gordain shook his head. A haunted expression ghosted over his features, and I immediately wanted to erase it.

Without thinking too much about it, I slid my hand into his and gave his fingers a squeeze. "Every time you talk about your job, you get the saddest look."

He huffed but didn't let go.

"I'm sorry for whatever it is," I added. "I'm not prying, but if we're friends, then I'm here for you."

"I'm meant to be the one there for you, after everything you've been through," he replied.

"We can be there for each other. Deal?"

Gordain broke the hold on my hand and drew me into a swift side-hug. It was meant in a friendly way, but I felt it all through me, missing it after it ended. I'd grown cold from standing still and I shivered.

"Deal. Let's get moving again. Last one home cooks breakfast." Gordain tapped me, then broke out into a sprint.

I grinned and took off after him. Not that I had a hope of winning. When I came to all things Gordain McRae, I was beat.

* * *

Ally appeared at the dining table just as we finished eating. He eyed the remainders of our meal and turned an outraged expression on his brother. "You ate without me? And bacon? You traitor. You never cook unhealthy foods for me."

Gordain and I had fallen into talking on the final stretch of the run, and I tagged the castle before he remembered we were meant to be competing. He'd served up bacon sandwiches and a carafe of coffee half an hour and one short shower later.

We chatted just like when I'd been here before.

Best breakfast I'd ever had.

"Ella had years of missing out, she deserves bacon."

"And I don't? Even though I've had to put up with your miserable face this last month?" Ally grinned.

"Yours is in the kitchen." Gordain rolled his eyes at his brother, the latter leaving the room. Then Gordain turned to me. "When we met Lachlan, and he mentioned James's baby, something bothered you. What was it?"

I'd plaited my hair after my shower and reworked it now. These things always looked gorgeous on videos of other people doing it, but my hair was thick and usually just ended up in chunky, uneven curls.

I concentrated on twisting the ends into the band. "I was thinking how different things will be for James's son or daughter. How they will grow up happy, you know?" Then, because I didn't want to dwell on my past yet again, I switched the conversation around. "You'll be an uncle, huh? Lucky kid."

"I know what you mean." Gordain stuck his hands under his armpits. "Callum and Mathilda's bairn will have the best of everything. Two devoted parents, three uncles fiercely guarding the wee lad or lass. A world away from the shitestorm that was our early years."

I didn't know much about Gordain's childhood, only that he'd lost his mother at a very young age, then his father when he'd been a teenager. "What was it like for you? Was your dad like Lachlan?"

Ally stumbled back into the room, manhandling the pitted oak door, a plate balanced under his chin and coffee spilling from his mug. "Our da? A vicious fucker. Nothing like Lachlan. In fact, if it wasn't for Lachlan, G probably wouldn't have survived to be the great ugly man he is today. Isn't that right, bro?"

With that bombshell dropped, he fell into a chair and took a bite from his sandwich, his gaze bright.

To my surprise, Gordain barely blinked. "Aye. That's a fact."

A buzzing came from across the room. Gordain stood and crossed to collect his phone from the sideboard. He frowned at the screen then excused himself, answering the call as he entered the great hall. "Lieutenant McRae."

"That'll be the base." Ally tipped his head at the door. "What are your plans for the day?"

"Your brother is giving me a driving lesson." Or I hoped he still was. We'd agreed it on the run back from Braithar. "You?"

Ally waggled his eyebrows. "I'm driving into Inverness to pick up a lass."

Well! "I didn't know you had a girlfriend."

"Jealous?" He took another bite of his sandwich.

I batted my lashes. "Devastated. How could you throw me over for another woman?"

"As if. Your head's been turned from the moment you stepped foot inside this castle."

My mouth dropped open. "What?"

"And he's a goner, too. Otherwise he'd be heading out each night on the prowl like he always used to. I was joking about that barmaid."

He winked at me, and I just stared.

Gordain joined us again, his expression bleak. "Change of plan with that driving lesson, Ella."

"Huh?" My cheeks must be flaming red. In the corner of my vision, Ally laughed at me.

"What's going on?" his older brother asked.

"Just getting Ella in a fluster. Look at her face. Chill, lass. Your secret's safe with me."

I gamely ignored him, addressing his brother instead. "No driving then?"

He blinked at us then held out his hand, helping me up from my chair. "We can still go, so long as you don't mind a diversion to the base. I need to drop by."

"Sounds good to me." I swayed, unsteady on my feet. Not by standing too fast, but by the fact that Ally was right. My head was totally turned by Gordain.

Hardly surprising for a girl who'd been locked in a gilded cage. He'd helped set me free, and all I wanted to do was find my wings.

"Then let's go."

* * *

The drive out took us through open Scottish countryside. Gordain brooded over something, quiet in the passenger seat, so I took to regaling him with stories about school.

"Etiquette lessons are really a thing?" he asked eventually.

"Yep. I remember one class where we sat at formal dining tables and ate an eight-course meal. We were judged on our conversation and on the correct use of cutlery." I dropped my voice to sound like the teacher of that particular lesson. "No, Elinor. That is a knife, not a saw."

"How old were you?"

"Maybe twelve or thirteen."

"I can't believe a place like that exists anymore."

"St Briavels is another world. Overall, the education they pedalled was excellent. I'm grateful for that, I guess, but the focus was on looking and sounding the part, with an assumption that you'd be in a public-facing role as a tasteful decoration. Maybe a princess or a wife to an important politician." I snorted a laugh at Gordain's stunned expression. "Ceremonial duties were the ambition for my classmates, but many of them came from families where women had little control over their own lives. The college's restrictions were harsh, which is why I was always in trouble. Richard knew exactly what he was doing when he put me into that place."

"Which was?"

I shrugged a shoulder. "He could forget about me there."

Silence held in the car. I watched the road. The flat ground leading to rolling hills. Forests and glens. Gorgeous.

"I hate the thought of you stuck there."

"I hated being there." I gripped the steering wheel. "Ten years. If it wasn't for Taylor and for the Hinchcliffes, our housekeepers at Belvedere where I used to go for the holidays, I wouldn't have a clue what love or friendship was."

I'd said too much. Cut too close to the bone. I felt it just as surely as I felt Gordain's discomfort. I fidgeted in my seat, my concentration frazzled by the unhappy memories. A sudden burst of claustrophobia had me nauseated.

I wanted to stomp my foot down and flee. Escape the trap and live wild.

Gordain shot me a concerned glance, but my chest was too tight to speak.

"Slow down. Take the next left," he murmured.

I followed orders, steering the car through the outskirts of a small town. Ahead, the gates for a military base appeared, high fences with razor wire lining the formidable entrance. We rolled in, and I stopped the car. Guards took our IDs and queried my purpose in visiting, then the roadblock lifted, enabling me to drive on.

"Park up here and get out of the car." Gordain pointed to a space beside an office block.

I followed orders, feeling wretched and not knowing how to shake it off.

I'd had this kind of desperation come over me before, though this was back when I had no chance of doing anything about it. I was free now. Why hadn't it gone?

Out of the car, the sea breeze lifted my hair. Gordain slammed his door and came around to my side.

Without saying a word, he swept me into a hug, hard and fast.

For a moment I froze, then I hugged him back. Strangling him with my arms. Burning up energy in a tight hold against his form.

We relaxed into one another. Not letting go.

"Didn't realise I needed this," I mumbled into his shoulder.

"From what you just described, you wouldn't know to ask." He released me, his expression unreadable as he stepped back. Then he glanced over to a row of low buildings. "I needed it, too."

I was a self-centred idiot. He had a host of worries, and I was stuck in the past, dwelling over things I couldn't change. I needed to be right here in the present. "I'll be waiting with another hug when you're done."

Gordain gave me a pretence of a smile then walked away, his muscles rigid.

On the drive up, he'd told me it would only be a brief visit, just so he could collect a letter, so I waited by the car and watched him go. The door to the office slammed closed behind him, and I heaved in a breath of salty sea air.

I sensed a pair of eyes on me.

A woman got out of an expensive car, parked across the

road from mine. She looked at the door Gordain had taken then brought her attention back to me.

"Good morning." I raised a hand.

"Huh." She drew in her nicely shaped eyebrows. "Who are you?"

"I'm Ella Fitzroy. And you are?" I smiled my trained super-gracious smile.

"Surprised," she said by way of an answer. Then she indicated with her head to the door. "Is Gordain okay?"

A strange feeling sank my stomach. She knew Gordain, and well enough, too, by her question. I ran a subtle gaze over her, assessing her with an eye my college style tutor would be proud of.

The stranger's jeans weren't high street. Designer, a classic brand, as were her boots. Her car was expensive but not flashy, and her tasteful handbag would've set her back a grand, easy. Her long nails, and her toned but not muscular arms, told me she wasn't a serving officer in her own right.

I hated that I knew this shit. How to take people apart with a swift assessment of what they displayed to the world. But it let me place her as likely a friend or relative of military top brass.

Had she dated Gordain? *Was* she dating Gordain?

Yeah, that feeling? Jealousy, no doubt.

I kept up my polite demeanour. "He hasn't been okay, but he'll be fine."

No matter what was going on, Gordain would find a way through it. He was the most competent man I'd ever met.

The woman's shoulders sank. "I was worried." She shook her head, not talking to me. "And now I see why he said no. No wonder."

She was talking in riddles, but I liked the sound of him saying no. "If you tell me your name, I'll pass a message on."

"I'm Autumn. But no need to pass anything on. Ella, wasn't it?"

I nodded and she popped open her car door again.

"Thank you, Ella. You've set my mind at rest."

"I'm glad to help," I replied, but the woman only bobbed her head.

She drove away, leaving me to guess what had gone on between her and the man I was waiting for.

6

HEAD SPIN

*G*ordain

"The disciplinary panel will be convened, and you will be advised of the date in due course."

I stared at the ranking officer, at his cool eyes. "Permission to speak, sir."

"Granted."

What could I ask? The letter I'd been handed, and the summary given verbally, was crystal clear. I faced a formal disciplinary hearing—a significant offence in the career of an airman—over the wing commander's complaint. The RAF took character seriously. You made commitments to the cause and if you acted outside of that, you were seen as unfit to serve. They'd put me on leave for an unknown period, though my search and rescue training started imminently.

Cold unfurled in my gut.

"I'm due to attend SAR training. Will the course be delayed until after the hearing?"

The officer behind the desk steepled his fingers and gave

an impatient sigh. "The course will proceed as planned. You will not be participating. The streaming has been revoked."

Fuck. I forced the expression from my face. My fate was sealed.

At best, I would have to go back to basics, lose the respect I'd gained alongside the coveted position. At worst... My career was over.

"Any further questions?" the officer asked, already lost in his computer screen.

"No, sir."

"You are dismissed."

Pausing in the soulless corridor outside the room, I slid on a pair of sunglasses, hiding from the world while I reeled. The unfairness grated. The fact that despite all the rigidity of the military, one man's malice carried more weight.

I thought this would go away. Or be considered a slightly embarrassing non-event. But no. The Wing Commander had thrown the book at me.

At the exterior door, I gripped the frigid metal handle, trying and failing to think of a single thing I could do to make this right. But there was nothing. I knew the drill.

Outside, Ella waited, a bright smile ready. It faded as she took in my expression. She'd promised me a hug, but I couldn't go there. All I wanted was to take and take from her. If I had her in my arms, I wouldn't want to let her go.

Ella wasn't mine to use like that. Nobody was.

She seemed to understand and instead climbed inside the car, then she remained silent while I sulked. She drove us off the base and into the wild Highlands with no need for me to instruct or help her; she could control the vehicle just fine.

"I think I'm going to be released from my contract.

Maybe even fired," I eventually forced out. It was the worst the commander could do and, judging on today, he'd probably go there.

She sucked in a breath. "Why?"

Christ, I didn't want to tell her what had happened, not now anyway. How could I explain something I didn't remember? It only made me sound less in control and more culpable.

After the event, I'd grabbed a quiet minute with Jordie to ask how long I'd been gone from the bar before they'd found me. It was incredibly unlikely, but if I'd had sex with the woman I was found with, I wanted to know about it.

His answer—twenty minutes—didn't help.

With no way of contacting the woman in question, I was on my own in the mystery. I'd gotten myself checked for STDs anyway. The tests had come back negative, but all of it was a wakeup call.

"I did something stupid. I was due to start an elite training course, and they've pretty much confirmed that won't happen."

My chest had a hole in it, and I was bleeding out. Not just for the job, but for the indignity and lack of faith the RAF had in me.

I waited on Ella's words like she could condemn me or free me.

"That doesn't sound like you, G."

Didn't sound like me? I slept around. I sometimes got drunk. Why couldn't it happen to me? A surge of emotion rose.

"Maybe you don't know me that well to judge," I bit out, my frustration overflowing and landing on the only near target.

Ella stared forward, her mouth slightly open and her

eyes wide in surprise. Ah fuck, I was taking it out on entirely the wrong person.

"I'm sorry—" I started, but she cut me off.

"You're right. I spoke out of turn. It's none of my business." Then she closed her mouth and made a show of concentrating on the vacant road.

And I stared out of the window, trying to work out what the hell was going on.

* * *

At the castle, Ally's car had been moved—now parked in a different spot. I recalled his mission to get laid and blew out a breath. "My brother might have company," I said to Ella.

She dipped her head, then, without answering, slid the keys from the ignition and hopped out of the car. I followed her across the car park.

At the front door, she stopped. Then she arranged her face into a pleasant smile. Totally fake. "Thank you for the lesson. I appreciate your time."

I wanted to call her on it. Or have her call me on my rotten mood. But Ella wasn't here to help me with my problems. She had enough of her own.

I was alone in this. No right to ask for a damn thing from anyone.

"I'm going to the gym. Grab yourself whatever you want for a late lunch. I'll have dinner ready at seven," I grumped, my muscles itching for release.

"Don't worry about me. I'll make something myself," Ella called over her shoulder, and she stomped away, her fake smile gone as she turned her back. "Look after yourself, Gordain."

Then she was gone. I was Gordain again and not G.

And I wanted to break things.

* * *

*I*n the tower gym, I took out my frustration first on the punchbag, then the weights. Music blared, and I hit my routine hard. Hurting myself. Punishing my body for taking part in something I didn't remember.

In the past, I'd got tattoos to remind me of bad times. Occasionally some good. I liked the sting of the gun.

It made me feel alive.

I was laid out on the bench, sweat pouring off me, when footsteps sounded on the stairs outside. Swiping a towel from where I'd slung it over the weights rack, I dried my face then stopped the music before it went onto the next track.

Ally swaggered into the room. Ally. Not Ella. My disappointment hurt more than the burn in my shoulders.

Two hours of sweating my balls off hadn't dented my addiction to all things Ella Fitzroy.

"What is it?" I tossed the towel to the end of the bench and scrubbed over my eyes with the heel of my hand.

"Condoms. Need 'em."

I stared at him. Then my brain caught up, and I snapped back into big brother mode. "You have a lass here, and you...?"

"Aye." He beamed. "And she's made a man out of me already. Hence the request."

"Right. Nice one." I jumped up and moved past him, jogging the stairs to my rooms on the floor above. Callum and I had remodelled the space into a liveable apartment the year after I'd joined the RAF. I had a bedroom, a wee bathroom with a decent shower but no bath, and a living room with a round wall against which we'd built a couch. Most of the windows were tiny slits, designed to shoot arrows out of.

I couldn't imagine living in a regular flat-walled house. Somewhere that was purpose-built and didn't have issues with crumbling stonework or centuries-old sloping floors. As a family, we were experts in castle repair jobs. It was what we knew.

That was half the reason I'd taken Ella to see Braithar this morning. To show her the place I used to run to as a lad when my father's beatings had become too much.

I sighed, pulling the light cord to the bathroom.

Ally followed me in.

"What's her name, the lass?" I asked, opening the cabinet under the sink.

"Kaylee. She's followed me for ages, and we've chatted a wee bit. Turns out she liked me for more than just my stories."

The twins documented their lives online and had a huge following. It had prompted Wasp's interest in more serious photography. Ally's posts, on the other hand, were more often stunts he pulled or pictures of his own face.

I located an unopened box and handed it over. "Good to know you're being responsible."

He slid the box into his back pocket, giving a nod as thanks. "You taught me well. There'll be no stray babies from this McRae. By the way, did you see Wasp's picture yet?"

I grimaced and checked my phone, finding the McRae family chat. The second shot was of him and Taylor on the airplane, both pulling baffled faces, their hands to their mouths covering fake shock. His comment was: *Has anyone seen my V-card? Seem to have lost it.*

"Can't believe you've both grown up," I said.

Ally grinned, but then his face fell. "Yeah, I sent him a picture of my bare arse in reply. But I didn't mean that. What about Ella? Do you think she'll mind?"

"I think she might."

"Do you want to tell her or shall I?"

This was what I loved most about my youngest brother —though a twin, he'd been born ten minutes after Wasp and always played the baby of the family—he messed around and got into trouble, but he was unfailingly honest about it. Never hiding his mistakes. Or those of other people.

I should learn from his example.

I blew out a breath. "I'll tell her. Is she downstairs?"

Ally shook his head, turning to leave. "No. She's been sawing away at her violin for hours. Real angry sounds. Did you piss her off?"

"I might've done." I followed him into the octagonal hall and to the top of the stairs.

"Then tell her about Taylor while she's already angry. She'll burn out and get over it quicker."

"Is your friend staying for dinner?" I called after him down the stairs.

"Aye. And for the night. Don't come knocking." Then he was gone.

* * *

*A*lly and his guest came down for dinner, draped over one another and flirting up a storm as they ploughed through the chicken stew I'd prepared. The lass gazed at my brother like he was a rock star, laughing at everything he said.

It was almost cute, if it wasn't nauseating.

Man, I needed to get out and get laid.

My lingering mood and my snapping at Ella had as much to do with her as it did my job. The work problem I'd had time to get used to. It sucked, but it was becoming inevitable. The Ella problem wasn't going away.

It was getting worse.

Every time I looked at her, my blood heated. Little details—the outline of her collarbone under her shirt, or the depths of her blue-green eyes—had me fascinated.

She was too young for me. My best friend's little sister. She needed friends and space to mess around with lads. To enjoy herself in her newfound freedom.

Christ, the thought had my blood spiking yet again.

I had to get out of here tonight. Find a bar. A willing body.

But first... I leapt up and grabbed a fork and a bowl of stew and marched out of the dining room, up the stairs that ran up the interior wall of the great hall, then down the bedroom corridor. The sound of Ella's violin filled the air. She'd got lost in her music.

I rapped my knuckles on the door.

The tune continued, so I rested against the wall adjacent to her door. Then, after a minute and no answer, I slid to the floor, her bowl warm in my hands. It was beautiful, the piece she was playing. Soaring for a while then angry and vibrant. A hint of desperation.

It had me thinking of flying. The urgency of reaching someone. Missions I'd flown where the likely outcome was of recovering bodies rather than saving souls.

Fucking poignant.

I closed my eyes against it, the rising music, the image of Ella feverishly playing the piece.

Hot. Sweaty. Her dark hair pulled back from her face.

I put the bowl to one side and placed my head in my hands.

Caught up in my thoughts, I didn't notice the playing had stopped until the door opened in front of me.

Ella paused in her step into the hall. "Gordain! You made me jump."

Yeah, well, Ella. You make my head spin and my heart ache.

I clambered to my feet, retrieving her dinner and offering it out. "Brought your food. I knocked, but..."

She took the bowl, her eyes bright but her actions cautious. "I didn't hear. Thanks. I meant to come down but I lost track of time. I was writing a new piece."

"It was beautiful."

"You listened?"

"I loved it."

We watched each other for a long moment. "I'm sorry—"

"I shouldn't have—"

Both of us spoke at the same time.

Ella gave a short laugh. "I'll go first because it was my mistake. I pushed you for something you didn't want to talk about. Just because I was getting a driving lesson and along for the ride didn't give me any right to pry into what happened at the base." She dropped her gaze. "Or to pout like a child after. I see that now."

"No." The words stuck in my throat.

She peeked up. "No? No what?"

"I... Ah, fuck. I snapped at you and you apologise? No to that. And no because I was the one acting out of line. Ye have every right to ask. I started the conversation." And I'd tell her the details. But not right at this second. I dragged in a breath. "I'm sorry, okay?"

Ella's cheeks tinged pink, visible even in the dim light of the hall.

I was so fucked over this lass. So utterly fucked.

So I needed to go before I did something stupid. "There's something I needed to tell you. About your friend."

Her eyebrows drew in. "Taylor?"

"And Wasp." I scrunched up my nose.

"Did she sleep with him?" Ella guessed, saving me the words. Then she tilted her head. "Were you worried about telling me? Aw, G. I already knew. She asked me if I minded, if I was into him." The pink on her cheeks spread. "I told her to go for it."

Ella had a way of looking at me. Like the way my older brother did, seeing the whole but noticing the different parts. What was missing or what was new. But where his gaze homed in on problems, hers sought something else.

I squared my shoulders under her scrutiny.

"I'm going out tonight." My words tasted sour in my mouth, but if I stayed, I had the strongest sense that I'd kiss her. And kissing Ella then quitting Ella couldn't happen in the same sentence. "Enjoy your dinner. Don't forget the invitation we have tomorrow to Braithar."

Ella took a step back. "I won't." She ducked her head. "Have fun on your evening out."

Yeah, like that was a possibility, but I forced myself to walk away all the same.

7

TENSION

Ella

The piece of music finally came together half an hour before I had to get downstairs and leave for the lunch with Gordain's relatives. Composing went like this. I'd get the scent of a melody, a soaring riff or small arrangement of strings, and I'd be off on the hunt.

I'd slept maybe three hours last night, working out the end-to-end composition. It was sixteen minutes of an angry pursuit. A chase over ground, a fast and furious tremolo, with an ultimate loss of the quarry.

With care, I placed Suki back in the case and wiped my bow before storing that, too, mulling over where I'd pitch the piece, once I'd recorded it. It would suit a film score, as most of my more recent music did. Or maybe a computer game—a huge market for classical music.

Of the few compositions I'd sold to date, I'd only heard one used in the wild—the background to an indie movie.

In time, I wanted my music to be everywhere.

With a quick glance in the mirror, I checked my reflection—I'd showered, dressed, and styled my hair into long curls an hour ago. *Good enough.* I left my bedroom and took a heavy, steadying breath, my mood marred by the face I'd have to put on to see Gordain today.

He'd gone on a date last night, I was almost certain. Or a hook-up, at least. After what Ally had told me about Gordain's habits of going out at night, it was all I'd thought about.

At midnight, frustrated and high on playing, I'd gone downstairs for an energy-boosting snack. The place had been dark, no sign of him around. And after his stressful day, it wasn't a far reach to imagine what kind of night he needed.

I wished I'd had the mettle to kiss him, like I'd wanted to when he'd come to my room, but my inexperience bore out. There was no chance I'd be enough for him.

Gordain wore his sexuality like a mantle. A raw force that radiated off him as he moved. He was effortlessly beautiful and strong. The slightest raise of his chin, a glint in his eye, was enough to flood me with heat. His confidence and strength were addictive.

Even in his bad mood yesterday, he'd watched over me, directing me in the car, his focus split but never broken. He'd just found out that his dream career was destroyed and yet he'd cooked dinner for the household. Brought me my meal.

I hadn't even minded him snapping at me, after I'd gotten over myself. His temper showed me that he was alive and hurting.

Today, I vowed to play the friend and not get distracted by wanting him.

At the top of the stairs into the great hall, I spied him and paused. Gordain waited by the fire, his gaze lost in the flames. Then he turned and noticed me, the side of his mouth lifting in a smirk.

"Morning. Get some work done?" he asked.

"Aye, she did. All night long, baby." Ally appeared behind me, a girl at his side. I hadn't heard his door despite the fact his room was only just around the corner from mine. "Luckily, we were watching films until late, so it didn't keep us awake."

"Hey," I said to his friend. "I'm Ella."

"Kaylee." She tucked her fair hair behind her ear, a shy look on her face.

"G, game on!" Ally stooped and grabbed a basketball from where it had been sitting in the hallway.

He tossed the ball. It sailed through the open space, down towards the huge fireplace. Gordain plucked it from the air then bounced it twice on the flagstone floor, the sound echoing. He raised an eyebrow in challenge.

"This is on," Ally crowed and clattered down the stairs.

Head-to-head with his older brother, Ally grinned wickedly and dove for the basketball. Gordain backed away, circling until he could make a break across the hall.

I tried not to see his smooth moves, the neat twist of his hips that had him evading Ally again, the two of them chasing about the floor. He lifted the ball, his biceps sharpening and his focus on the opposite wall.

Good *God*, he was attractive.

There could only be one reason for his improved mood. I was *not* thinking about that.

Ally leaned in and whispered something, and Gordain smirked wider, whispering one word back. He feinted left, but his brother anticipated him and stole the ball. Kaylee, beside me on the landing, gasped and hung over the rail, her attention rapt.

Ally made a run and launched the ball at a protruding stone I'd never noticed high on the wall. "Boom!" he yelled as it hit home, and he raised his arms in a cheer.

Gordain applauded, a small glance up to the stairs telling me he'd let that win happen so Ally could impress his girlfriend.

Except his gaze lingered on me.

"Ally's so talented." Kaylee sighed.

"Ella, ye coming?" Gordain stopped at the bottom of the stairs.

I gave him a nod, totally cool and in control.

In my dreams.

Outside, a gentle sun warmed my skin. I held up my keys. "Ready for another ride?"

Gordain shook his head. "I have something else planned. Follow me." He walked backwards a few steps.

I trailed after him, puzzled. "It was sweet what you did for your brother, letting him win."

"Who said I let him win?" He took the corner of the castle.

I caught up. "But you did. I'm glad to see you're a little happier."

Gordain not having his sunny outlook was just wrong, so there was some small benefit to him getting... No! Not thinking about it.

We walked toward the garage, and I asked the question I'd been determined not to ask. "Have a good night last night?"

Gordain paused, midway through opening the side door. "Aye."

"Great." My stomach turned itself into one big knot, and I fought back the stupid, stupid jealousy that overtook me in a wave.

He'd slept with someone.

It had put a smile on his face like I never could.

I stepped after him, not paying attention to my surroundings, misery mixing with the sheer envy.

Then I blinked, because Gordain's motorcycle gleamed in front of me. He waited beside it, his hands on his hips.

"I spent the evening out here tuning up my bike. What did you think I'd been doing?" Humour lit his eyes.

He was teasing me? My lack of sleep had my emotions in a whirl. That was the only explanation I had for why I suddenly felt worse rather than better.

He'd been here the whole time I'd been hacking out an angry composition.

Not screwing some willing, experienced woman.

"Why didn't you?" My voice came out tiny.

"Why didn't I what?"

"You know what I'm talking about. Go out."

The humour left Gordain's expression, and he palmed the back of his neck. "Maybe because of the look on your face right now."

I stared at him.

He dragged in a breath. "Fine. Because of the look on *my* face right now."

My body had frozen up, and I gave my head a gentle shake, keeping my attention on him. A tender warmth emanated from his gaze, but there was longing there, too. Banked but fierce.

Tension stretched out between us. Tangible and warm.

"Okay," I said calmly, the only acknowledgement I could muster. I was so out of my depth. It had never bothered me before. Not when I'd only imagined kissing him. Now, my mind worked overtime. Last night, I'd pictured him fucking another woman. Resigned myself to it.

If I put myself into that picture, became the woman in his arms...I'd have no idea what to do.

"Okay," Gordain repeated back, the word quiet but the weight of his gaze pinning me to the spot. "We need to go if we're going to be on time. We can... We'll talk more later, aye?"

"Let's do this thing." I tilted my head at the bike.

Gordain wheeled it outside, and I carried the two helmets that sat on the workbench. He went back inside and emerged with his leather jacket.

He stood in front of me and, wordlessly, put it around my shoulders.

I slipped my arms inside, in a kind of trance, held by the power of the energy between us. We put our helmets on, and I secured mine under my chin. Then Gordain threw a leg over the big bike and looked back at me. I palmed his shoulder, climbing on behind.

Then I slid my arms around his waist, snug against him.

This felt so *right*.

"Hold on to me, Ella," he murmured, then the bike purred between my thighs.

And we were away.

Gordain drove us out of the McRae estate with care, avoiding potholes and going slow. This wasn't what I expected, not from a hot pilot. He should be gunning the engine and making me scream.

"I thought you'd try to impress me by going fast," I yelled to Gordain, pressing my fingers into his t-shirt so he knew I was saying something.

"Then the journey will be over quicker," he replied, turning his head so the sound of his voice carried. Then he reached back and took hold of my thigh, pulling me tight to him.

I grinned and rested the helmet on his broad back, then linked my fingers over his firm stomach. I didn't have the guts to slide a hand under his loose t-shirt. To touch his skin.

Maybe I could manage that on the way back. Because something huge had shifted between us, and I had to work out what it was.

* * *

*L*achlan and his wife were waiting outside Castle's Braithar's imposing entrance when we pulled up. Gordain brought the bike to a halt and helped me off. I dragged the helmet from my head, and he held out a hand for it, stowing it on the seat next to his.

"Guess all the effort I put into my hair was wasted." I ran my hands through my curls, shaking them out from where the helmet had flattened them.

"You look beautiful, like you always do," he said quietly, and I could only swallow my surprise as he took my hand in his and led me to meet his relatives.

He thought I was beautiful.

It took everything in me to summon my manners to get through the visit.

Over the meal, Marianne, Lachlan's wife, told stories of how Gordain had spent half of his childhood in their castle. I snuck glances at Gordain, imagining him as a boy, a sweet little grey-eyed child.

Then my heart ached, as how could anyone want to hurt him? From the comment Ally had made about his father being an abusive asshole, it made sense that Gordain used this place as a sanctuary, and the couple clearly doted on him. He was in the pictures on the sideboard, alongside two girls which I guessed were their daughters. More, he was at home here, his posture relaxed and his smile easy.

Marianne watched us both. Gordain had introduced me as his friend, but the woman had tipped him a wink, and it had him smiling. Whatever had been exchanged between them was presumably about me.

"Ella." Marianne pushed her glorious mane of red hair over one shoulder and turned her attention on me. "You said you were going to university in September. What will ye study?"

"Music theory." I took a sip of water.

"You're a musician?"

"I play violin, some piano. A little bit of most instruments."

She raised her eyebrows. "Impressive. Will you join an orchestra?"

"No. Though I chose a performing art college, which means I have to perform, but it has the best composition component with amazing tutors. That's my area of interest." The third part, musicology—the history and research part of my degree—sounded kind of dry, but it was necessary if I wanted good grounding for a career.

"You don't like performing," she said.

I sensed Gordain's gaze on me as I shook my head. "Not much. But it's a mandatory part of the whole. The main issue is that I'm not good enough—"

Gordain drew a sharp breath. "What? How can you say that?"

I gave him a grin. "It's okay, I'm an average performer because I didn't study the hours I should have. My school didn't allow it. Concert-level fiddlers train for hours a day from childhood. I'll never get to that standard but I can be good enough for what I want to do."

He looked outraged that I could be so casually dismissive about myself. Even if it was true.

"What career do ye want when you graduate?" Marianne asked.

"I write pieces and sell them. But my idea is to set up a company, eventually, and maybe write directly for studios. Film scores."

I bit my lip—I'd never told anyone, bar Taylor, about my dream. But Gordain's attention on me suddenly filled me with pride. He was impressed, I could tell.

Marianne leaned in. "You're already making money out of this?"

"A little, and I have an idea of how to do better, but I know next to nothing about business. I'll work on the idea while I'm at university, then give it a try."

"And wait three years suffering through the performance part of the course? Why not go for a term, see the extent of what you need to know, then hire the right people to teach you?"

I blinked at her. As much as I'd despised my school, I'd still turned up for my lessons and taken my exams. I'd seen it as my due. Maybe I hadn't been as rebellious as I thought. But university would be different—the students would be career-minded, and I'd be spreading my wings.

"I ask," she continued, "because I studied business management but quit when I knew enough to run my business. I'm self-employed, so the qualification didnae mean anything. Plus the other students were wee arseholes, only interested in getting drunk and screwing each other. It didn't help that I was a few years older, perhaps. Maybe you'll nae be so bothered."

"That might be part of the appeal," I joked, though it really wasn't.

Lachlan changed the subject, and I was glad. Marianne's view suddenly made my decision feel like another cage.

No. I'd chosen this. It was what I needed.

For pudding, we ate individual strawberry and cinnamon tortes made by Lachlan. The man was chief of the clan, and massive, so the idea of him creating the delicate pastries was an amusing one.

As I was taking my last delicious mouthful, Lachlan put his arms behind his head and addressed Gordain. "Ye ken old Mack is selling up."

Gordain put his fork down with a clink. "No. Why?"

"Retiring."

Gordain looked at me. "Do you remember I told you about my first flight? Mack runs the flight school at Inverness airport. It was him who took me up. And I borrowed the heli from him to fly to Belvedere."

To save me. He didn't say the last bit, and it felt like a secret between us.

After a beat, he turned his attention back to Lachlan. "Who'll take over?"

The older man shrugged. "So far, no one. Plans are that he'll run the final private pilot training course in a fortnight then close up shop."

"That's a travesty." Gordain shook his head. There was something in his expression, like he'd had an idea.

I made a mental note to ask him about it later.

"Ella." Marianne stood and placed her hands on the table. "Come, I'll give you a tour of Braithar."

Gordain and Lachlan walked behind us, talking about their friend while Marianne showed me the ground floor. Braithar was a beautiful place inside and out, with a spacious great hall made of stone and timber, gorgeous acoustics from the high ceiling, and a sweeping staircase leading to a wide balcony. Every room was light and airy.

It would make a wonderful recording space. An even better home.

Outside the front of the castle, our hosts hugged us both, telling us to come back on my next visit.

"And Gordain," Lachlan added as we climbed onto the bike. "Two years and ten months left, lad."

"Until what?" I asked, settling against his back, the sensation of being so close to him again heady.

"Didn't he tell you? Gordain has an option to buy my castle. One day, if he's lucky, he'll be the one showing you around, aye?"

Marianne and Lachlan waved, and Gordain drove me away. But on the bridge over the river, below Castle McRae, he pulled over, stopped the bike, and dragged off his helmet. His movements were jerky, and there was a fever in his eyes. His fingers found the fastening to my helmet, and he helped me remove it.

And I readied myself for whatever it was Gordain was about to do.

8

BEGGING FOR CRUMBS

*G*ordain

"I was found in a darkened room in a bar on the base," I said, my voice coming out in a rush and the gravel under my boots grinding where I forced myself to stand my ground. "There was a half-dressed woman draped over me, and it was her father, the wing commander, the most senior officer there, who walked in on us."

Ella scrunched up her nose, the excitement in her eyes dialling back.

"All of which is behaviour not becoming of an officer, especially not a young one who fought every step of the way for recognition of my strength of character and not my age. That's why they revoked my award of the search and rescue training."

Silence held between us, then, "I'm so sorry, G. You don't deserve that."

I was a dog begging for crumbs. I lapped up Ella's words, half afraid that she wouldn't give an opinion, seeing as I'd snapped at her yesterday.

She continued, her expression neutral, the light summer breeze playing with her hair. "Why is it such a big deal that you were hooking up? Why would they let you go because of that?"

"I wasn't hooking up with her." There was no way anyone would believe the next part, but I had to say it anyway. I desperately wanted Ella to accept what I was saying as true. "To this day, I have no memory of that part of the evening. I remember the training mission we went on in great detail, the fucking greenhouse the heli turned into in the hot sun, my pounding headache when I hit the bar, and the single, cold pint I drank. I didn't even finish it. The woman in question talked to me, and I walked away. Next thing I knew, I was in the middle of that scene."

Horribly exposed, I braced myself against the low stone wall of the bridge and stared up at the sky.

"Then that wasn't your fault."

I glanced down, and Ella bit her lip, her cheeks pink again.

"You fought it, right?"

"I did. I assumed it would go away."

"But it hasn't."

"And it won't."

Understanding dawned in her gaze. She raised a finger. "Answer me this: Do you want to stay in the military?"

I squinted at her. "It's been my life for six years. I started out at sixteen. Callum had to sign my papers—he was my legal guardian after Da died. The RAF invested so much in me..." And yet they were turning their back on me.

"Would you stay if you couldn't fly helicopters?" she pressed.

"Not for a second." Was that true? Christ, it was.

Ella brushed her hair from her eyes. "Isn't that the

answer? You're sure they're going to kick you off the course, then fuck them. Quit. Take the training course Lachlan talked about. Fly private helicopters. Take back control."

"You don't miss a thing, do you?"

"I could see you thinking something over. That was my guess."

It was a real option, as I could let my RAF contract expire. Jump before they pushed. But the wrench of saying goodbye to my military career cut deep, even merely considering it. I swung around and walked a few steps away, my hands linked behind my head.

Accepting this made me a failure.

Nothing like the man I was supposed to be.

"Gordain?"

"God knows what you must think of me right now," I said as I turned back, but then I stopped because she wasn't looking at me like I'd let her down.

Her gaze held hunger, alongside care and all the fucking things I wanted to see when her eyes were on mine.

"Don't assume anything. And don't walk away."

"Tell me what you're thinking," I urged, my muscles going rigid where I clamped down the impulse to grab her.

"That there's a pull between us and it's only getting stronger."

I stood there like a fool. "Yeah?"

"And I really want to kiss you. Or for you to kiss me. Either's good."

An engine sounded behind me, then a car horn blared. I leapt forward and grabbed Ella, pushing her against the bridge wall.

A familiar beat-up old Land Rover careened down the road then stopped alongside us. Ally, alone in the car, heading in the direction of home. "What are you doing here? Did you break down a hundred yards from the door? Ooh!" He waggled his eyebrows, his elbow resting on the open window. "Is this a lover's tryst?"

"Shut up, Alasdair," I grumbled, releasing Ella.

"Your secret's safe with me. But Els? James is trying to get hold of you. He texted me to see if I was with you. Maybe you should give him a call."

"Oh! I haven't checked my phone for hours." She patted her pockets. "I must have left it in my room."

"Let's get back," I said, my mind scrambled but the interruption definitely unwelcome.

Inside a minute, I dropped Ella at the front of the castle, my smirking brother too close for us to continue our...conversation.

One thing was for sure, I'd do anything Ella Fitzroy wanted. She'd asked me for a kiss. It would be rude not to deliver.

9

AT EACH OTHER

Ella

A smirking Ally hovered in my bedroom doorway, his eyes dancing with delight. "Did ye kiss my brother?"

"No comment."

"But ye did."

"Go away." I forced back my smile and found my phone on the heavy old dresser. On screen waited an email from the lawyers and two missed calls from my brother, no voicemails. I caught the gist of the email as I dismissed it—confirmation that my university fees had been paid—then dialled James's number. I turned my back to Ally, an eyebrow arched.

I was only partially mad at him for the interruption; I still wanted that kiss.

"I'm bored now and need someone to talk to," Ally said.

The call connected but went straight to voicemail, asking me to record a message. I hung up, tapping out a quick text to say I'd try him again later. Other than telling me they'd landed safely, he hadn't been in contact.

"What happened to Kaylee?"

He shrugged. "One-night stand. Well, a day and a night."

"You're not going to see her again?"

Ally gave a dramatic shudder and brushed his arms off. "No! She's a sweetheart, but I'm starting as I mean to go on, like my brother. Play the field, learn my skills." He lifted his hands above his head and raised his shoulders to an imaginary beat.

Way more than I needed to know. "Poor girl." Then something he said suddenly leapt out at me. "Do you mean Gordain?"

"What?"

"The brother who's the hit-it-and-quit-it guy?" I already knew the answer but asked anyway.

Ally frowned and stopped his ridiculous dance moves. "Yeah." Then his eyes widened. "But he's never been serious about anyone before," he added in a rush. "I didn't mean—"

"Ah, stop, I don't care. It's not like I want anything serious." I gave my own pretend shudder. Gordain and I weren't even a thing; there was nothing more to it than mutual, temporary attraction.

Ally's gaze gentled. "So you were at each other earlier."

I trusted Ally. Despite playing the fool ninety-nine percent of the time, he had a good heart. Suddenly, I didn't want him to see me as pathetic.

"I was about to kiss him. Or him me, so yes. But I'll be going to uni soon and catching up with the rest of the human race in screwing around."

"Gordain is your practice man? Does he know that?"

"Did Kaylee?" I shot back, irritated by a niggling feeling that, though nothing had happened, I was doing something wrong by Gordain.

Ally peered at me. "I was upfront. You should be, too."

With that, he turned on his heel and left me to mull over his words.

* * *

Ten minutes later, and I'd crossed the great hall and entered the narrow passageway at the back right-hand corner. It came out at a set of spiral steps, and I climbed them, my heart thudding. Then I stood outside the door to Gordain's rooms and dragged in a breath.

"Here goes nothing," I said to myself, raised a hand and knocked.

"Come in," he yelled over the music playing.

I pushed the door, slipped through, then leaned back to close it with a thud.

"Ally?" Gordain called again, his voice coming from a room adjacent to me in the little hallway.

"Guess again," I replied.

The music stopped, and a door opened. Gordain appeared in the frame, backlit by a bright light and with shower mist settling around his bare feet. He fastened a white towel around his waist. Otherwise, he was gloriously naked.

Water ran down his inked skin. My mouth dropped open.

Neither of us spoke.

A heavy tension grew. Gordain rolled his shoulders, a barely perceptible move, and his gaze took me in.

"Want me to put a shirt on this time?" he asked, his voice low, almost taunting.

"Don't you dare." I gathered my courage and took a

couple of steps until I stood before him. My hand shook, but still I reached out and pressed a fingertip to the tattoo of flight wings on his right pectoral muscle. "Which was your first?"

Gordain blinked, closing his eyes for a long second. Then he took my hand and moved my finger to his biceps to trace over an image of two stags. "This one. I got it when I was sixteen. The McRae coat of arms."

"Ours has a lion," I murmured.

He gave a short laugh. "Makes sense. Fitzroys and bravery go together. I've learned that much."

Except I wasn't feeling very brave. More young and foolish. Even so, I couldn't deny the force of attraction that pulled me into this man's orbit.

Taking his hand with me, I drew my finger through the water drops that clung to his collarbone. My breathing came short, and heat flushed my cheeks. Every muscle of his beautiful body was honed and hard. Each drawing on his skin skilfully done, all in black or a dark blue. I mapped a compass, then a swirling pattern like the rotors of a helicopter in motion.

He let me explore, his body taut where he held himself still.

I flattened my palm over the bare patch of skin right above his heart. "Nothing here?"

"Not yet. Never had anything so close to my heart that I needed to make it permanent."

Gordain released my hand and took my upper arm gently in his grip. I finally raised my gaze to his face. His eyes flared, their ferocity burning into mine.

Oh boy.

"Can I ask a dumb question?" I said.

He lifted his chin once.

"You're single?"

"Aye."

We were close. Very close.

"And you're never serious about relationships?" Because I had to be sure. I couldn't set myself up for a fall if I knew how this would go from the first.

"Never had anyone I wanted to be serious about," he replied.

"Okay." I chewed my lip, no idea how to take this to the next step despite him being right there, his mouth inches from mine.

"Any more questions?"

"N—" I said but before I even finished my *no*, Gordain pulled me in by the waist, and his mouth landed on mine.

Oh *God*.

Instinct had my eyelids shuttering. My entire focus became the warmth of his lips moving over mine. It took a second for my senses to fully awaken, but then a small gasp escaped me, and my blood surged. I kissed him back, urgently, holding on to his biceps for dear life.

Our mouths fused.

I wanted to be good at this. I was so, so out of my depth.

Still, it was the hottest thing that had ever happened to me.

"Ella," Gordain murmured.

He pulled his head back, and I opened my heavy eyelids to find him staring at my lips, intensity in his gaze. He brought his hand to cup my chin and laid a soft kiss on my cheek. One on the corner of my mouth.

A self-confident smirk crept onto his face. "Is this what you imagined?"

Torture, or torment. Oh, so gentle. "Uh-huh," I managed.

"Good." Then he kissed me again, harder.

This time, I opened my mouth under his. A quick study.

Ours tongues touched, and Gordain made a sound of pure, masculine hunger. His careful control evaporated. Urging me to take a step back, Gordain pressed his body firm against mine until my shoulders hit the wall. I parted my legs around his knee, and he pinned me to the stone. His thigh wedged between mine, right at the juncture of my legs. All the while our tongues slid together, him leading, me following.

In the past, when I'd dreamed about this, I hadn't guessed at the wave of heat, the heightening of every sense, the surge of my blood. I fucking trembled under his kiss.

I wanted to claw at him. Drag him closer still.

Reading my mind, Gordain hoisted me, somehow keeping the towel around his waist. I wrapped my legs about his middle and circled his bare shoulders with my arms. His hands gripped my backside. He hauled in a breath, his gaze hazy. Then he blinked, as if he realised who I was and what we were doing.

No way. This wasn't about to stop.

I drew my fingers over his buzzed-short hair and tilted his head up. Now it was my turn to take what I wanted. I pressed a soft kiss to his top lip. His light stubble scratched my skin.

I liked the roughness of it. The manliness of every inch of him. His hard dick—what a surprise that was—pressing against my core. I was dizzy with want.

My second peck had him growling then plundering my mouth once more.

If I could shut off my brain, I'd happily let Gordain carry me to his bedroom, lay me out, and thrust inside me. My body needed it, craved the release.

But the rest of me wasn't ready.

I'd chosen a man who I knew wouldn't push me beyond where I wanted to go. For now, I was content in our hungry kisses. In learning how his body felt.

All the while, I was so, so aware of the gulf of experience between us. From the noises he made, and how hard he was, something was working for him. Or maybe he was just horny and this was how guys could be.

Except there was no way I could be good at this.

And my fingers were calloused from my violin.

Was that a turn off? It couldn't be sexy.

My cruel insecurity had me lose my beat, and the kiss turned sloppy. I pulled away and hid my face in his neck, all of a sudden embarrassed, tripping myself up with my thoughts.

"What's wrong?" Gordain asked. He nuzzled my cheek, trying to get me to look at him.

"I'm just… I wish I was better at this," I said into his skin.

"Are you crazy?"

"No. I've only ever kissed one boy before. And he told me I was terrible." It had been on one of the rare trips Taylor and I took into the village near our school. She'd flirted with a boy, and I'd tried and failed at my first kiss with one of his friends.

"Ella, look at me."

I did, peeking into his gorgeous eyes. Dove grey now. His eyelids were low, his gaze hot. He rolled his hips, rigid against me. "Can't you tell how much I'm enjoying your kiss?"

His compliment brought a smile back to my face, though I still felt awkward.

"That boy was an idiot," Gordain continued. He kissed my neck.

"I'll get better. Maybe after I've been at university and had some practice, I won't be so hopeless."

"You don't need to get better—" Gordain halted midway through his sentence. A flash of emotion crossed his features, and he closed his mouth.

It looked like hurt, his fleeting reaction.

From somewhere in his apartment, a buzzing sounded.

"What's that?" I asked.

The buzzing came again, and Gordain lifted his head. He blinked, and his features hardened.

"My emergency radio. Need to put you down, lass. Keep your eyes up in case I lose the towel."

I complied, instantly missing the closeness.

Kissing Gordain McRae was the stuff dreams were made of. Unimaginably erotic. Teasing and satisfying in equal measures. More than enough for this sheltered girl.

For now, at least.

Gordain reinstated his towel and stepped into the snug lounge. From a shelf stacked with books and DVDs, he collected a tall black radio with an aerial. I'd seen it elsewhere in the castle but never thought to ask what it was.

"Mountain rescue. I'm on duty when I'm home," he said, frowning as he pressed a button. "Gordain McRae."

A voice barked back, asking him to confirm his availability and location. He did, his body held tense.

"One adult male, one adult female, one confirmed injury. Evacuation procedure. Ben Crathie. Pick up en route."

Gordain answered then signed off and brought his gaze to mine, all action in his moves, no hurt now, just solid edges. "I need to go. I'm sorry."

I followed him into the hall then waited outside his bedroom, giving him privacy while he dressed. The devil in me wanted to sneak a peek at him, but our moment was over.

Besides, I was sure I'd ruined it.

Gordain exited his room, dragging a waterproof jacket over a long-sleeved sweatshirt. He was in the zone, ready to go.

"I don't know how long I'll be out. The mountain we've been called to can be tricky."

"Be careful." I wrapped my arms around myself, shuffling out of his way.

He grabbed his phone and the radio from the den then returned to me. "We'll talk tonight."

Talk? That didn't sound good. "I'm sorry I made that weird. Just look after yourself out there."

"You didn't make anything weird, Ella. I did." Gordain shook his head and strode away. "See you later."

Then he was gone, his bootsteps drumming down the stairs, away from me.

* * *

Ally joined me in the kitchen, hours after Gordain had left. I'd made chicken pasta—one of the few dishes I knew how to cook—guessing that Gordain would be likely exhausted and in need of feeding when he got back.

Except he'd been so long already. Worry dogged me.

The younger McRae took a bowl and ladled himself out a huge portion of the meal.

"Smells amazing," he said, spooning it into his mouth. He sat at the kitchen island and seized the tub of freshly grated cheese, dumping a handful on top of his food. "Who knew you could cook? You can stay."

I couldn't raise a smile. "Ally, what normally happens on a mountain rescue?"

Ally slowed his chewing. "You mean what does my brother normally do? He's in the back of the heli. He's not licenced to fly the rescue helicopter yet so he goes out on the winch to pluck people who are stupid enough to get stuck up in the mountains."

The kitchen had grown dark as the evening drew in, and I flipped on the counter lights. It should've made a cosy glow, but it only reminded me that Gordain was out there risking himself in the failing light. I drummed my fingers and glanced at the round clock for the fiftieth time.

"Are you worried?" Ally cocked his head to one side. "I thought you weren't that into him, he was just a practice guy."

"He's still my friend." And my brother's best friend, at that. "Shouldn't you be worried, too? He could get hurt."

"I'm kidding." He pushed his bowl back and clambered off the chair. Then, with surprising tenderness, he gave me a side-hug. "Gordain's been to a war zone, ye ken. They packed him off for a tour when he started his pilot training. I spent months waiting for a phone call to tell us he'd been shot down."

"But the call never came," I decided, blowing out a breath.

Ally shook his head. "Wrong. It did. His Chinook got shot out of the sky. We only found out about it after he'd been rescued, but it gave us all nightmares for weeks."

God! "Was he hurt?"

"No. The pilot managed to land on a slope and slide it to the bottom. We're not meant to know the mission details, but they all survived to be rescued. Gordain was copilot. He knows his stuff."

He ruffled my hair and sat back in his seat, commencing his assault on the food once more. "That couldn't hurt him, and this won't either. We're mountain men." He puffed out his chest. "Even if Gordain lost the heli, he'd know how to find his way to civilisation again."

His words didn't help my worries.

All I could do was wait.

10

MOUNTAIN RESCUE

*G*ordain

A fierce gust of wind battled against me, channelled by the ravine, and I swung out wildly on the winch cable, still meters from the ground but nearing the rocky shelf that was my target. The heli pilot was an arrogant moron, and I was in trouble being on the wrong end of his inexperience.

But beggars couldn't be choosers in the mountain rescue team—we were all volunteers, and I had no right to complain. It only cemented my own failures—had I started my rotary training, I'd have been qualified to fly the RAF's team in no time. Instead, I was just one among the civilian personnel.

Below, the woman we'd come to rescue huddled at the back of the cliff, barely visible in her black coat and dark jeans. In the failing light, I was lucky to have spotted her, waving her phone's torch around on the mountainside. We'd already picked up her boyfriend and taken him to a waiting ambulance. His twisted ankle had stopped their hike, and I'd had to bite back my advice.

They had no map, no water, flat shoes, and dark clothes. And they'd separated. All no-nos for hiking in the Cairngorms.

Even Ella had known not to jog an unfamiliar track in the fog. She had more sense at eighteen than this pair of thirtysomething hill walkers put together.

Another gust drove me towards the rocks, and I gestured an impatient instruction to the heli, the rotor noise making radio contact impossible. The pilot had me too close to the cliff.

I swung again, dropping several feet, this time crashing into a granite overhang. My upper arm took the brunt of the impact, and my head rang from the ding to the helmet.

Fucking ouch.

I groaned out my frustration, adjusting my cable now I was on the shelf, and carried out the rescue as efficiently as possible. It wasn't badly hurt, but my arm ached, particularly when the woman shrieked and clutched me as we winched skyward.

In the helicopter, I checked her over again, but her worst complaint was dehydration from her hours stuck in the dark crevice. She'd be fine with water and rest, so we strapped in and headed off the mountain.

The manoeuvre, on my part, was textbook, even if my mind was half occupied with the kiss that had rocked my world just a few hours before.

One part of it ran over and over in my thoughts. Ella thought her lack of experience a problem—it wasn't. She was gorgeous and smart, and I didn't want anything more than she was willing to give.

But she'd set the scene, specifically making sure I wasn't after anything permanent.

I could've kicked myself for my answer.

What if I'd told Ella the real thoughts I'd had? That although there were good reasons why we shouldn't be together, I wanted to ignore them.

None of it made sense, but it wasn't like I was getting on my knees and proposing, so why shouldn't we see if there was more to that kiss?

One thing was for sure, I'd misled her when I'd said I'd never wanted more with anyone. Maybe, for the first time, I did.

11

KISSING LESSON

*E*lla

By eleven, there was still no sign of Gordain. No news and no letup from my gnawing fear. I paced in front of the great hall's fire, keeping the flames burning with fresh logs. Ally had sent Gordain a message, but there had been no response. He sat in the opposite seat, making occasional conversation, but my anxiety seemed to have infected him, too.

I went over mine and Gordain's last conversation, and our kiss. I wanted more of it, that was for sure. I wanted more of Gordain full stop. But it was a weird feeling. Hadn't I declared to myself that I didn't want a boyfriend? Not at age eighteen and with zero real world experience.

Richard used to have a name for me—*the girl*. He rarely used my name, and if he did it was Elinor and not Ella, but most times he'd overlook me and talk to whoever I was with. My headmistress or a tutor. *What are you doing about the girl? How much is it going to cost for the girl?*

It made me feel, even at sixteen or seventeen, like I was

an infant, not a fully fledged person with ideas and thoughts of my own. I'd had no decision-making power, and I was never, ever consulted. Even now, with my uncle still able to access my finances, I felt like I was being second-guessed at every stage. I'd heard nothing from him since James kicked him out, but that couldn't last.

My phone dinged in my hand, and I snapped it up to stare at the screen. An email.

I sighed, shaking my head at Ally whose gaze had also whipped up, and resumed my pacing. He went back to his own device.

Then I looked at my screen again, registering the sender's name. *R. Fitzroy.*

My skin crawled. I opened the message from my uncle.

Elinor.

This morning, I received notification of your university tuition fees. I have approved them, though your choice of degree is frivolous. I trust you will appreciate this goodwill, as you must know how little you deserve my attention. In due course, I will be in touch, and you will return the favour.

Yours, R. Fitzroy

I read it again, cold in my veins and anger bubbling from his tone. From his fucking expectation that he still had the right to talk to me. That I owed him anything.

Why the hell had the lawyers contacted him? I swallowed my outrage, knowing that they had no choice, but even so.

"Everything okay?" Ally asked.

"It's nothing." I deleted the email and slid my phone into my pocket.

I couldn't handle my uncle if even thinking about him had me nauseated. Or chilled with fright. No, I hadn't changed at all in the months I'd been free. And until I could tackle that man, I never would.

Which made thoughts of Gordain easier.

I forced the two halves of my feelings into two separate boxes.

The first—full-on sexual desire for Gordain. Temporary, probably. Perhaps in response to my...self-service problem. It couldn't be more, or if it was, I couldn't trust it. I didn't know myself at all. Too much had changed recently, and I was still responding to it.

The second—caring about him as a friend. He'd always be in my brother's life, so I would have him around. I wanted that so much.

An engine roared outside, and my heart sped. Ally leapt to his feet and strode to the door. He opened it and peered out into the pitch-black night.

"It's him," he said, a grin lighting up his face. He gazed for a second, his shoulders sagging, then he made for the stairs. "I'll let ye greet him in private. I'm going to bed."

Ally vanished. I twisted on the spot, frozen as Gordain appeared in the doorway. He shot the bolts of the heavy castle door then turned, and spotted me by the fire, alone now in the dark.

"You waited up for me?" he said. His jacket was torn, and he held his left arm gingerly, like it hurt.

I opened my mouth, but nothing came out.

We stared at one another, and my pulse thrummed in my ears, tension building.

"Fuck it," Gordain muttered, and he strode over.

I met him with willing arms, my lips warm on his cold ones. We pulled one another in and, though I was careful with him, he was anything but with me.

Gordain banded me to him, the smell of the outdoors clinging to his skin. All other thoughts rushed from my head.

"I worried," I said against his mouth.

Gordain pulled back, gazing at me. "Really?"

"I thought something terrible had happened. Are you injured?" I ran my hand lightly up his arm, over the thin sweater.

Gordain shivered, rolling his shoulders back. "It's nothing. I got battered by the rocks on the second rescue. I'm braw."

I drew a deep breath. "Shower and shoulder repair first, or food?" Then I held up a hand. "Actually, go on up. I'll bring you your food, then take a look at you."

Gordain gazed down at me, his head tilted. "All the time I was out, I had one thing on my mind."

"Oh yeah?" I didn't get a chance to ask more because he swooped back in and stole another kiss. One that left me breathless.

"Hurry up and follow me upstairs," he said, his voice low.

I'd never heated pasta so fast in my life.

In Gordain's snug living room, I placed his bowl of food on the coffee table then clicked on a lamp. Noises came of him moving between his bathroom and bedroom, then, after a minute, he appeared, dressed in a t-shirt and shorts.

He made a beeline for the food, dropping down on the couch next to me. He ate, and I tucked my legs underneath me and shuffled to face him.

"You are an excellent chef," he said, halfway through the meal.

"How do you know Ally didn't make it?"

Gordain gave me a look and set his bowl aside. He took a quick drink of the water I'd brought, replaced the glass, then, without pause, dragged me onto his lap.

One hand wedged into my hair, and the other gripped my waist. Gordain made a hungry sound and laid a kiss on my throat.

Oh *God*.

"I'm meant to be checking over your arm," I said, twisting to give him better access.

"Then check. I'm not stopping you." His next kiss landed higher, just below my ear. "But while you do it, tell me about the arsehole who ye kissed last."

"That's bothering you?"

"Aye."

I rolled up his t-shirt sleeve, trying to concentrate while Gordain continued his distraction technique.

"He was just a boy I barely knew. It was my first kiss, and a bad one."

In the dim lamplight, a red-and-black bruise spread over his shoulder. There were no cuts that I could see, but it must hurt.

I sucked in a breath. "We should put something on that."

He made a sound of disagreement. "Kiss me again. I won't remember my own name, let alone that wee dent."

I brought my gaze to meet his, suddenly unsure again. I was on his lap, and he wanted me to lead. Should I...move?

"That first kiss," Gordain murmured. "It was also your only kiss, aye?"

I gave a self-depreciating grumble.

"Then practice some more on me." With one finger, he lifted my chin. "Don't overthink it. Your kiss sends me wild. Try it again. That's all we're going to do, so take your time and make it good."

I swallowed and braced myself against his chest. Then I touched his cheek, tracing over his rough stubble.

"Want me to shave first?" he asked, his voice quieter.

"No. Why do you cut your hair so short?" I asked. It was only slightly longer than his scruff.

He shrugged his good shoulder. "I got into the habit in the RAF."

I wanted to ask more questions, but I was procrastinating. So I dipped forward and pressed my lips onto his.

Gordain took a sharp inhale but held his head still, giving me control. His hands found my hips and settled, not grasping me or grinding me onto him, just gently letting me explore.

We sat in the cosy dark and let our mouths become acquainted.

I grew bolder. Tentatively, I nudged his head back to give me a better angle, and I licked his lips. Gordain moved with me and opened his mouth. Our tongues met, and I jerked, the shock of how utterly sexual this was new and electric.

I went back for more.

The kiss turned hot and wet, and I learned just how much Gordain liked me stroking his tongue with mine.

"Christ, Ella," he said, low and rough, but still he restrained himself, letting me set the pace.

Beneath me, he grew hard, only his shorts and my soft leggings between us.

My confidence skyrocketed along with my pulse, and I shifted ever so slightly so I could rub the persistent ache between my legs on his hardness.

Gordain gave a strangled noise of pleasure.

"Is this okay?" I asked.

"Aye, lass. Work yourself on me. However ye want me, I'm yours."

I should've felt self-conscious again, but Gordain's encouragement gave me a fresh wave of pleasure that had me dragging in a breath. "I haven't been able to... I mean, for months..."

He stilled. "Ella?"

"Yeah?"

"Do you want to come?"

So much it hurt. With my face burning, I gave a tiny nod, and Gordain grinned wickedly.

"Then let me help ye out."

He stood, lifted me with ease, then laid me on my back on the couch and fitted himself between my legs. His mouth met mine once more, but it was his cock that had my full attention. He lodged himself right up against my clit and, with a sweeping kiss, he rolled his hips, pressing in just the right spot.

Oh God!

I squeaked, getting more pleasure from the base of his cock through two layers of clothes than my own hand and multiple tries.

He moved his hips in steady motions. Holding himself over me, he kissed and grinded on me with exacting pressure.

"Don't stop," I whispered.

Gordain didn't let up. Faster and faster. Driving me insane with lust and blooming pleasure across my body. My nipples hardened, desperate for touch, and my insides clenched, empty. I wound up, tight, tighter, like a spring.

"Ohhh." I broke the kiss, arching my neck and screwing my eyes closed.

Gordain upped his assault, his lips on my neck, nipping lightly with his teeth. The effect was so overwhelmingly erotic, I lost my mind, blown away with sensation.

"Gordain!" I yelped as if warning him of the precipice I was hanging over.

"Let go, Ella," he commanded and thrust again and again.

I exploded.

Waves of pleasure spiralled through me, and I gasped, dragging him down into my arms. My body pulsed, bright lights shimmered behind my eyelids, and I clutched him, rigid as I saw out the aftershocks.

"Thank God, at last." I groaned, my head spinning.

I opened my eyes, expecting a smug grin. But if anything, Gordain looked wild.

"Your shoulder!" I released my hand from where I'd clamped him to me. I'd held on to him hard.

"What shoulder?" Gordain didn't budge. Instead, he took my mouth in a blistering kiss. Then he leapt up and strode out of the room. "Be right back. Don't move," he called before the bathroom door slammed.

I lay still, my bones melted from the spectacular orgasm. If Gordain could do that without us even taking our clothes off, what could he do in a bed with no restraint?

I could hardly imagine.

More the point, what was he doing in the bathroom?

After a minute, he returned. He sat and pulled my legs onto his lap then grabbed up his bowl, finishing the last forkfuls of pasta, his movements buoyant and an infectious smile tweaking his lips.

"Did you just..." I gestured with my head to the door. "I could've..." Except I wouldn't have a clue how to touch him, let alone do it well. At least now, I wasn't embarrassed about learning on him.

He lifted his chin. "This was about you, not me. But

there was no chance I was getting to sleep next to ye tonight without taking the pressure off."

Fresh heat spread through me at the thought of him touching himself. "I'm sleeping with you tonight?"

"Aye. Unless you don't want to."

I did. The nasty taste Richard's email had given me returned, and I craved the safety of Gordain's arms. I gave him a minute nod.

Gordain stood and collected me in his arms and carried me into the hall. In his bedroom, he laid me out on the bed and grabbed a t-shirt from a drawer, handing it to me. Then he gave me a minute to change before he returned and climbed into his big, comfortable bed next to me. Gordain killed the light, dragged me onto him, and laid a soft kiss on my hair.

We settled together in the dark, just our breathing filling the space.

A year ago, I couldn't have imagined this—being in bed with a man I'd fantasised over. Weirder still, how well we fitted.

"Stop overthinking things, Ella," Gordain mumbled. "We're just sleeping."

So I slept.

* * *

I woke hot, my thigh over Gordain's and my head on his uninjured shoulder.

Gordain slept on, his breathing even and deep. He was an early riser, so I could only imagine how exhausted he must have been when he'd got home last night. Still, he took care of me, with his skilled body and his swoonworthy kissing lesson.

With care, I slid to the side. Gordain's bedroom, like his lounge, had little slit windows, with glass but no curtains, so there was just enough of the early morning light to see his sleeping form. I took my fill, memorising his handsome face, his rugged jaw, and teasing mouth.

"You staring at me?" He stretched both arms over his head before bringing them back to encircle me.

"I was."

"Like what you see?" In a flash, Gordain rolled on top of me and gazed into my eyes.

I held my breath. The two boxes I'd put him into weren't so clear-cut in the light of day.

He pulled back an inch, registering my expression, confusion replacing the contentment on his face.

Someone hammered on the door.

"Wake up! Everyone's on their way back!" Ally yelled. "You've got fifteen minutes until they're here."

"Oh shit!" I shoved Gordain off me and leapt from his bed. The morning chill nipped my ankles. I sought my clothes.

Gordain rose to rest on his elbow. He drew his eyebrows in and glanced between me and the door, no urgency in his moves.

Then I paused, because there was nothing wrong in me being in his room, not that I'd share the details with anyone.

"Not sure why I'm rushing," I said. "Ally startled me."

Gordain sighed. "Here." He leaned and grabbed a blue hoodie from the chair. "It'll be chilly in the castle as ye flee to your room."

"Thanks." I pulled it on then made for the door. I gave him one last glance.

Gordain only watched me, his posture rigid and his eyes dark.

I left him there, regret stinging me, and I had no idea why.

* * *

*A*fter a quick shower and a change of clothes, I returned downstairs to the great hall. Noise rose to the rafters from the twins reuniting, and two of Callum's estate workers, burly men I'd seen around the grounds, talked to the laird about pressing business. I couldn't see my brother or Beth. Gordain stood at the edge, and his gaze found mine. I offered him a small smile. It bounced off his indecipherable expression.

Then Mathilda said my name, pulling my attention away. "Ella. I need to talk to you."

She directed me to the den and closed us in.

"Where's my brother?" I asked. "Why did you all come back so soon?"

The woman twisted her mouth, and it was only then I registered the pain in her eyes. "Beth is unwell. She took ill at the hotel on our first evening."

I clasped my hands to my mouth. "Is she okay? Is the baby okay?"

"She's in hospital in Manchester with your brother. We rushed home. The baby's fine. No need to panic." She closed her mouth and opened it again, deep concern apparent in her pause. Mathilda's hands travelled to her belly.

A rush of fear swamped me.

"Can I call my brother? Do you think that would be okay?" My hand shook and I extracted my phone.

"Of course. He'll be waiting for your call. He tried you a couple of times. He reminded me that you have your driving test later. After that, Callum and I will see you home."

I thanked her and dialled James. He answered on the first ring. Mathilda left the room, giving me privacy.

"Ella, I'm sorry, I should have sent a text."

"Don't be ridiculous! Tell me everything." I hated it, the formality between us, the distance Richard had created, straining mine and James's relationship. If for a minute I'd considered telling my brother about the contact I'd had from our uncle, the thought now left my head. He didn't need more stress.

James gave me a brief rundown of how Beth's morning sickness had worsened significantly, to the point she couldn't eat or drink anything. My brother had panicked and called out a doctor who'd advised that she should come home with a drip in her arm and a nurse to care for her. Not that James would leave her side.

"She's going to be okay," he said, strain apparent in his voice. "It's just an extreme form of morning sickness. But she was just so ill and weak... I was beside myself. With what happened to Mum and Dad..."

He stopped, and my heart gave a thump. Our parents' deaths might have been a decade ago, but that didn't diminish the loss.

"I'm so sorry," I replied. "I'll come home."

"We should be back tonight. The doctors are just making sure she's okay," he said. "Oh, and Ella, call Howard Marks. We found out more before Beth got sick, but he's better placed to tell you than I am."

I made a promise to do so, and we hung up.

I called the lawyer on autopilot, not really thinking about whether this was the best time to hear any news.

"Lady Elinor Fitzroy," Howard greeted me.

"Just Ella, please," I mumbled, my mind far away.

Howard gave me an update on the latest they'd found

out on Richard's investments. The evidence James sought had been there, so at least the trip had some small benefit.

"Are we going to take him to court?" I asked. How much pressure would that add to my brother?

"That is in motion, and Richard's businesses will be frozen in due course. But there's also the matter of your guardianship."

I perked up. The order that gave my uncle control of my money for years longer was my greatest source of anxiety. "Please say you've cut him off."

"No," the lawyer said, his tone apologetic. "But we have put forward papers to have the order made over to your brother. It's complicated and is likely to take many months—"

"What else can we do?" I interrupted. I didn't want James to be bothered by me, to have to manage my affairs. I wanted independence for everyone's sake. "There has to be another way."

"The only immediate route is for you to be married. It would give you legal majority by way of a loophole in the guardianship order. These things are antiquated by nature and therefore make the assumption your husband would become your guardian." Howard dropped the words like a bomb.

He'd briefly mentioned the idea in a conversation just after James had inherited, but I had dismissed it right away.

"But I don't want to get married. I don't even have a boyfriend."

The man grumbled and puffed on the other end of the line. "I cannot advise you to break the law, but if you were to consider a temporary arrangement... Without telling me the fact, of course. That would meet the criteria."

I blinked, my mouth open.

A temporary marriage which would get Richard off my back. Which would take the burden of looking after me off my brother. Which would enable me to be independent of my asshole of an uncle.

"Tell me more."

12

CUT IN TWO

*G*ordain

Ella had been a long time alone in the den. I stood across the hall and waited, only half listening to my brother receive a briefing from his estate workers.

"Gordain." Callum summoned my attention back. The men had left.

"Aye, sorry. What?"

"Angus couldn't complete the cabling work as the parts hadn't been left for him."

I racked my brain. Callum had given me two instructions, and I'd carried both out. Then I remembered a last-second comment he'd sent my way. Fuck it. I'd been too lost in Ella to remember everything. How unlike me. What a screw-up.

"You asked me to run to the DIY store. I didn't do it."

"Ye didn't. It doesnae matter."

Good thing he was the laird and I was not.

"No. I'm sorry. That's entirely my fault."

Callum looked between me and the den door. Then his

gaze narrowed. "Mathilda and I will be seeing wee Ella home this afternoon."

"Right. Or I can do it."

"Aye, ye could." His gaze turned shrewder still. "What about after that? I have work to plan and I'll either include you or I won't."

Callum was hedging the question of what was happening with my job. It wasn't like him to be indirect. It was time I told him.

"I'm going to leave the RAF." The words fell from my mouth. I stood in the great hall, my brother's castle, almost on the very spot where six years ago I'd told him I was signing up, and watched my life fall apart.

"That must have been a hard decision." Callum hesitated, stuck, perhaps, between giving me the arsekicking I needed and being a good older brother. "What will ye do instead?"

"Private pilot training. I'll fly civilian. I'll probably have to leave the Highlands for a while." Ella had been right—the course Mack offered was a good choice for me now, but the jobs in that area were mainly in England, serving the bigger cities.

I was being cut in two.

"And the lass?"

There was no one in hearing range, Mathilda being busy with the twins, but I shot a fierce gaze at Callum. He knew me too well. Understood my staring at the den door too well.

"She'll go home and to university. That's all there is to it."

"Aye." My older brother inclined his head, his bafflement and frustration now clear. "Then it's best if ye dinna see her home."

That was it, my humiliation was complete. My brother didn't trust me anymore. Our family had suffered the worst kind of shite, and as a consequence, we were so close, so attuned to one another. His slight affront floored me.

Even so, he was right. I gave him a curt nod and strode away, calls to make and a life to dismantle.

The hardest part surprised me. It wasn't my job or leaving home—I'd worked away for years now so that didn't matter.

It was Ella.

Because my lust had turned into feelings for her.

And they were wrong, and pressing, and would be a fucker to overcome.

I couldn't see her again.

* * *

*E*lla found me in the garage, where I was keeping out of the way until she'd left for home. She knocked then leaned on the doorframe, her expression cautious. She held a piece of paper in her hands. Fluttered it.

"I passed," she said. "My driving test. Mathilda went with me."

It should have been me who'd taken her, but it was better for all if Ella and I spent the least amount of time together before she went. Not that my heart didn't swell to see her.

"I knew you would." I dropped my wrench and straightened from my crouch at the bike.

"I'm about to leave. I'm going to drive home on my own. I've persuaded Mathilda and Callum." She waved her hand. "Don't make me have to persuade you, too. It's daylight, and the roads won't be busy. I've passed so am legal. I'm going to do it."

"It's too long a drive," I groused.

"I'm going to do it anyway."

We stared at one another in a sort of showdown. She swallowed, and I tried not to see how achingly beautiful she was.

"There's something else I wanted to ask you," Ella added, taking a step inside the garage. She glanced over her shoulder then brought her big eyes back to me. She spoke in a rush. "I had a call with James's lawyer earlier. He told me that if I was married, I could be free of Richard."

I drew back. "Married?"

"It's that or it'll take months and stress James out more because he'll have to take over my guardianship. With Beth being sick, I thought..." She trailed off, and her cheeks pinkened.

I took a steadying breath. Because marriage? How could she get married? "Why are you telling me this?"

"I wanted to ask you..." She shook her head, her black hair tumbling over her shoulder in pretty curls, then tried again. Strain apparent in her expression. Every word forced. "Will you marry me, Gordain?"

I'd never thought I'd hear those words, never had any interest in using them myself. But now, from her, they felt so different than I'd imagined.

Pretend. Say yes and have her.

But there was only one answer, because she didn't mean them the way my fucked-up brain wanted her to. "No."

"No?" She widened her eyes. "It wouldn't be real. Just in name only—"

"Yeah, I got that." I folded my arms, my fucking heart bursting.

"Still no. Right." Ella's gaze dropped to the floor. "I'm sorry, it was stupid of me..."

I wanted to reassure her but if I opened my damn mouth, I'd tell her how I felt, and that was so messed up. None of it was real and, in a few weeks, it would be gone. I'd be in a new job and over this.

She'd have long forgotten about me.

"I'd better go. See you around." Ella gave me one last look, trying and failing to hide her hurt. Then she walked away.

I didn't even say goodbye.

13

ST BRIAVELS, IT WASN'T

E^{lla} Streams of students passed me, the halls resounding with the noise of hundreds of people going to their first class of the new term. Greetings were hollered, coffee chugged, and junk food stuffed into gaping maws. A woman with a shaved head veered around me, sending me daggers for getting in her way.

St Briavels, it wasn't.

But that was good. Right?

I drew in a deep breath and trod on to my lecture hall, easy to find—I'd already had orientation, right after I'd arrived in Manchester.

Heading in through the open door, I climbed the stairs then slid into one of the few remaining seats. To my left, a man slouched in his chair, messy brown hair in his eyes and one leg partially in my floorspace. He didn't move it. I sat gingerly, crossing my legs the other way.

A woman took the aisle seat. "Fucking early tutorials. What a bunch of bull." She pulled her laptop from her bag and opened it, a number of chat boxes already active. "What's your name?" she said at the screen.

It took a second to realise she was talking to me. "Ella," I replied. At boarding school, we'd been taught the correct way to introduce yourself, and I stifled the urge to give her a winning smile and a polite set of information-prising questions. My roommate in my digs didn't know anything about me, certainly not my title or where I lived. I intended to keep it that way. A fresh start.

"Topaz." The woman pushed her bobbed peroxided hair behind her ear with multi-coloured fingernails. "Don't even ask."

All right then.

At the front of the room, a woman marched in. She reached the lectern and cleared her throat. The babbling noise stopped, and the milling students sat.

"I am Professor Maran, first chair violin with the London Festivus Orchestra. You lucky few who have made it into my class either by skill or luck should understand one thing." She swept her gaze over the room, and an awed silence greeted her. "I am a new appointment to the university and did not have a hand in your acceptance into this unique and privileged opportunity. If you think being a big fish in your small school pond has my interest piqued, guess again."

Beside me, Topaz gulped.

The professor continued, "As department head, I have established my own priorities. The hours my predecessor put aside for instrument practice are not sufficient. You'll find a new schedule in your inboxes with an increased performance requirement for your first term. We will start as we mean to go along."

More performance? It was only meant to be a third of the course, including instrument practice. I figured that would mean one or two live performances—there wouldn't be time for more.

Professor Maran went on to give us her in-depth career background and her high expectations of us. Nearing the end of the session, she tapped her laptop and pulled up a slide on the screen. It outlined a task. "From this moment on, you'll be working in groups of four, preparing your first assignment—a performance in four weeks' time. Your immediate neighbours now are your working partners."

Four weeks?

"Guess that makes us work buddies," I said under my breath to Topaz.

"Lucky you, choosing the seat next to mine. Planned that nicely," drawled a voice from my other side.

Twisting around, I frowned at the rude guy. "Why did you say that?" My words came out too loud and directly in a pause where the tutor drew breath.

Professor Maran's attention landed on me like a ton of bricks. I sensed it even across a room of people.

"And you are?" she asked, staring directly at me.

Oops. "My name is—"

"Stand, please," the woman ordered.

Heat painted my face. I rose. "Ella Fitzroy. It's a pleasure to meet you."

The professor glanced at a paper on her desk. Then she tilted her head, regarding me once more. "Ella, can you tell me what you are doing on my course?"

"To learn. I intend to have a career in music."

"I see. Musicians are ten a penny. Just look around you. After graduation, half of your fellow students will have jobs in coffee shops and not even a sniff of an orchestra seat." She peered at the paper again. "You are far from being an excellent performer. How do you intend to stand out?"

I resisted the urge to wither under her scrutiny. "I don't plan on approaching any orchestras, if that's what you mean. That isn't why I'm here."

But as the words left my mouth, I regretted them. The professor had introduced herself by her achievement—first seat violin was a highly sought-after position. I'd just made out it wasn't worth my notice. "What I mean is—"

"Orchestras approach you, not the other way around. And the point I am making is that each of you, from this moment, needs to develop your professional reputation. In your case, Ella, I recommend you don't lie about your name. It's an asset few have."

I gaped. "I didn't lie—"

"Elinor, Lady Fitzroy, is the correct way to address you, according to my helpful notes. Fitzroy is the name of the dukedom, correct? Not a legal surname."

A ripple of nervous chatter came from the other students.

"Earldom," I mumbled. Then I cleared my throat. "We use it as a surname."

"Ah, my mistake." The professor's eyes gleamed, her badass new teacher routine nicely underway. She turned her attention to a new victim in the other corner of the room, and I sank back down, my face on fire.

"Nice one, Your Highness," the man next to me said. "Way to make our group look bad before we've even played a note."

"Ignore Donovan," Topaz whispered to me, with a glare to my space-invading neighbour. "The rest of us do."

"You two know one another?"

"Orchestral summer camp," Topaz added. "Unfortunately for me, we were in the same section. As was Ivor." She indicated past Donovan to another man, heavy-set, with his attention fully on the tutor. He'd be the fourth in our group, I guessed.

And they all knew one another.

I was the outsider all over again. So much for an anonymous beginning with equals. With a swift, forced smile at Topaz, I returned my attention to the front.

University was starting out nothing like I'd expected. But that was good. I needed the change, the kick up the backside, the expanded horizons. I'd make the best of it.

* * *

Six weeks in, and my *make the best of it* plan was laughing in my face.

Ivor regarded me over his music stand, his small eyes narrowed in annoyance. He gave an exasperated gasp. "How can you not know Wieniawski *Violin Concerto no. 2*?"

"I do know it. It's pretty, but I've never played it." I dropped my bow hand to my hip, trying to keep cheerful despite yet another chorus of *you don't belong* from our group's resident snob.

Ivor wasn't a bad guy, but he was perpetually frustrated with me. Last week, after our horrible first performance was done, I'd dyed a chunk of my hair blue. It was my little act of rebellion after nearly choking onstage—I'd needed the release of doing something wild.

Ivor had huffed and puffed about acting like a professional—a valid point, if we were looking for employment. And he took great offence at the fact that I was more or less self-taught.

The frequent debate in our group was over the best teaching technique—the Russian school or the Suzuki method. I knew enough to follow the conversation but I hadn't lived the same life my course mates had.

When I'd described the fortnightly tutorial I'd had at St Briavels and the online course I followed, even Topaz had winced.

And because the world hated me, practically the entirety of my first term now had to be dedicated to practice and performance. For the first stage show, Professor Maran had given us the evil task of making a piece of music she chose fit our quartet's specialisms. We had Ivor on clarinet, me and Topaz on violin, and rude Donovan surprisingly proficient on the piano.

It hadn't gone well.

For the second, due just before the Christmas break, we got to choose our own for our group to perform.

I badly wanted to put forward one of my own pieces, but our classes had so far barely touched on composition. That would be in term two in January. I could hardly wait.

"Look, Ivor," I said. "It's not a good piece to choose. We barely scraped through the expo with the Beethoven mangle. This time, we should try something different. Try and stand out. Don't you think?"

Ivor shook his head, his jowls wobbling. "I wasn't putting it forward for us to play, I was merely pointing out a piece that you could—no, *should*—have in your repertoire by now."

He was always doing this—telling me off for what I didn't know.

"I actually have a suggestion for our next piece." I raised a hand to gather the group's attention.

"Oh, here she goes," Ivor muttered.

"How about *The Gravel Road*, from *The Village*? James Newton Howard."

Blank faces stared back.

"It's a beautiful, moving piece." Poignant, actually. It had made me cry when I'd listened to it yesterday. It made me think of Gordain, and missing him overwhelmed me once again.

It had been months since our time together at the castle, and I knew he was doing okay—my brother had told me he'd taken the private pilot training and passed. I also knew he'd stayed with James and Beth at Belvedere for a weekend after he'd gone for a job interview.

I wondered in which city. I wondered if he liked it. I wondered if he thought about me at all.

I hadn't asked James anything.

Even so, my heart wasn't so willing to give Gordain up.

My idea of dating and having fun? Not so much of that had happened. I was too busy to feel lonely, but listening to that piece of music had taken me right back to being held in his strong arms.

"I Googled it. A film score?" Topaz looked up from her phone. "That isn't going to fly with Prof. She's a traditionalist through and through."

"Yes." My blood warmed. "And that's my point. Everyone is going to choose pieces she'd play, not thinking about their own strengths and standing out."

Not that I wanted to draw her fire, but I'd rather play a piece I loved.

Ivor and Topaz looked at Donovan.

He raised his head from his slouch at the piano. "Really? I have to play arbitrator again? Fine. We can do that or we can choose an easy Mozart quartet. Even her ladyship will be able to learn one of those." He threw a smirk my way. "Vote, people. Mine, which will keep the professor sweet, or the little lady rebel's, which shits on the classics."

Ivor sniffed and fiddled with his clarinet. "Mozart."

"Mozart. Sorry, Ella." Topaz shrugged.

"Done. Ivor, choose a piece and email a first pass at how we can divide it up." Donovan stood and stretched his arms behind his back. "Ella, I'll walk you up the road."

He stalked off, and I looked at Ivor. "I'll help with working out the piece."

Ivor sniffed. "I'd be most grateful. Thank you."

Stowing away my violin and bow, I turned to Topaz. "You coming?" She lived two floors down from me in Halls.

"Nope. Got a date. Have fun with Donovan." She made big eyes, and I pulled a face, then followed our mercurial pianist outside.

Donovan waited at the street door. Night had fallen, and the yellow streetlights cast shadows over his features.

Where Ivor wasn't my fan, and Topaz was fun, if flaky, Donovan was one to watch. Depending on his mood, he either played the asshole, tearing casual strips off people—mainly me—with his nicknames and sarcasm, or, he was intensely quiet, ignoring people and missing practice once or twice.

He'd also asked me out.

I'd said no, and he'd covered it up by saying he'd meant drinks for the group. That sounded fun, but one-on-one? Not with him.

I started the walk back to my dorm—five minutes from the practice hall through Manchester's Castlefield district. Filled with canals, bars, and old, imposing buildings, it was a bustling part of town.

Except for this deserted back street.

Donovan moved, too, though keeping a step ahead of me.

"Did you want to talk to me about something? I've got a

call I need to make," I said, telling a partial truth. I had a video chat planned with the twins tonight, but not for an hour.

"These pieces you keep bringing up, from films and whatever, is that where you want to work? A musician for hire, schlepping up to studios?"

"Not exactly."

He glanced back but kept moving, maintaining his position just ahead of me on the pavement. "Then what's the big plan?"

I shrugged. "I'm working on it."

"You know the pay for session musicians is shit. And no one would know your name. And, to be honest, you aren't all that hot. I mean, you're not bad, but in a competitive environment? Nah. Who's going to hire a young girl? Fancy name or not."

"In my version, I'm the one doing the hiring," I snapped. Why I'd just told him that, I didn't know, but I was sick of being the outsider in the group. The one who hadn't been classically trained and didn't covet an orchestra seat.

Except I did. My own orchestra.

In the past weeks, through talking to older students, I'd increased my knowledge about music practice and theory, and I'd had some thoughts on my business idea. I'd need access to a large pool of musicians, plus space to record and practice. And in my head, I'd become more of a writer/manager than a performer, which made sense the more I thought about it. I had so many buzzing ideas for pieces of music but I couldn't do it all. I'd hire conductors, technicians, producers.

From his inside jacket pocket, Donovan took out a packet of cigarettes, lit one, then offered it to me.

"I'll pass." I waved him off, wrinkling my nose. No to the death stick and double no to the fact it had been on his lips.

"Sorry, your ladyship. You know, you have a real stick up your arse." He blew a plume of smoke into my face.

"God!" I coughed and stopped walking.

"I'm only messing with you. Don't be so uptight."

Yeah, because I was the unreasonable one here.

"Is there something you want?" I said, my tone short.

We'd reached a lane. Still, there was no one around, no cars passed on the wet road, and there were no lights in the tall buildings around us. I even hoped for Ivor to come up, blustering about something else I didn't know.

But no. We were alone.

I shivered in my coat and raised my shoulders. Donovan smiled around his cigarette, but it wasn't a kind expression.

"I'm going to The Griffin," he said, naming a local student bar that I'd been to once or twice with Topaz.

"Yeah? And I'm going home. Like I said, phone call." I stared him down, suddenly aware of how much smaller I was than him. No man had ever truly intimidated me before, other than my uncle. The new feeling had me shrinking away.

Donovan snorted, then he tore his cigarette from his mouth and tossed it to the ground, a flare of sparks catching in the breeze.

Something showed in his eyes. Frustration, maybe.

It looked closer to dislike.

"Whatever. Take care on the way home, princess," he called and strode away.

Unnerved, I fast-walked the rest of the way home, returning to an empty room, Jessica, my roommate, absent. I was freaked out, cold, and wanting comfort.

After a thirty-second shower in the communal bathroom, I dressed in sweatpants then dragged Gordain's hoodie over my head. I'd kept it, and hidden it from my brother, and though I was about to talk to the twins, there was no way they could identify it on a screen.

I sat on my narrow bed, pulled my sleeves over my hands, then raised the material to my face. It still smelled of him. Just.

And I was the saddest loser around.

My phone buzzed and I jumped. Taylor's name appeared on the screen.

We'd spoken more and more in the past weeks, rebuilding our friendship.

"Ella, are you sitting down?" On the screen, she danced around, bright sunshine at her back. "I'm calling from sunny LA, but ask me where I'll be on the first weekend in December."

I sat up more. "Where?"

"England! London, more specifically. Can you travel? I want to meet up. We can go to a club, Christmas shop, sightsee together."

My heart leapt, as that was exactly what I needed. A friend intervention. Except I had a prior engagement. "I'd love to, but there's one small problem. Actually, two large blond problems. The twins are coming to Manchester to see me. That Friday is end of term, and they're coming to see me perform."

James and Beth had wanted to come, but my sister-in-law's pregnancy hadn't gotten any easier on her, and they couldn't stray far from home. Somehow, the twins had found out, probably through Callum, and they'd made the arrangements to come see me so I wouldn't be alone.

Taylor gave an easy shrug, her white bikini strap bold

against her tanned bare shoulder. "Then I'll come to you. It won't be a hardship seeing Wasp again."

And with that, I had an exciting plan on the horizon. With my failure, so far, to find my wings at school, with the weird exchange with Donovan earlier, I needed friends more than ever before. There was only one person whose presence would make it perfect, but I doubted he'd want to be within a hundred miles of me.

14

———

HEART ACHE

*G*ordain
"The problem with helicopters is that they don't want to fly. They aren't like planes, happily soaring along. A 'copter wants to plummet to the ground. Every bit of that hunk of metal is trying to obey the laws of gravity and smash it and you to pieces. Your job, kid, is a fight from takeoff to set down. And it's much, much worse on a dark rainy night."

"Mhmm," I hummed, only half listening to Leonard as I waited for our manager to return. Of the fifteen pilots on rota at Sky's the Limit, my new employer, Leonard, had decided to take me under his wing.

Lucky me.

I'd been on a tour with the RAF, countless missions—both training and actual rescues—been shot at, ran a team, got stuck in a crashed heli in hostile territory, aced my civvy training, and I was getting lectured by Leonard. A man who didn't like flying at night.

How life had changed.

"You've got to have big balls, mate. Great big hairy balls.

Do you know what I'm talking about?" Leonard eyed my locker. The picture taped to the inside of the door.

"No problem there." I slammed the locker shut and dragged on my leather jacket, the problem of my balls ever on my mind.

They were blue as the fucking sea I'd flown over this morning.

Evan, the manager, returned. "All arranged," he told me, handing over a clipboard and pen. "You know you're the youngest pilot ever to work for us, let alone take the North Sea flights."

"Suits me. I've got no commitments." I signed off his form, committing myself to the most challenging assignment our team had, then bid my colleagues goodbye and strode out of the small office and into the cold December afternoon.

The twins were on their way to meet me. I hadn't seen any of my family for months, sticking my head down and focusing on work, work, work. I had a rare night off ahead of starting the six-week turn on the oil rigs the company served. I'd be isolated and cut off, but that was fine. My aim each day was to be tired enough so I could sleep without going over and over Ella's kiss.

Having her in my bed.

Her fucking proposal.

"That your girl? In your locker?" Leonard traipsed alongside me.

The picture was of Ella on stage, her violin under her chin and a fierce look on her face as she played. Ally had sent it to me, and I used it as a good luck talisman, checking in with her before each trip then again before I clocked off. Not that she'd ever find out. She was out there, living her dream life.

She was winning, from what I could tell. I hoped she was happy.

"No," I replied, harder than I meant. Then I relented, because today was a good day, and I needed to relax for once. I lifted my chin at Leonard, and we crossed the tarmac to my bike and his car. "Got to have something to keep you going."

"I hear that. You're pushing yourself too hard. I mean what I said about the job being a dangerous one. Stay safe up on those rigs." Leonard popped his door then called a farewell.

I got on my dangerous bike, leaving behind my dangerous job, and went to meet my kin.

* * *

The twins arrived at my apartment—a functional space with little by way of decoration—that I shared with two other pilots. Our shift patterns meant there was generally someone sleeping or filling up on food at any one time. The next two days, though, had both men away on overnighters, so the twins could use their rooms even without me there.

They launched through the door, crashing into me in giant bear hugs.

"Christ, who's been hitting the gym?" I held Ally at arm's length then grappled his biceps. He'd put on muscle tone. Wasp, too, when I turned to look at him.

The boys grinned at me and commenced overlapping tales of all I'd missed in the months since I'd moved down south. Mathilda was huge—the twins we now knew she was expecting two months off being born. Callum was beside himself, hovering over his wife twenty-four seven.

My heart ached over Wasp's description of work Callum and Lachlan had jointly commissioned on border land between the two estates. I pictured the site as plain as day—Ella and I had run through it.

Wasp took himself off to the bathroom. Ally waited for him to be out of earshot, then his eyes gleamed, and he came back to me. "Go ahead, ask."

"Ask ye what?" I ran my thumb over a jagged fingernail, worrying at it.

"How she's doing."

I grimaced. "I don't want to know." He meant Ella, obviously. Knowing real details would make me involved in her life, and I was trying to be anything but.

"Liar. You're in the same city as her. You must have flown over her or driven past her a hundred times."

That was true. Manchester was my new home.

I had a vague idea of where Ella went to university—hard to avoid knowing the city when I flew people in and out in my glorified taxi service. But I didn't know where she lived or where she hung out. I'd never sought her out and nor would I. The job here just happened to be the better one of the three cities I was offered. "Wouldn't know it if I did."

Ally eyed me. "She dyed her hair blue."

"What?" I stared.

"Ha! Look at you, all not bothered. Give it up."

I rolled my shoulders, pulling my t-shirt tight across my chest, then glanced to the window like the nonexistent view could save me from the scrutiny.

"What the actual fuck." Ally pounced on me, his hands on my left pec. He poked at the metal bar under my shirt. "What's this? Oh my God. You got a piercing?" He whooped with laughter.

I shoved him off. "Aye, I did."

"Let me see."

"No!"

"If you don't, I'll just assume it's a kinky version with a spiked end."

We stared at one another.

"And," he added with an evil grin, "I'll tell everyone we know."

"For Christ's sake." I relented and dragged up my shirt, displaying my chest. Being five years older than the twins, I was used to being climbed on and teased. I'd taught them to drive and I'd trained them to be strong and how to fight. Being an older brother was a responsibility I didn't take lightly.

There were limits, though.

"Why?" He made a face of disgust, eyeballing the plain titanium barbell.

"I was going to get another tattoo." Of a fucking lion, of all things, right over my heart. The stencil had looked like the Fitzroy lion. It had been a dark day, and I'd been miserable, craving release by the addictive pain of a tattoo gun. Thank fuck I hadn't done it.

"I changed my mind at the last minute and got the piercing instead."

"Was the tattoo going to say 'I love Ella Fitzroy'?"

Fucker. "No. It said Alasdair Maddock McRae is a pain in my arse."

He dropped back on the couch, laughing it up. Wasp joined us again, and Ally sobered. "Come see her play."

"Who, Ella? Aye, do!" Wasp leapt on the idea. "You said you weren't working. Got a better plan? We've come all this way, and it'll suck if you aren't with us. You've only got one night before you go."

"I don't—" I started, but my brother continued.

"She's got some problem with a guy in her group, Tay told me about it. He's acting strange with her."

"Strange how?" My hackles rose.

"Nae sure. Taylor said she thought he was flirting, but aggressively."

"Is... Is Ella seeing him?" I hated asking. Hated that I'd one day hear of her boyfriend. Her happiness.

"No. She doesnae like him. We should go and put on the heavies. Three of us will be more menacing than two."

I'd had no intention of going to Ella's performance. The twins were meant to spend an afternoon with me then the weekend with Ella and Taylor, coming back to my place to sleep.

But the thought of some guy giving Ella grief... "Who is he?"

Ally grinned an idiotic wide-mouth grin. "Better come with us and find out."

I couldn't ignore Ella in need, but even if I had to see her, she didn't have to suffer seeing me.

15

NERVES

*E**lla*

Outside the theatre's heavy blue velvet curtain, the audience babbled, chirpy tones and laughter floating through to the staging area.

Holy crap.

I waited with my group for our turn to go on, my stomach a mess of nerves, and my bow clenched so hard in my fist the wood was bending.

"Fucking hell, Ella. You're a wreck." Donovan stood in front of me, smart in a black suit, but his lips in his permanent sneer. "I swear to God, if you fuck this up for us all by being so precious..."

I glanced up at him then swallowed. "You'll what? Throw a fit on-stage? Leave me alone, Donovan. I can't help my nerves."

"Make me," he replied, his eyes gleaming.

Ugh.

"Ella, maybe we can try deep breathing," Ivor cut in, taking a position at my elbow. In the past month, he'd thawed towards me, hopefully due to my work rate. I might never be the consummate performer, but he'd heard a couple of my own pieces—and seen my Melody Fitzroy profile on MusicLinkt—and he'd been impressed.

"Okay." I blinked at him and copied his breaths, mine not as dramatic as his—Ivor adored being on stage, and everything was a performance.

"Doing great, hun!" Topaz cheered me on from the side, her long white dress a contrast to her new punky hairstyle.

My nerves receded a tiny bit. At least I had two friends here, plus the three in the audience. Taylor, Wasp, and Ally had sent encouraging messages from their seats.

My brother and Beth hadn't managed the trip, Beth's pregnancy keeping them at home. There was only a month to go before my niece or nephew was due. I'd be home after the weekend and, if the baby was born in my winter break, I'd get to spend time with them and help out.

I couldn't ease the anxious edge I carried, not only for tonight but for the impending birth of the baby, too. At least this was the last performance I had to do for a while. Thank the gods of Christmas for that.

I kept my gaze on Ivor and breathed out.

"You're up." A cheerful group trooped down the corridor and passed us, a spring in their step now their piece was done.

Which could only mean one thing—it was time to play.

We entered the stage and took our places. Staring blindly, I bowed to the tutors, my short white dress flowing and my hair dyed back to black, and set up. My group looked the part, at least, with the men in tuxes and Topaz and me in white, but I could hardly see past my shaking hands to appreciate the effect.

Ivor had chosen Mozart's *Eine Kleine*—a lovely piece and

easy to adapt to our quartet, but basically elevator music. Too familiar, not challenging, and a bore-fest for the crowd.

Oh God, the *crowd.*

My pulse whooshed in my ears.

For unknown reasons, Gordain's face popped into my mind. Who was I kidding? It did about half a hundred times a day. I pictured him out there and focused on that and only that.

Okay. Better.

I breathed through my nose.

We started the music.

The weird thing was, as the short piece progressed, I thought I actually *did* see Gordain. But a version without the shorn hair. So alike, but it couldn't be him. He wouldn't come here, I was certain.

The lookalike shadow leaned against the aisle wall in between two raised sets of seats, straight ahead of my right-hand stage position. They watched me, whoever they were, modelling Gordain's broad shoulders and single-minded concentration.

Their focus didn't shift from me, and the rest of the crowd dimmed as I concentrated on keeping the shadow in view.

I played for that individual alone.

It being a short piece, we finished it neatly. Overall, it hadn't been a horrendous performance. Polite applause rippled around, then my name was yelled from the back of the theatre. Ally. I'd recognise his holler anywhere. I spotted him and gave a thankful smile to my friends.

When I looked back to find my shadow, he'd gone.

We made our final bow to the row of professors then left the stage, returning to the waiting room. I packed away Suki and my bow with a sense of utter relief spreading through me.

"We did it! And I didn't die," I said with a grin to my group.

Ivor sniffed. "It was passable, and that was the most we could hope for. Well done, team."

"Well done?" Donovan stalked over. "It was shit and you know it. You," he poked a finger in my direction, "can do better. Next time, keep your focus on the piece and not on your buddies."

My cheeks warmed. In private, or in a recording booth, I was better, that was true, but overall, I thought I'd done well. I hadn't fallen to pieces, thanks to the shadow. "I wasn't that bad. And my attention was exactly where it needed to be."

Donovan gave me a look, one that was becoming familiar. A judging, almost provocative gaze, as if he wanted a fight but didn't want me to think I was worth it.

Well, that was easy to handle. I pivoted on my heel and strode away.

Taylor had given me insight into Donovan's shitty attitude. She said there was a type of flirting where the man tried to dominate the woman by putting her down. Giving her negatives all the time so she'd lap up the occasional positive and become grateful for his attention. Putty in his hands.

I might be naïve when it came to men, but I was learning fast. I could spot emotional manipulation and I wasn't having any of Donovan's.

I paused at the door. "Ivor, Tope, I've got friends in the audience. We're going to a club. Want to come?"

"Party!" Topaz cheered. "I'm in."

"Maybe for just one drink." Ivor wrinkled his nose. "As long as we drop our instruments off on the way."

I agreed, and we left, leaving Donovan to stew in his own juices. He didn't ask to come, and fuck was I inviting him.

Now term was over, I hoped to never have to work with him again.

* * *

*P*erhaps inevitably, Wasp and Taylor disappeared almost as soon as we got inside the noisy club. At my dorm earlier, where she'd arrived in good time to give me moral support, Tay had prewarned me she planned to talk to Wasp. And by talking, I assumed she meant kissing. We'd had a good couple of hours catching up, and she was here for the whole rest of the weekend, so I didn't mind. Tonight was about having fun.

After a round of drinks, Ally and I took to the dance floor and shook our stuff, leaving Topaz and Ivor debating grades.

I'd had a glass of wine.

It was the end of term.

I hated university so much the relief of it being over for a month had me flying high.

Most of all, being among real friends, even if two had scarpered, gave me a sense of safety I hadn't had in a long time. In the middle of the hot and sweaty dance floor, I threw my arms around Ally's neck and hugged him, hard.

He let me cling onto him like a limpet and, God help me, I wished he was his brother. I'd have given anything for a hug from Gordain now.

"You okay?" Ally pulled back and mouthed against the pounding music.

I just stared, and he gestured with his head to a seating area on the far side of the floor.

"Emotional moment," I replied, as soon as it was possible for him to hear.

Ally sat on a bench and pulled me down next to him. "Is something wrong?"

"No." But it wasn't true. In the midst of friends, one person's absence hit so hard it hurt. I couldn't explain that so I distracted us both.

"You're getting a lot of attention." I poked him in the chest then gestured to the women and men who couldn't keep their gaze off him.

Ally had grown beautiful in the past few months. His loose, sleeveless t-shirt revealed carved biceps and forearms. The angles of his face had sharpened since last summer. His dark-blond hair fell into his eyes, and his wide, laughing mouth looked ready to charm at any second.

He wasn't even eighteen for a few more months, yet the doormen had ushered him past without an ID check.

He'd been handsome when I'd first met him. He was going to be devastating as a man. Not quite at Gordain's level. Not for me anyway. But that didn't stop heads turning as people passed our alcove.

"And you're cramping my style." He swept his hair back, his smirk telling me he was only half joking.

"Got your eye on someone?" I watched the sea of faces, the undulating bodies on the dance floor. People writhing against one another. Simulating sex in a crowded room.

"We'll see how it goes," he said with an easy shrug. "What about you?"

I blinked at him. "Me? Pick up a stranger?"

"I meant are you seeing anyone?"

I pulled at my dress. The fine material clung to me from the club's humid air. "You know I'm not. Taylor tells Wasp everything, he tells you, so don't tell me you don't know."

"You're still hung up on my brother?" Ally's gaze gentled. "Your relationship is the only secret I've ever kept from my twin. He probably knows, if you told Taylor, but we've never discussed it."

"What relationship?" I laughed to hide my dismay, because I wanted that word to be true. For there to have been more between us than one evening of kisses and scorching chemistry. And at the same time, I didn't.

I still hadn't found my wings.

I still hadn't lived.

Had I?

"Maybe I should take someone home tonight," I added, bitterness in my tone.

Ally slung his arm over my shoulder and sighed, resting his head against mine. He didn't reply. Perhaps we both knew how little chance there was of me even kissing a stranger, let alone anything more.

I had no interest, not for any one of the milling faces.

"Go fish." I clambered to my feet, my calf muscles aching from my heels. "I'm going to find Ivor and Topaz. Talk shop for a while."

Ally dropped a gentle kiss on my hair, but his attention was across the room, and he peered as if spotting his next conquest. "Maybe someone better will find you first."

"What if there isn't anyone better?" I replied, half to myself.

But Ally was gone.

I left the seating area and wound my way through the throng to the opposite side of the dance floor. There, I entered a corridor. I'd been seeking the bathroom but, the farther the passage curved around, the more obvious it was that I was in the wrong place. At the end, a sign on a door read *Manager's Office.*

Definitely wrong. I turned to head back to the bar, and almost walked right into a hard body.

"Sorry!" I squeaked automatically, raising my hands.

Then I saw who it was.

Donovan stood in front of me. Apart from us, the corridor was empty, and we were out of sight from the main area of the club.

"Here you are, princess. I've been looking for you."

My mouth dropped open. "Why?"

"Unfinished business."

He'd followed me here? I recoiled and side-stepped.

He copied my movement, blocking my path. "Next term, I'm asking for you to be removed from my group."

"Suits me," I replied, folding my arms across my chest.

"What? Didn't you hear? I want you gone."

Instead of answering, I just glared, discomfort unfurling in my stomach.

Donovan tilted his head, sizing me up. "Like that, is it?"

My temper rose, fast and hot. If he'd followed me here to mess with me, I wasn't playing. My instincts were right, and this guy was a creep. He'd been an asshole to work with, and I wasn't having it. "I'd rather not work with you again anyway. You bring us all down and you're rude to everyone. I was going to ask Professor Maran to split up the group."

Donovan sucked in a breath. "You think you can do what you want. Must be nice to have rich parents to buy your degree. What are you even doing on this course? Why not just have Daddy the earl throw handfuls of cash as you play your mediocre pop music? Save the rest of us the hassle of dealing with you."

I gaped, his words so gratingly unfair they left me momentarily speechless.

A big mistake.

Donovan snapped out a hand and pressed it on the wall behind me. Then he boxed me in with his second hand the other side of my head.

His eyes darkened, and he leaned forwards.

"What do you think you're doing?" I uttered. Alarms roared in my mind.

"Why are you fighting it?" Donovan asked.

"What?"

"You want me," he stated, far too close.

My breath came out as a tiny, surprised puff. "Are you joking?"

"You play with me. You seek me out almost every day—"

"Because we share nearly every class!"

"—then you told Ivor not to listen to me. What am I supposed to think about your teasing? It's all been a game. You did this. You wound me up, and now here I am." He gestured down his body.

I didn't follow the motion. "Donovan, get off me."

"Princess, put your hand down and feel—"

"I said get off me!" I yelled.

Donovan's face contorted, his gaze dropping to my lips.

I held my breath for a second, terrified that he was going to try to kiss me. Readying to jam my knee between his knees. Or poke his eyes out with my fingers.

But then, Donovan was gone.

Snatched by the scruff of his neck and forced to the floor.

Gordain stood over him, a terrible expression twisting his features. His fist smashed down on Donovan's face.

16

I WILL END YE

*G*ordain

The arsehole at my feet howled, outrage mixing with a healthy dose of fear. I'd dropped him on his back and now had him pinned with my knee to his chest and a tight grip on his long hair.

Easier to teach him a lesson this way.

"Didnae ye hear the lass's instruction?" I asked, swallowing my urge to break his face. "She told you to get off."

"Who the fuck are you?" he said, his eyes wide.

"What does that matter?" I smacked his head against the concrete floor.

At my shoulder, Ella hovered, her hands clutched to her mouth. Our gazes connected, and my world shifted. Righting itself. Like it always did when I was near her.

Except now, I was boiling with fury over what I'd just seen and heard.

"You don't know what you were breaking up," the man said, drawing my attention back to him. "That was between me and her. She wanted it."

"You have got to be kidding me," I growled.

"Wanted it? I wanted it?" Ella chimed in, advancing to peer at him, her expression fierce. "I don't want anything to do with you. How hard is that to understand? But you kept pushing."

"What do you want me to do, Ella?" I asked. "Because I really want to break him in two. You decide."

In the RAF, I would've pulled my punches, obeying the order to maintain the honour of my uniform. But there was nothing honourable about letting a man get away with threatening a woman. Scaring her.

I hadn't resisted the first punch, but now it was up to Ella.

"You know him?" Ella's attacker bucked, trying to escape. "I thought you were fucking that other bloke you were with. If you're so easy, why not me?" He grimaced, like he knew what was coming.

He was right.

Ella gasped at his words. My anger surged. Overflowed.

I lifted his head by the hair and swung my fist again. My punch landed squarely on his face, his nose making a nice crunch.

"G!" Ella yelped.

I pulled my arm back to hit him again. Red-hot rage infected me. Blood lust. He'd meant to hurt her.

"No, please, mate," the man whimpered. He tried to scramble away.

"Please?" I glared at him, pinning him harder. "Did ye hear her say no? Maybe next time you'll listen if I beat it into ye."

Behind us, footsteps landed, and I spared a glance to see the twins and Taylor arrive.

In a second, Ally crouched one side of me and Wasp the other, shadowing me, having my back.

"Fucking hell." The man on the floor whimpered, blinking away tears as he glanced between us.

"Yeah, meet Ella's army," Taylor sneered. She put an arm around Ella. "This the guy who's been pissing you off all term?"

"Sure is," Ella replied.

A door opened beyond her. At the edge of my red-tinted vision, a suited man paused. "God! What's going on?"

"Help!" the arsehole pleaded. "Get them off me."

A hand landed on my shoulder. Ella's.

"Actually, this man was protecting me," she said, a tremor in her voice. "Are you the manager?"

"I am," he replied.

"The man on the floor followed me to this club and threatened me. My friend is teaching him manners."

The manager replied, his tone soothing to Ella, but I couldn't hear past the blood rushing in my ears. He'd followed her. He'd *followed* her.

Anything could've happened.

I stared at Donovan, my grip tight and my body primed to do him harm.

"I wasn't going to do anything," he said, his voice pleading.

"If you go one step near her again, I will end ye," I said through gritted teeth.

"We all will," Wasp added, a low and menacing tone to his voice like I'd never heard before.

"I won't. I swear. I promise."

"I mean it. If you even look at her wrong—"

"Gordain?" Ella's voice punctured my red mist.

I raised my gaze to her.

"The manager is going to throw Donovan out now. You can let go."

With a last meaningful squeeze, I released him and stood, instantly taking hold of Ella like she belonged to me. She came willingly into my arms, and I didn't look at anyone else to see a surprised expression.

For the first time in months, all was right with the world.

Donovan staggered to his feet, his gaze firmly on the floor and nowhere near Ella. The manager muttered something and led him away.

"Els, are you okay?" Ally asked Ella.

But Ella took a step back and just stared at me.

"Uh, guys? Let's give them some privacy. Ella, catch you later," Taylor said, and she ushered the twins away.

Ella and I were left alone and, for a moment, neither of us said anything. Instead, we just watched one another.

I took a second to scan her. Earlier, at her performance, I'd been stunned, caught up in her playing, in how gorgeous she was in her white dress with her black hair loose and spilling down her back. A vision. An angel. Now, my adrenaline held me in check.

Ella raised her chin. "I'd ask what you're doing here but I don't care."

"Did he hurt you?" I managed.

"No. I'm pretty sure he was going to try to kiss me, but I had a knee aimed at his balls so he'd have thought better about it." She gazed at me, examining my features. "Even so, I'm glad you found me. Even gladder that you punched him. If anyone deserved it, he did."

I dipped my head in acknowledgement but didn't say anything more.

The moment shifted. My fire banked.

Ella folded her arms over her white dress. Her gaze turned shrewd. "Actually, I lied. I do want to know what you're doing here. How did you happen to be in the right place at the right time?"

"Would you believe luck?"

She raised one dark eyebrow.

That would be no, then.

"Why don't we go somewhere and talk?" she asked, then led the way down the corridor.

* * *

We left the nightclub and entered the dark, rainy evening, no sign of our backup army. I sent a quick message to my brothers to say we were leaving —they had their own key to my apartment, and Ella did the same with her friends.

I shrugged on my leather jacket. "Where shall we go?"

"My dorm is just down the road, and my roommate has gone for the Christmas break. We'll have privacy."

I fell in alongside her, and we made the short journey without talking. Inside the student block, Ella led me to an elevator. It climbed the floors, and we watched one another from opposite sides. Her blue-green gaze inched over me. Mapping me for differences, perhaps.

The mood changed again.

My temperature steadily escalated.

I'd had the idea I was seeing her home, but maybe that had been naïve. Something more was going on. With a fierce grip on the handrail at my back, I shifted my weight, my attention fully on her.

The elevator dinged, and Ella took a staggering breath. We exited and moved as one, down the hall, pausing at a door while she fumbled with a key.

"Dammit," she muttered, and I reached around and steadied her hand.

"Thanks," she said as the lock disengaged. "This is your fault anyway."

"My fault?" I followed her into a small room with two narrow beds, two desks, not enough space to swing a cat. I thought my apartment was a box, but this place took the biscuit.

Ella dropped her bag on a desk, dislodging a pile of music books, and slid off her coat. "Yeah, your fault. I haven't seen you in months, and you happen to appear at the right time and place? Then there's this." She pointed between us.

"I know." The chemistry. The wild attraction. It hadn't dimmed one iota. Electricity ran over my skin, and I shivered.

"Why don't you start with what you're doing in Manchester. Did you come to see the twins?" She popped her hands onto her hips in an attempt at bravery, except hurt played out in her voice. "Did you mean to avoid me?"

I winced and rubbed my jaw. "I live here."

Ella recoiled. "Since when?"

"Months ago. Since I started my new job."

That gaze that had been so heated, dimmed, the realisation that I'd dodged seeing her plain on her beautiful face. She plonked down onto her bed. "Obviously the twins know."

"They're staying at my apartment this weekend."

She nodded, her eyes not meeting mine. Her shoulders slumped, and she reached beside her pillow to grab an item of clothing. Then she thought better of it, shoving it back.

Too late. I'd already spotted it—my hoodie.

My pulse shot through the roof.

She'd kept it. And in her bed, of all places. The thought momentarily floored me.

"Thank you for tonight. I'm glad you were there." Ella entwined her fingers. "Actually, I'm glad for another reason. I've spent the whole term going over and over what happened between us." She peeped up. "At the end. What I asked you."

"Your proposal." I pulled out the chair and took a seat, shedding my coat. "I've thought about it a lot myself."

She winced. "Did you ever tell anyone about it?"

"No. Do you even need to ask?"

"You had every right to. I embarrassed myself. I seem to keep doing that around you."

My heart ached for her. Always thinking she was doing wrong. Always assuming the worst. "Ella, look at me."

She raised her gaze from where it had dropped to her hands. Energy shot between us. She sat taller.

"Why do you think I turned you down?"

"Why? Because it was ridiculous. What possible reason would you have for accepting me?"

I tried again. "Why do people normally get married?"

She frowned. "Because they love each other."

"You needed a marriage in name only. My heart wouldn't let me go there. It already wanted more."

A beat. I just watched her.

Ella gaped, realisation dawning. "You... You had feelings for me, G?"

Strange, how one lass had the power to destroy me. All of a sudden, the busy, packed life I'd created for myself became a sham. The wall-to-wall shifts, the money I'd been saving for God only knew what—a future?

There was no future if Ella laughed in my face now.

I'd been treading water.

It became painfully apparent.

I raised my chin to confirm the fact.

With an expression of pure wonder, Ella rose. She didn't take her gaze off mine as she closed the distance between us. Stopping between my open legs, Ella raised a hand and traced my jaw. Then she pushed her fingers into my hair—grown out of the buzzcut and long enough for her to grip.

"Brown at the roots with honey-blond highlights. I might have known you'd have incredibly sexy hair."

I closed my eyes, letting her control me. Own me.

Ella cleared her throat. "I've asked you this once before but I'm going to ask it again. Are you seeing anyone?"

"No." It took every bit of willpower I had not to grab her and pull her onto my body.

Nothing had changed from before. The sheer want was still the same. The lass was still eighteen and had barely lived.

"I hurt you," she decided. "I'm just piecing it all together. I talked up my freedom and coming away to university. I kissed you, a lot, and spent the night in your bed. All while chattering away about spreading my wings."

I adjusted myself on the chair, gripping the hard sides, my groin tightening at the memory of the last night we'd spent together. "Everything you did was right. Is right."

"Gordain McRae. Open your eyes and look at me." Her turn to make the demand.

I complied.

"I'm sorry," she said, a gentle expression on her beautiful face. "No wonder you steered clear of me."

"I wanted ye to live that freedom you craved. I still do."

"What if I've had enough of it?"

I gave a half-laugh, because it hurt to even imagine us

together. I'd pushed away the thoughts for so long. "After a few months? You haven't even tried."

Ella regarded me. "And if I did? Try? What then?"

My breath left me.

She continued, "If I somehow fast-forward time to a point you consider me worthy of you, what do I need to have done?"

"Worthy of me?"

"Answer the question."

Involuntarily, my hands left their grip on the chair and took her hips, her white dress hitched high on her thighs. I dug my thumbs into her flesh, and Ella gave a little moan. It went straight to my cock.

"You'd have spread your wings and flown. You'd have looked around and come back. Ye wouldnae be settling for me."

Like an idiot, I'd said it, admitted what I wanted. Her. But the version of her not wondering if she was missing out.

The words hung between us, then Ella dropped onto my lap, her lips millimetres from mine, and said, "Done."

Set loose by her single word, we attacked one another. Hands grasping the other tight, lips meeting in an explosive kiss. Ella's mouth opened, and I thrust my tongue inside, stroking hers.

She met me move for move, grinding down on me, almost hurting where I was so hard and ready to go.

I wanted the pain.

We shouldn't be doing this, especially as we'd just agreed she wasn't ready, but that couldn't stop our momentum.

"I want you so badly," Ella said against my cheek. "I've missed you and thought about you and needed this." She kissed over my face and around to my neck. Then she lightly bit my earlobe.

My blood roared.

I stood, holding her in my arms, then knelt on the bed. Ella dragged me down onto her, and we rolled on her narrow mattress, legs intertwining, mouths fused. Months of nothing but my own hand had me acting without thinking. At Ella's prompting, I raised up on an elbow and dragged my t-shirt over my head then tossed it to the end of the bed.

She gazed at my chest with hunger. "You're pierced."

"New."

She raised her gaze to mine in question.

"It was that or another tattoo. I'd needed…" Sex was what I'd needed. Her body on mine. But I wasn't going there.

"Interesting," she replied and leaned in, enclosing her mouth over my nipple.

"Ah, fuck." I dropped my head back, mind blown with her forwardness. Before, in my tower, she'd been bold but clearly intimidated. Now, she was pushing boundaries.

Ella tongued my piercing, rolling it around.

She reached for my belt buckle.

My fever spiked and had me moving. Taking control, I fitted myself between her legs, her dress rucked up around her waist, now, with her delicate white underwear on display.

"Have you been taking care of yourself?" My voice came out with a hint of a growl. I seized her thighs and pushed her legs wider.

"Every time I've been alone, it's been you I had on my mind when I did this." Ella palmed her breasts through her dress.

"Then it's my turn to get you off." Without pause, I

ducked my head and pressed my mouth right over her clit, through her lacy briefs.

The scent of her filled my nose, and I inhaled, instantly harder than ever before.

More, my body roared. I twisted my finger under the strap of her pretty underwear and dragged them down her long, smooth legs.

A groan ripped out of me at the sight of her. Bared to me.

"You're so beautiful." I leaned up to kiss her gorgeous mouth one more time, then moved south to get to work. Spreading her wide open with my hands, I placed my mouth directly on her clit and sucked.

Ella yelled my name.

I sucked again, harder, and ran a finger down, pushing inside her.

She bucked under me.

The second I lay my tongue on Ella, I was a goner. Her taste was everything I'd been missing. "I knew it. So fucking sweet."

I licked her, hard, and she moaned and writhed. I fucked her with my finger, adding another, sliding through her wetness and caressing her.

Between my mouth and hand, I worked her, my dick hard and aching in my jeans, my world her pleasure.

"Gordain!" she cried, and her hips jacked, moving in time with my hand.

I sped up, loving her little noises, every sharp inhale and breathy swear word uttered. Then, finally, she exploded. Ella dug her nails into my scalp, gasping soundlessly, her orgasm tightening around my hand, her body arching up.

She dropped back onto the bed, breathing heavily. I withdrew my fingers but licked her once more, lazily, loving my task so fully I didn't want to stop.

"Your turn." Ella sat up and reached for my belt.

I grabbed her wrist. "We're not going there."

"I'm returning the favour," she said and laid her lips on mine, kissing me and shaking off my grip.

"God," I said with a groan, helpless as she unzipped me, freeing my cock.

"I've never done this before so I'm working it out as I go." Ella grasped me in her fist and gave me a hard stroke.

"Oh fuck." My head spun, pleasure spiralling.

"Tell me if I do anything wrong," she said then ducked her head and enclosed the end of my cock with her hot mouth.

My roar could be heard on the moon. Crashing back against the wall, I took hold of her head, helping to guide her first attempt at a blow job. Not that she needed my help —every move she made was heaven-sent.

I bit my lip hard enough to taste blood.

Actually, I needed to taste more of her.

Two could play at this game.

"Shift around," I ordered through gritted teeth.

Ella lifted her head in surprise. I lay out alongside her with my head at her waist then hauled her above me, her thighs over my shoulders.

"Oh!" she said with a sharp inhale.

I licked into her with easy strokes.

Ella got with the programme quickly, and her mouth took my cock once more.

Her moans as we worked together were the best sounds I'd ever heard. It was all I could do not to explode into her mouth.

Then she got daring. Still stroking me with one hand, she explored my balls with the other, kissing down my shaft to reach them. Then she licked me, flicking her tongue, copying my movements. "Is this good?"

"Everything you do is good. Just don't stop."

Ella made a pleased sound and continued her exploration. Driving me crazy.

I wanted to fuck her so badly it almost hurt.

I had never needed to come so hard.

"Get back on my cock," I ordered, and Ella complied, her heat and suction returning.

But if I was going down, she was going down faster.

With my tongue, I drove into her then slid three fingers inside her at once, moving my mouth to suck hard on her clit.

Ella yelped and bucked, her teeth dragging over my cock.

I jerked in surprise, and my balls tightened, the slight pain kicking off the start of my orgasm.

I worked her faster, needing her to get there first. Ella moaned and tightened around me once more, riding my hand and face, chasing her pleasure.

Then she deliberately used her teeth on me, this time on the ridge as she drew her mouth over my cockhead.

Fuck. Me.

I knew I had a thing for pain, the tattoo gun, the piercing, but I'd never explored it in sex.

Ella had me dead to rights.

She did it again, and it was all I could do to hold myself together. I upped my assault on her, stroking into her and teasing her clit with my tongue.

"G! I'm coming." She groaned and slid my cock back inside her mouth, over her teeth. Deliberately rough.

Every vibration of her orgasm pulsed through her into me.

Then mine caught up.

"Ella!" I yelled, dropping my head back and trying to push her off me. She didn't budge. My cock pulsed. My balls emptied. There wasn't a thing I could do except lay there and come so hard I saw stars.

Ella choked, then laughed and got right back to it, continuing to work me, but gentler now. And she swallowed me down like a champ.

The last of my throbs played out, and she raised her head. Then she lay a sweet kiss on my cock.

I almost whimpered with the pleasure.

"That," she said, moving around me and lying out at my side, "was hot."

"Uh," was all I could manage.

Ella giggled. "Are you okay?"

"Dead. Went to Heaven," I managed.

She laughed hard now, shaking the bed. I smiled with her and slid my teeth over my bottom lip. Then I pulled her face to mine and kissed her, long and hard.

In unison, our phones buzzed.

"Ignore," Ella said against my lips.

"Agreed." We kissed, slow and dirty. Wet tongues, mixing up the taste of one another. I'd never known anything so earth-shatteringly sexy.

My phone buzzed again. "Fuck," I complained.

"Check it," Ella said. "If one of the twins is locked out of yours, he'll only break a window to get in."

I grumbled agreement then kissed her one last time and sat up, tucking myself away. I stretched to grab my leathers and fished for my phone.

"Work," I said, reading the screen. The message gave me a change to my flight time. "Fuck's sake."

"What's that?" asked Ella.

"There's bad weather coming in. I'll need to leave earlier than planned."

"Where are you going?" She turned her big eyes onto me, and my fucking heart melted. Of all the times this could have happened.

"I've got six weeks working on oil rigs."

"Six weeks?" She blew out a breath. "You're going to miss Christmas at the castle?"

I shrugged. "I took the shift so people with families could have the time off."

"You have a family."

"They won't miss me too badly."

The heat between us rapidly evaporated. With a small frown marring her brow, Ella reached to take her phone from her bag.

She gave a quick inhale, her hand to her mouth. "Beth's in labour."

"No!"

"She's early, though. James will be in pieces. I better go home." She pulled at the hem of her dress, inching it down her thighs.

Then she seemed to decide something, bringing her fierce gaze back on me. "You're wrong. Everyone will miss you. I'll miss you." She shook her head. "If you're insisting on me living before you'll see me again, you're going to have to give me a list of all the things I need to do. I get that I can be better at this." Her face flushed, and I guessed she meant bedroom activities. "So, what, am I dating?"

"Date, see who's out there, but don't sleep with anyone. You don't need practice. That isn't what I meant at all." The words were out of my mouth before I could stop them, because fuck, this was her life, not mine.

Except I didn't want any other man touching her.

Ella's embarrassment lifted, and she gave me a coy smile. "I'll text you with updates."

We had each other's numbers but we hadn't used them since I'd flown in to get her from Belvedere all those months ago.

Such a simple thing, but it felt like a milestone.

The springs creaked as I climbed from the bed, taking my cue to leave. "I willnae have much signal for weeks."

"Then I won't expect to hear back until you do." She sat in the messy sheets, hair tousled, cheeks pink, never looking so lovely. "But I will hear from you, G?"

"Aye, ye will," I replied, and somehow, after keeping away from Ella for months, she was back in my life.

And I was maybe back in hers.

17

THE VISCOUNT SAYS HI

Ella

Baby Sebastian James Moncrief Durant, Viscount Ashlyn, was born at two in the morning, almost a week after my sister-in-law's labour had started. The doctors had delayed proceedings for as long as possible, but he'd been determined to enter the world.

I'd fallen in love in a tiny heartbeat.

Now, a week after Christmas, my newborn nephew stared up at me with round eyes—the Fitzroy shade of blue and green. He made a perfect O with his mouth, yawned, and snuggled in his blanket, content and happy in his warm, safe world. I raised my phone and took yet another picture. I was obsessed.

Sebastian was getting used to breaking the heart of everyone who met him. My brother and Beth had brought him home two nights ago, and a new era reigned at Belvedere. A happy family lived here again.

I planned to do everything in my power to keep it that way.

With a couple of clicks, I sent the latest picture to Gordain with the caption "The viscount says hi."

I stashed my phone, and my brother emerged from his bedroom door, his black hair chaotic and his face crinkled in sleep. I'd given him and Beth a chance to sleep in together by babysitting, though I hadn't left their apartment.

"Do you remember Dad used to call you Ash?" I said quietly over the baby's head. Viscount Ashlyn was another title James held, and it was traditionally used by his eldest son until he inherited his father's earldom.

James rubbed his unshaven jaw. "I do. A lot of memories have resurfaced since Sebastian was born."

He sat on the sofa next to me and reached out to take his son. My brother was a dad!

We managed the transfer carefully, the baby making a face at his father that had us both grinning.

"I wanted to talk to you about decorating your rooms again," James said softly. "Make the space properly yours. How do you feel about it?"

Previously, I hadn't been interested in the colour of my walls or what kind of flooring I walked on. It seemed a waste of money. Now... Things were different.

Not only had the baby transformed how Belvedere felt, but I wanted the roots. The connection to my family.

"I'd like that." I smiled at my nephew though spoke to my brother. "I'd like that a lot."

"Good. I'm inviting Gordain here in a couple of months. He's going to help with the painting."

I raised my gaze. My brother was giving me a look.

"About Gordain." I chewed my lip, considering how to start this conversation. He was my brother's best friend, and I had no idea if me dating him was going to cause a problem.

"Are you seeing one another?" James asked, his tone neutral.

"No. But I'd like it if we were."

James frowned at his son. The baby's eyelids drooped as he sank into a nap. "Am I a barrier between you?"

"I don't think so. More that I'm too young and unreliable for him." My tone came out glum, and a flash of pain crossed my heart. "Did he say something to you? How did you know there was something there?"

"He didn't say anything. I haven't seen him in a while. It was Beth who warned me last year. She said he watched you like I watched her and not to be surprised if the two of you were an item soon."

"Do you mind?"

The corner of James's mouth lifted. "Of course not. He's the best man I know."

"You don't think he's too good for me?"

James shuffled, threw an arm around me, and pulled me into a little family hug. My heart swelled, and it almost hurt how badly I needed this.

A decade of missing out on family warmth sunk in.

"No, Ella," he said simply. "How can you ask that? You're the best, too."

And that was that.

* * *

A week later, I had my bags packed, ready to return to university. I still hadn't heard anything from Gordain, but I wasn't going to let that stay the case for long.

After hugging my family goodbye, I got on the road. This term was going to be different. For all the months I'd been in Manchester, I hadn't achieved any of my learning goals.

Now, like Gordain, I had my aim in mind. It was just going to take a little time and manoeuvring to get there.

My phone buzzed right as I was exiting the estate. I put my earpiece in.

"My Lady Elinor." Howard Marks, my brother's lawyer, came on the line.

This time, I didn't object to the use of my title. It was mine. Why shouldn't I use it?

"We've had an interesting development in your guardianship case," he continued. "Your uncle has been in contact with my office today. Multiple times, in fact."

Richard was back? I swallowed. "I thought he'd gone to ground."

"So did we. But there's a good reason for his reappearance." Howard cleared his throat. "It seems the last payment due to him failed."

"What does that mean?"

"Every month, as per the arrangements your father made, he receives a stipend for your care. This month, no payment was made. The coffers are dry."

I gaped, then pulled my car over at the side of the road. "How is that possible?"

"We believe that over the years, the charges he has made on the accounts have been excessive."

"He spent it all?"

"Every single penny."

I hadn't expected a fast resolution to the problem of my uncle retaining my guardianship, but with him going quiet, it had become less pressing. So much else had happened and, aside from that one email, I'd heard nothing. It had been easy to pretend he didn't exist. "What did he say on the call?"

"He complained about the fees for your university

tuition. He demanded it be refunded and your brother pay it instead."

I shook my head. "Why go after such a small amount? It's tens of thousands when he's blown millions. How long would that last him?"

Howard harrumphed. "With his lifestyle, not long. Which means he may have found himself in dire straits. I feel obliged to warn you to be vigilant. He was unhappy about the development and even less happy that we refused the refund."

"Don't worry about me. Thank you for the warning." I made my farewells, needing to immediately call James.

If Richard was going to tap anyone for money, it was him. I had nothing left. He'd taken every last penny.

If he came for me, it would only be blood I could give.

* * *

At university, I moved digs, swapping with Topaz's roommate so I could change floors, in case Richard had my address. I spoke with the building's security, feeling like a fraud for being alarmist.

Then, after two weeks with nothing happening, I finally relaxed, added to by the joy of learning Donovan had transferred to another course, telling Ivor ours wasn't challenging enough for him.

Gordain finally replied to my messages, back in signal range for the first time and returning to Manchester in a few days. I told him that, to satisfy him, I'd go on one date with someone else. Just one. After that, he needed to either give me a list or a time limit.

I had my plans. Life was too short to wait.

18

YOU WEAR YOUR HEART ON YOUR SLEEVE

*G*ordain

The heli's rotors hacked through the sea air, driving us from the North Sea towards the Scottish mainland, and a band tightened around my chest the closer we got. Our route took us over Lossiemouth, my old RAF station.

We had to refuel before continuing south.

We were going to land at the base.

I'd had no say in the planning, being a passenger on this return flight, and since quitting the air force, I hadn't seen any of my old colleagues. It was inevitable now. We were minutes out from landing, the runway lights, brilliant even in daytime, visible ahead.

On my phone, I exited the conversation with Ella I'd been rereading, and started a new one with Jordie, my old pilot buddy. *You around?*

Stranger! Where are you? came his immediate reply.

Landing at Lossie for fuel. ETA 10. Meet you in the pumps? I typed back. As a civilian, my movements would be limited. I'd stick with the heli and her crew.

Can't wait, came the response, and I grinned at my phone then braced myself for landing.

Jordie jogged up before the blades stopped turning. He hauled me from the door and bellowed his welcome, thumping my spine.

He looked me over, poking a finger at my company jumpsuit. I did the same to him, instantly transported back to a time when he'd be meeting me from a mission and we'd be heading to the bar.

"It's been too long," I said, my words almost lost to the stiff breeze.

"Whose fault is that? You've been skimpy with your replies. I'd almost given up on you." He grinned, his square jaw jutting out.

I grimaced. "Sorry." It was true. I'd worked and worked, throwing myself into thinking about anything other than my lost career, my separation from my family, and of course, all things Ella.

"Whatever. You're here now. You've got time for coffee," Jordie decided, and he dragged me away with an arm around my shoulders. Just like old times.

* * *

Jordie dropped into the seat across from me in the airfield's small office. Technically, I shouldn't have been allowed in, but no one batted in an eyelid. In fact, the more familiar faces I saw, and punches to the shoulder I received, the more at home I felt.

"Sucks what happened to you, McRae," one new recruit called—I recognised him from training I'd given a year ago. "Hope you nail the bastard."

I stared after him. I thought I'd be despised on the base. For letting down the uniform. For walking away.

"It's perfect timing you coming this morning." Jordie nudged a steaming mug across the table. "Big news. Wing Commander Phillips is under the cosh."

I blinked. "What does that mean?"

"Top brass is investigating him. He's suspended as of a few days ago. But to be honest with you, after the shit he's rumoured to have pulled? That guy is outta here."

"What is he accused of?"

"Embezzlement, awarding contracts to his family firm. You name it, they're throwing it at him."

I gaped. "But he's a wing commander. Untouchable."

"I bet he thought so, too." Jordie grinned evilly. "The man is out of luck. You should post evidence for what happened to you. But you'll have to hurry. The trial is in a couple of months, but they are compiling the case now."

"Fuck." I dragged my fingers through my hair. "I should. He forced me out. This was my life, and that fucker made me quit."

"Would you come back, if you could? We miss you here."

I swung my gaze to Jordie. Ella's face flashed in front of my eyes, and I had the strangest thought of how much I'd miss her if I was sent away again on a tour. How much she'd hate it. We'd never see one another.

What was that about? We weren't even together. I'd seen her once in months.

"I... I'm nae sure. It was my life, but it was all or nothing, ye ken? I've been out of it for so long. Life is different."

Jordie blew on his coffee, the steam spiralling. His gaze turned speculative. "It's hard when you've got someone at home waiting for you."

"I bet."

"How's the better offer?"

I drew my eyebrows in. "The what?"

"The woman you threw me over for? You still seeing her?"

Ah. At the end of the summer, I'd turned down Jordie's invite to go to his wife's party. I'd done it for Ella. "No. I never was."

The clock on the wall gave me ten minutes until I had to get back to the heli. Fuck it. Jordie had been in my shoes once. If anyone had experience in this arena, it was him.

"Your wife. She was young when you met her," I stated.

"She was." Jordie inclined his head. "How old is Ms Better Offer?"

"Eighteen. Her name is Ella."

"You're, what, four or five years older? I don't see the problem."

I hadn't been prepared for this conversation but I pushed anyway. Ella's last message informed me she was looking for someone to take on a date. And if I didn't like it, I only had myself to blame.

I hated it. With everything in me.

Yet we still weren't in the same place. If she decided against me, it'd scar me deep. Ella Fitzroy let loose in my head reaped all kinds of damage, and I hadn't yet got over our last encounter. If any man was at risk from death by a woman-shaped distraction, it was me.

"Because I'm not a casual dating kind of guy," I said then swigged my scalding coffee, burning my mouth.

"You want commitment," Jordie diagnosed. "Got it. I didn't have that problem. On our third date, my wife told me I was the only man she'd ever want, and that we'd be getting married. I snapped a salute and asked her what kind of ring she wanted."

I chuckled. "She knew her own mind."

"Certainly did. Mine, too. I'll give you one piece of advice. If you can't do casual then tell her what you can do. She'll either want it or she won't."

I heaved a sigh. "And if she won't?"

Jordie leaned over and clapped me on my shoulder. "Then come back here and shoot up shit with us. It was good enough for you once, and if you plead your case, you might get the chance of another try."

* * *

With the heli fuelled up, I said farewell to Jordie and readied to fly back to Manchester. I checked my phone before boarding. A message waited from Callum along with missed calls from him and the twins.

Come home. Meet the new bairns.

Then he sent a picture that had my jaw dropping. My older brother in a hospital gown with a tiny baby in the crook of each arm. *Born this morning, came home this afternoon,* he wrote. *Braw, and wee, and with a pair of lungs on each you can't imagine. Cannae wait to meet their uncle.*

"I need to go," I yelled to the pilot.

"Why? Is there a problem?" he asked.

I had the rest of the day off, so it wasn't an issue for me to make my own way back, and Castle McRae was only an hour down into the Highlands.

"Two wee bundles of trouble." I held up my phone, my mind already across the airfield, ready to beg, borrow or steal a car to get back to my family.

"Cute! Hop in. I'll drop you off on the way," he replied with a broad grin, and just like that, I was going home.

* * *

One scenic flight later, I paused at the castle's heavy oak door with an aching heart. Months ago, I'd left the place feeling like the worst kind of letdown. I'd rebuilt some of that damaged pride but I'd missed my family more and more as the months passed. It was time to make changes.

I swung open the door and marched in.

Callum stomped across the great hall, meeting me halfway.

"Gordain!" He threw his arms around me, crushing me to him.

I did the same, smacking him hard on the back. "Congratulations," I mumbled.

"Ah, ye should see them! Bonniest wee bairns you ever saw. The lass has the loudest yell."

"One's a girl?"

"Aye! A girl and a boy."

I pushed off him and stared. Twins had existed in our family going back centuries, but always boys. A pair of twins was the reason the estate was split down the middle, carving up the land that Lachlan and Callum separately owned.

"No! We've never had that. It's always been lads."

"I know! Come meet them."

Callum slung an arm over my shoulder and guided me across the great hall, filling me in on the grisly details of the birth. We jogged up the internal staircase and then up the narrow stairs to the solar. Inside, the older pair of twins sprawled on the couch, gazing into a cot.

"Hey, bro. Asleep," Ally mouthed, pointing down. "Wake them, and Mathilda will kill us all."

I tiptoed over and peered into the cot at the two smallest

members of my family. God, they were adorable. Fair, fluffy down for hair, and scrunched-up faces.

"Lennox and Skye," Callum said, gazing over my shoulder. "They're more than happy to meet their oldest uncle."

I parted my lips in surprise. Lennox was my middle name. "Well, hello, sweethearts," I whispered to the sleeping bairns. "Aren't you bonnie?"

Mathilda shuffled out of the bedroom, bundled up in a dressing gown and moving gingerly. I wrapped her in a hug.

"They're perfect," I said. "You did good."

She immediately began to cry. "It's perfect now you're back. We heard the helicopter. Oh, Gordain. We've all missed you so much."

"That's the hormones talking," Ally said softly. "She cried at me bringing her a glass of water."

"Seriously, though." Callum pulled his wife into his arms. She snuggled down, her face weary and her eyes closing, though her head remained cocked towards the cot. My brother raised his chin at me. "I've wanted ye home. It hasnae been the same."

Mathilda elbowed him in the ribs.

"And I'm sorry," Callum added. "I was an unhelpful fucker when ye left. I should have been a better brother."

"Language," Mathilda chided without opening her eyes. "Babies present."

"They're not even a day old! They cannae ken swears from anything else I'm saying," he protested then laid a soft kiss on his wife's head.

I choked, welling up, overwhelmed by the scene. It was time I confided in my family. About my problems with the RAF to start with. Then, in time, about Ella. I'd always acted alone, shouldering my problems, taking myself off to lick my wounds. Maybe that was my problem.

I didn't want to be alone anymore.

* * *

A quick phone call secured me the night off, and I spent the afternoon alternating between which bairn needed cuddles more.

Over dinner, I told my family about the wing commander and the true reason I'd left the RAF. Then and there, Mathilda made me write out my complaint letter. It had been cathartic, both getting the facts on paper and telling it to a room of shocked supporters.

No one doubted me. Through their eyes, I saw how badly I'd been treated.

After, Callum and I walked the bairns around the great hall to get them to sleep. The front door creaking open had us both swinging around.

Lachlan poked his head in. "Lads!" he barked. "There ye are!"

We both hushed him, flapping arms and pointing at the dozing twins.

"This is them? Would you look at that!" He crept in, resting a big hand first on Lennox then on Skye, who I held.

"We heard they'd arrived," he said, smiling at the bairns. "I'll pay a formal visit, ye ken, with my lady in a few days, welcome the wee lad and lass to the clan. But I was passing and had to stick my head in."

"That might be one of the last families you do this with. Perform your welcome blessing," Callum intoned, his gaze on Lachlan but his words carefully placed. As chief of the clan, Lachlan carried out a lot of ceremonial duties. Not always willingly, but he showed up.

"Why's that?" I asked.

Lachlan cleared his throat. "A couple of days ago, I came to see Callum about giving up my position as clan chief. He'd be taking up the mantle earlier than planned. Likely by the summer."

I bounced my gaze between the two men. "Why?"

Lachlan sighed. "I know ye had an idea to buy Braithar, and we gave you a time limit, but I want to give up the castle sooner. Our girls have moved away, and the drive to Marianne's farm is too much now. I want to retire there in the new farmhouse we've built on the moor."

"We have a deal. Three years," I exclaimed.

Skye mewled, and I jogged her gently, a surge rising in my body, telling me to be anything but calm.

"Aye, nothing's decided. But regardless, I'll give over the chieftainship to your brother earlier than planned."

It was farther and farther, my dream. I'd saved money, but it was nowhere near enough.

Da used to taunt me with the fact that Callum would one day be chief of the clan. *Laird Never McRae,* he called me, like I cared about the title.

Skye cried out, a wee wail that cut through the air.

Lachlan winced and waved a hand. "That's my fault. I'd better go. See ye, Callum. Gordain, we'll talk it through another time."

He left, and Callum and I traded twins, my brother slipping Skye into his shirt. She settled against his skin, her little face relaxing again in sleep.

"We'll hold him to the agreement," Callum said, his voice low and reassuring. Whether for me or his daughter, I wasn't sure.

I lifted my chin in a semblance of agreement, but my cage had been rattled and my attention broken.

I paced the hall, my gaze on Lennox's scrunched-up red

face. Already, he looked so much like my brother, his da. A miniature version.

Callum strolled beside me. "Over dinner, you talked about that scene in the bar. When you came to with that woman draped over you, you were afraid you'd had unprotected sex, aye?"

I swallowed then nodded. "I hated the thought."

"Because of the risk of having an unwanted bairn?"

I studied his face, his stern brow over a gentler gaze. Lachlan's visit had prompted thoughts for us both.

"Da hated me," I said, the words misshapen and bitter in my mouth. "I was so sure I'd never want kids. I didn't think I'd ever want a girlfriend."

"Until recently."

"Aye."

Silence held in the ancient space.

"Seen much of Ella in Manchester?" Callum asked.

"Once. I'm surprised the twins didn't tell you." Heat rose in me at the memory of what had happened in Ella's dorm room. It shifted a little of my gloom.

At my shoulder, my nephew snuffled, and I patted his back under his father's watchful gaze, fixing my mind on less stimulating thoughts.

"Aye, they mentioned something."

I heaved a sigh. "I've no idea how this will turn out, but if in time Ella decides she wants me, I'm waiting for her."

Callum stopped in front of the fireplace. He held my gaze, scooping up a log and tossing it into the flames. "Ye sent her a picture of the bairns yet?"

"No."

He straightened and stood beside me, shifting Skye so her face was visible. "Take the shot while they're sleeping."

I slid my phone from my pocket and took the selfie. Me with my older brother and the babies.

"If that doesn't melt her heart, nothing will." Callum peered at the picture and nodded his approval.

I sent it, bumping up her last message about dating. Fuck that. What the hell had I been thinking suggesting it?

My stomach squeezed. What if she was on a date right now?

"Why do ye think it's her heart that's the problem?" I asked, replacing my phone.

"You've always been the same. All or nothing. You wear your heart on your sleeve."

Except I hadn't. I'd kept parts of myself closed off from Ella. Deliberately protecting myself. "What would you have done if Mathilda had been seventeen when you met?"

"Taken it slow. Told her everything there was to know about me and let her decide if I was for her. Which is exactly what happened."

"You've told Mathilda everything?" There was so much shite in our family history. Our father's abuse. The certain twist of fate that led to him hating me while he obsessed over Callum.

All stirred up now in my head since Lachlan's visit.

"Aye, every last thing. Why I have a sword tattooed down my spine. Why ye have the slashes on yours."

I'd never told another soul that story. Only the four of us brothers knew.

And Mathilda, too, apparently.

I stared at my brother, and he watched me gently.

"This is what you do when you ye love someone. Ye hand over your darkest secrets and trust them to keep them safe for ye."

"I want that." My damn heart kept aching, and I rubbed my free hand over the spot.

"I thought as much. I'm glad for ye."

"You are? I thought—" He'd disapproved. It had been clear on his face.

Callum shook his head. "I was wrong, and it was none of my business. I'm sorry. If ye come and tell me that you and the lass are together, I'll be happy."

So would I.

* * *

In my tower apartment, I left the twins—glued to my side since the bairns and their parents had turned in—watching a movie in the snug, and stepped out into the hall to call Ella.

She picked up on the first ring. "Your name on my screen gave me heart palpitations."

"Don't go on a date." My voice came out too fast, before I'd even said my greeting.

"G—"

"I can't handle it. I know what I said but I have another proposition for ye."

Ella paused. "I'm listening."

"See me," I said, hoarse. "We'll go slow, but I'll take you out. Don't search for anyone else."

Then I swallowed, remembering the very reason I'd told her to go out and look elsewhere. "Unless you want to. Your choice. I'm just saying, I'm an option."

"Yes," she said quickly. "Yes to you. No to anyone else. We'll do it however you want to do it."

"Good." I gripped the phone, my other hand at that ache in my chest.

"Aye," she replied. "'Bout time you saw sense."

A laugh escaped me. It hadn't just been me. She'd wanted this. But something had changed for her, too. A cacophony sounded in the background of the call. Instruments.

"Sorry. I'm at a recording session."

"What have they got you working on now?"

Ella took a deep breath. "Actually, it's one of my own pieces."

I stood straighter. "You're recording your own work with an orchestra?"

She laughed, a happy, light sound. "Yes! There's six of us. Ivor and Topaz from my old group, then a few others I pulled in who had the right sound. I've made so many changes this term, starting with asking to focus on production and recording. One tutor is supporting me, the other thinks this is a temporary thing. It's not. It's a practice run for where I'm heading."

"You're living your dream. I'm so proud of you."

"Almost. I just need one other thing to click into place." She paused. "When are you here next?"

She meant me. I couldn't stop my grin. "I'll be in Manchester tomorrow evening. But I've got two weeks of night flights." I'd had to trade my shifts in order to get the day off to spend with my family.

"I'm recording all day. How are we going to see one another?"

"How about I take you out for breakfast?"

"Yes! I can't wait to see you."

I couldn't, either, and after we hung up, making a date for the morning, I was pretty sure I wouldn't sleep much until I had Ella Fitzroy back in my life.

* * *

For two weeks, Ella and I met almost every morning. Short, rushed meetings, but never missed. I'd be coming off shift and she'd have crawled from her bed to meet me, the long recording sessions on top of her classes wearing her out. Not only had she persuaded the university to let her direct her own learning and create a recording outfit using their facilities, but she was also putting out pieces to sell again. She had contracts with other musicians and was making money.

Her drive, and her single-minded determination, fired me up more than ever.

We kissed goodbye each time, a chaste peck on the cheek that hinted at hunger and fire. But all in good time.

My past had been one-night stands, instant gratification with nothing of feelings or care. My future could be so different.

Even if work got in the way.

I had another stint offshore—a twenty-one-day trip back out to sea. Ella understood, but I could see how much she hated me going. If I'd still been serving in the RAF, my tours would take me away for months. Hard to ask someone to wait for you when life was passing them by.

The day I left, Callum called me. I'd had a letter come through to the castle. At my request, my brother read it out over the phone.

"It's about your case against the wing commander. They are inviting ye to give evidence at his hearing."

Holy fuck. "When?"

There was a pause as he read. "In a month."

"I'll be at Belvedere. I've got two weeks off." James and

Beth had invited me for a visit. I was going to help James with some work around the place.

"Perfect timing."

It was. I hadn't told Ella about the trial yet, not wanting to put too much hope on the letter I'd sent. Nor had I confided in her about the baggage I carried—the shite Callum said I needed to trust her with. I'd been serious about taking it slow.

Still, as I boarded the heli, heading out for my stint on the rigs, I shot her a text.

Come to Belvedere for the weekend when I'm back.

It was time to move things up a gear.

It's a date, she replied.

19

CLAIMING

*E*lla

I packed for my visit home with nerves guiding my every move. Gordain was there. Waiting for me. Holy fuck. We were happening.

Tossing clothes haphazardly into my bag, I ignored the *bonging* of my laptop, producing reminders for actions I hadn't taken. And wouldn't take.

Going away this weekend left me in a bit of a pickle with university. Despite the excellent term I'd had so far, with my shift in focus to recording and all the huge advances I'd made in that area, I was still supposed to have another performance piece underway.

The deadline was next Friday—seven days' time.

I hadn't even joined a group.

Professor Maran had emailed me to insist I give her an update—the title of the piece I'd be performing, or the people I was working with, at least.

I hadn't answered.

See, not only had I gotten the bug for recording again, I

was writing. Endlessly. Which left little time for anything else.

Last summer, Marianne, the lady of Braithar Castle, had suggested I ditch the bits of the course I wasn't interested in, but could I really just not show up? Piss off the woman responsible for a big chunk of my overall mark? It could mean she failed me for the year.

I needed to work out how much I cared.

I dropped my gaze to my bag, flipping in sleeves of a shirt that was making an escape bid. I'd made my decision. This weekend was the last chance I had to realistically hit that target.

And I was using the time to go see Gordain.

He was more important. How he made me feel outranked my final mark for the year. A grade that meant nothing if I didn't intend to apply for jobs with other people.

Leaning over, I snatched the new underwear I'd bought and stuffed it into the bottom of the bag. It was time to get this show on the road.

* * *

My sister-in-law waited on the steps of Belvedere, Sebastian in her arms. I flung myself out of the car then ran to them, kissing Beth on the cheek.

"How's my nephew? Gimme!" I grinned like a crazy lady, scooping the baby up in a hug. "You're getting so big! Look at all this dark hair. You're so beautiful," I babbled.

Beth chuckled. "He's smiling at you! He's only just started doing that."

"You're so clever," I told the baby then peered at his

mother. Her pregnancy had been the worst, so seeing her up and walking around took a big weight off my mind.

"How are you feeling?" I asked gently.

"A million times better now the puking has stopped. I need to nap a lot but I think that's normal. Who knew pregnancy could be so hard?"

"I am never, ever having babies." I shuddered.

Beth blew out a breath. "Sounds good to me. It isn't all sunshine and unicorn dust. Now, come in. James and Gordain are waiting for you upstairs. They've been working hard on getting your rooms ready and are just finishing up." She tipped her head, curiosity in her looks. "Gordain mentioned something. He stood up after dinner the first night he was here and said you'd been dating. Like it was a formal announcement. I think he thought we'd be surprised. Or that maybe James would get all big brotherly and tell him to watch himself."

"He did, huh?"

Then it was out in the open. I couldn't help my spreading grin. Gordain had claimed me to my family before I'd arrived.

I'd made the right choice this weekend.

Wait until he found out the little claim of my own that I'd made. He was going to go nuts.

"He made the point that you weren't serious," Beth went on, climbing the short flight that led into the entranceway. "But then he spent days fretting over paint colours for your bedroom. Funniest casual relationship I ever saw."

"Your guess is as good as mine there." I snuggled the baby and followed.

Upstairs, we made our way to my suite of rooms. Before, it had been mostly bare, not decorated since maybe my grandparents' day. Old wallpaper, expensive for its time but ugly and faded now, had adorned the walls. Gold leaf had embossed the ceiling cornices.

Beth pushed open the door with a ta-da gesture, and I stepped into a new world.

Dark, polished floorboards led to cream couches in the lounge. White, gauzy curtains drifted in the breeze from the tall windows. The walls were pale and uniform, the fussy designs painted neutral.

Modern and chic, but classy, too.

I turned a full circle, taking it all in. Lamps. Floor-to-ceiling book cases. A piano and a music stand at the end of the wide room. If a designer had taken a peek inside my head, they'd have seen this room. How did my brother and Gordain get it so right?

"I can't believe my eyes," I whispered.

"Guys?" Beth called.

My brother and Gordain appeared in the hall that ran off the living room. Both had paint-splattered clothes and dusty marks on their faces. James stepped forward, his attention on me as he watched for my reaction.

I suddenly felt emotional.

"Ella! We didn't hear your car." He advanced and embraced me in a careful hug. "Welcome home. What do you think?"

I hugged my brother back with my free arm. "I love it."

"Really?" He pulled back and examined my features. "Because if there's anything you don't like, we can change it. I want you to be happy here."

"I will. I am. I wouldn't change a thing." I spoke to my brother, but my gaze sought Gordain. As his did with me.

My hero waited in the doorway, a casual shoulder against the frame. But there was nothing casual in his stare.

The way he looked at me made statements and asked questions.

It showed his concern and how much he needed my approval for all his hard work.

Hunger abided there, too.

I swallowed but didn't break eye contact.

"What's that, Sebastian? You're sleepy? James, let's take him to his cot, give Ella a chance to settle in." Beth spoke to my brother then took the baby from my arms.

"I don't know how to thank you enough," I said to James, bringing myself back to the room.

"You don't need to. Welcome home." He patted my shoulder.

Beth herded James out of the door and closed it behind her.

Leaving me and Gordain alone.

For three weeks, I'd barely heard anything from him. Now, he was here, in my space, hot and dusty from working on making a home for me.

On slow feet, I moved until I stood in front of him. "Hi."

Gordain just watched me.

"I heard you told James and Beth that we were dating."

He raised a shoulder. A tight movement. "It was the right thing to do."

We stared at one another. He didn't elaborate.

"Well, I'm glad, because if we're a thing, it means I get to do this." I invaded his space and placed both my palms flat on his broad chest.

He stood firm.

"And this." I stretched both arms up, encircling his neck. Holding that intense stare in his grey eyes. Showing him rather than telling him how I loved what he'd done.

Gordain ran an arm around my back and brought me closer still.

A thrill shot through me. I fought a smile. The corners of his mouth tweaked, too.

This was killing him, I could see it.

"Did you think about me? In all that time you were away?" I traced over the soft hair at the nape of his neck. Teasing with just the tips of my fingers. A barely there pressure.

Something huge was changing between us, the mutual attraction acknowledged, but we hovered at the edge of a vital step.

Sex, for sure. But other stuff, too.

"Maybe."

Hooking my arm around his neck, I pushed against him, bringing our bodies flush. My breasts pressed on his chest, and the masculine scent of him filled my nose.

Oh God, his smell.

How could I be addicted to that? Our time being up close and personal had been so limited. Yet I knew that mix of musk, bodywash, and a hint of aftershave.

He dipped his head, his gaze heavy under lowered lids. Sexy as hell.

"Maybe I missed you, too," I said, almost on his lips. "It's possible that every night, I went to bed dreaming of you. Waking up in a sweat. Hot. Wet."

Gordain broke. He groaned and turned us so he had me against the hallway wall. "Want to take a guess how much I missed you?"

"Enough to work on my rooms during your holiday?"

He chuckled, his gaze taking me in at close range. Roaming over my features. Settling on my mouth. "Hard work is my way of relaxing."

"That makes no sense."

He rubbed the tip of his nose on mine, fascination in his gaze.

"You going to kiss me or what?" I sassed, but nerves bubbled up. I'd buried myself in work, trying to not notice the gaping hole in my chest from him being away. It was too apparent now, with painful edges only he could heal.

"Maybe. Callum told me something I didn't know about myself. That I was an all-or-nothing kind of guy."

"What does that mean?"

"That I need to stop myself pushing so hard. Let things come to me rather than needing it all, now."

"Because…" I let the words sink in, trying to understand. "You want everything? But for it to come to you?"

The intensity in his gaze stole my breath, telling me all I needed to know.

"Yes, Ella. Which is exactly why I'm trying to take things slowly."

Lord above. I hadn't thought I feared anything anymore, but the words I craved suddenly terrified me. How could I let someone so close when they had no reason to stay? What if slow for him meant it eventually petered out?

What if it didn't?

"No pressure." He examined my face.

I blinked at him. Then I leaned in and pressed my lips to his. Just gently.

Going to him.

Giving him the *hello* I'd dreamed about.

Gordain made a sound of pleasure, his lips warm. Then he moved, angling his head, making more of the kiss.

My pulse sped up. "I missed you. So much," I said against his mouth.

Then there was no more time for talking.

Our kiss was the first since my dorm room. We'd placed warm lips on cheeks on our breakfast dates, and hugged, but nothing more. Now, Gordain held me tight, a possessive arm at my back, his hand on my head. I touched his face, caressing his skin, rough with a slight hint of stubble.

This kiss answered a question. We were taking this further. Thank fuck for that.

Our tongues met in a flash of electricity, and I shivered. He held me closer, tasting me, teasing me, letting me know what he needed.

I pictured what it was he'd asked for. The good things he wanted going to him, rather than him chasing them.

Yeah, I could do that.

With a frustrated gasp, I gave him all I had, attacking his mouth in a rhythmical assault, showing him what his *slow* meant to me.

He was here in my home. We had two days and two nights. I planned to make us closer than we ever had been.

Gordain reciprocated, hunger in his moves, a dangerous edge that spoke of desperation and of him holding back.

His fingers dug into my skin.

This weekend was going to be so good.

Finally, we slowed, catching our breath, our foreheads together.

"Wow," I whispered, opening my eyes to his gorgeous face.

"I haven't even shown you the bedroom yet." Gordain's mouth moved into a smile, the effect dazzling.

I giggled. "Maybe we should save that until later."

Gordain choked on a laugh, looking boyish and shy, as much as such a masculine man could. "Aye."

He released me, and I righted my clothes, taking a step back.

"I'm going to offer to make dinner. Come with me?" I held out my hand.

Gordain took it, and we left my rooms. We interlaced our fingers as we walked down the hall, and my meaning was clear. I was claiming him right back in front of my family.

* * *

James and I cooked side by side in his and Beth's kitchen. We'd invited the Hinchcliffes, our honorary grandparents, to make a real family event. Our first since... God, since our parents had died. Life had finally moved on, and it felt great.

Midway through serving up, when I returned to the kitchen to collect the huge bowl of fluffy pilau rice, made to go with our sweet and sour chicken and homemade spring rolls—I'd expanded my repertoire in the past year—Mrs Hinchcliffe poked me on the shoulder.

"What's that peeking out at the back of your neck?" She lifted my hair. "I thought I caught sight of something. Ella! You have a tattoo!" she said, scandalised.

"Hinchie! Hush, it's a secret." I pulled down my high collar to show her.

A few days after Gordain had left for his three-week assignment, I'd passed a tattoo parlour, and an idea had sprung into my head. Then I'd gone home and researched designs before finding the perfect one.

I made an appointment, getting a lucky cancellation, and had it done the next morning.

"Is it a stag? My goodness." Her local accent thickened if she disapproved of something.

I twisted around and hugged her. I loved it, the stylised black stencil, the stag's proud antlers twisting up my neck.

With my thick hair worn down and my collar up, it was almost unnoticeable.

Naked, it would stand out.

The thought of Gordain seeing it in the heat of the moment had me breathless.

"Well, at least it's pretty. Do you remember your mother's tattoo?"

I stared at her, then a distant memory glimmered. It came back in a rush. "On her hip. What was it, a car?"

"It was! Lord knows why she got it, though your father was always into his motors, so I imagine it was a tribute to him." Mrs Hinchcliffe smiled fondly.

"Wasn't it blue and white?"

"You're right. The colours of the Scottish flag, to celebrate her heritage. No wonder you went and found yourself a Scotsman."

"Aye, that I did," I said in my best attempt at a Scottish accent.

She tipped me a wink then took the bowl of rice. "At least yours is tasteful. Just don't go covering yourself with them."

Mrs Hinchcliffe returned to her chair at my brother's table and took over cuddles with Sebastian. She and her husband called him Little Lord, just like they had done my brother. Neither of us had remembered it until it had popped out of Mrs Hinchcliffe's mouth earlier in the evening.

I loved it. My family being here, safe, and together.

I absolutely wanted the meal done so I could sneak into Gordain's bedroom and jump his bones.

He'd showered and changed before dinner, and the fresh scent of him was sending my senses into overdrive. He sat next to me, smiling and making conversation, telling stories of flying that had Hinchie gasping with fright.

While he talked, I had a funny thought. Last time he'd been away on the oil rigs, he'd got his piercing. A reaction to being...frustrated. Needing release.

Would he have gotten another?

I squinted, checking out the lines of his grey shirt trying to spot the outline of a barbell.

He caught me and gave me a quizzical glance.

Heat stole over me, and I hid my smile behind my water glass.

Gordain dropped a hand and took my fingers in his, under cover of the table. His casual thumb stroke was enough to give me palpitations.

"Keep looking at me like that, and I'm not going to be able to get up from this table," he murmured, his eyes flashing with heat.

I squeezed his hand, a promise in the press.

Finally, the meal was done. Beth took Sebastian to his cot, and James shooed everyone else away from clearing up. I gave a fake yawn and said my goodnights.

Then I changed clothes, sat behind my door, and counted to a hundred.

Gordain McRae, coming, ready or not.

20
———

HORNY TOWN

*G*ordain

I paced to the door of my dark bedroom. I'd killed the lights, readying to leave, then found myself stalling.

If I went to Ella's room, I knew what would happen. All the talking I wanted to do would come second to the scorching heat that ignited whenever we were near each other.

The idea of taking it slow was about to be written on paper, caught on fire, and the ashes scattered to the breeze.

I'd dreamed of being inside Ella more times that I could remember.

It was what had led to my second piercing being done.

The last night before offshore duty, I'd found my way to a piercing studio. Handed over my cash. Now, I had a smooth, silver cock ring, right *there,* where the only person who'd ever see it would be her.

Though, knowing my fucking brothers, they'd find out somehow.

A light tap sounded at my door.

I swung it open.

Ella waited on the other side, her hand to her hip over a long shirt—the only thing she had on, covering her to the top of her thighs—and the other on the doorframe. She pressed her lips together, banked fire in her eyes. "I'm nervous."

Instantly, my worries evaporated.

Stepping into her space, I wrapped my arms around her. "I didn't ask you to come here for anything other than your company. I figured we needed time together. Space to talk away from work and studying."

Ella nodded and dropped her forehead to my chest.

I took a deep inhale, and her scent flooded my nose. My good intentions dropped to the floor. In a moment I was back in horny town. I tilted Ella's chin up so I could see her eyes.

That fire was burning bright.

"Problem is, I don't think we'll be able to sit opposite one another and chat. Do you?" Gently, she propelled me back into my room, then closed the door behind her with her foot.

I gave a grumble of agreement.

"It's been murder sitting next to you all evening." She kept walking me backwards.

I let her lead, enjoying where she was taking this.

"I wasn't kidding when I said how much I missed you." Ella's expression shifted from sheer determination, revealing a flash of something more vulnerable. "Every morning I'd wake, and for a split second I was full of light, knowing I'd see you for breakfast. Then boom, back to reality with you gone."

"I know." The same had happened to me. Our breakfast dates had easily been the highlight of my day.

In two days, Monday morning, I had the hearing with the RAF, and Jordie's question popped up into my mind. Would I go back into the air force? I'd be away for a lot longer than a few weeks on a rota.

"You know what I did to get through the day?" I lowered my head to connect our gazes. "I'd reread the messages you sent and looked at pictures of you." Like a lovesick teenager.

"You did?"

"At work, I had a photo of you in my locker. I took it with me on offshore duty. Had it in my heli cab."

Ella fixed me with that fierce gaze. "So here's the thing. I want to be clear on what we are. This slow thing, the push and pull...it's going somewhere. The idea of me looking around to experience the world. Dating other people. Waiting."

"That's over. I don't want that either."

"Then we're dating. Official. No half measures." She seemed to hold her breath.

Joy and fucking fear shimmered inside me. I held my muscles taut, the power I was about to hand over holding the potential to tear me to pieces. "I don't think I can do casual. If we're together, I won't be able to stay away from you." I turned us, backing her towards the bed. "I have no experience with relationships but I know what I'm like when I'm around you."

"Wanting everything." She ran her fingers up my arm. "Wearing your heart on your sleeve."

"Turns out an all-or-nothing kind of guy can't change."

"Good," she replied. "Because I'm an all-for-you kind of woman." Ella's hands slipped down my body to find the hem of my t-shirt. She raised an eyebrow at me, slowly lifting the material.

I let her strip my top half. She inhaled, her gaze roaming

over my chest. At my tattoos. My piercing. The blank skin over my heart.

Then she touched the barbell in my nipple, and a grin took her lips. "I thought you might have the other done."

I laughed softly. "I considered it. Turned out something else caught my eye instead."

Ella's mouth dropped open. "What?"

"Wait and see." I swooped and kissed her, pulling her down with me as I went.

We landed on the quilt, Ella astride me, her bare legs either side of mine. The last time we'd done this, I'd led. This time, Ella pinned me.

"Hands on my hips," she ordered.

I complied, taking handfuls of her flesh. The long shirt rode up. I slid my hands underneath, tracing the line where her underwear should be.

Nothing there.

Oh, holy fuck.

"You skipped along the hall in just this?" I tugged at the shirt.

"Hush," she replied then continued her exploration. "Tomorrow, I want a picture of you bare-chested. I want to memorise this art. The patterns on you. I dream about them." She dipped and laid a kiss to the curve of my shoulder, over the whirring rotor blades pattern. Another to the stags on my pec.

She licked my nipple piercing and I nearly shouted.

"Good thing about being in a big house. No one can hear you scream." Ella's mouth curved wickedly.

"You'll be screaming in a minute," I replied.

She laughed, but there was an edge to it.

Our humour fell away.

Ella gave me another long, slow kiss, then she sat back, grabbed her shirt, and stripped it off.

No bra, either. *Holy hell.*

I'd never seen her naked. Her gorgeous long legs, sure. Her pussy, yeah. Not all of her. There was just enough light in the room to reveal her perfect form, her gleaming skin.

Her full tits. Fuck me.

Her hair fell in curls past her shoulder and around her body, black as night and soft as silk. I twisted it around my hand.

She dropped forwards, following my gentle pull.

Hunger had me taking her mouth hard. With one hand at the back of her head, I gripped her hip. Then, dizzy with need, I broke our kiss so I could admire her again. I brought both hands to her rib cage, pressing my thumbs in as I ran my hands up to palm her breasts. Two gorgeous handfuls I needed to taste.

Oh Christ.

Under her, my cock throbbed.

"You're beautiful," I murmured.

A soft smile broached her lips. "You're beautiful, G. Everything about you. Did you know that?"

Our mouths met in heat and building urgency. Ella's tongue flitted over mine, and her hands slid around to my back.

Then she raked her fingernails over my skin, just lightly.

I jolted. The sensation was…interesting. "Again."

She obeyed, scratching harder this time.

Fucking hell. It lit me up.

I flipped us, rearing over her but holding still. Confused.

"You like pain," Ella informed me. "At least a little bit. I noticed it before when we…were together. I might have obsessed over that."

"Don't want to think about why right now, but yeah, that turns me on," I grumbled. I brought my mouth to hers, then kissed her cheek, under her ear, her neck. Moving down her naked body.

Ella squirmed.

I kissed the swell of her breasts, then took her nipple in my mouth, palming the other, rolling it between my fingers. Her sharp inhale sent blood to my cock. I was already hard, had been before she'd shown up at my door, thoughts of sex dominating my mind. But we weren't going there tonight. Not fully. Ella still had little experience as far as I knew, and there was no rush.

I repeated the words in my head like a mantra, sucking on her, making her feel good. She writhed underneath me, her hands coasting down my body until they met my waistband.

"Take your jeans off," she asked, dragging in a breath. "I want to see you. Play with you."

Play. Sex had never been fun for me before, but it was with Ella. And I wanted her to see my new piercing. To get the look of shock on her face.

I made quick work of removing the rest of my clothes, settling next to her, fully nude.

Except for the ring through the end of my cock. Thick and glinting.

"Oh my— What is that?" She bolted up. "G! Jesus." She reached out a tentative finger and touched the ring. "Does it hurt?"

"No." My head swam at her touch.

"It's a piercing! Is it healed?"

"Yep."

"Have you, um..." She glanced away, her hand dropping to her knee. "Tried it out?"

I blinked. That shock I was seeking? Seems it was all mine. "Do you mean have I slept with anyone in the past month? God, Ella."

Her gaze came back to mine. Caution held her features, but she didn't elaborate.

"No," I choked out. "I haven't."

I badly wanted to tell her how I hadn't so much as looked at another woman since I'd met her. But that was a slippery slope into feelings and emotions, and the going-slow part of my plan didn't allow that.

If she knew how I'd steadily fallen deeper and deeper in love, starting the first moment I'd laid eyes on her, that would kill off the fragile moment for sure.

I loved her.

I loved her.

And I needed to get used to the idea myself first, before springing it on her.

I lay back and put my hands behind my head, my broad body exposed, my cock bobbing for her attention. The weight of the ring was new, but the rest was my greatest fantasy come to life.

I rolled my hips. "This is all for you. What do you think?"

Ella snapped her mouth closed. "Remember our first night together? You used your dick to, um…"

"Make you come?"

She blinked. "I'm wondering what that would feel like with the hard ring." Then her boldness returned. "Can I touch?"

"You'd better."

She took hold of my cock and ran her thumb over the end.

Christ.

I threw my arm over my eyes. Pushed my shoulders into the bed.

Then heat and warmth enveloped me, and I groaned at Ella's mouth enclosing my cockhead. She tongued the ring and pulled gently.

The sting of pleasure nearly knocked me out.

"Good?" she asked.

"I think I died and went someplace hot this time," I mumbled.

Ella snickered then returned to her exploration. This time, I lifted onto an elbow and watched my cock disappear into her mouth. I reached out and ran my fingers into her hair, taking control of her head. Guiding her movements.

Getting the most incredible blow job I could imagine.

"Oh fuck," I told the ceiling when it became too much and I couldn't watch anymore.

Ella hummed, and it nearly sent me over the edge.

"Not coming like that," I growled, and I rose, flipping her onto her back.

I dropped a kiss on Ella's thigh. I pushed her legs wide apart and kissed higher until I met the centre of her.

So fucking wet.

"You like the piercing," I stated. I licked her, long and hard, loving her taste.

"Yes. I want you to fuck me with it. I want to know how it feels. But..."

"Not tonight," I finished for her.

She nodded, maybe relieved.

"I've got you, don't worry," I added then reared up and brought my mouth to her nipple again.

And fitted my cock between her legs.

I sucked her and slid my hardness over her slick softness at the same time.

Ella gasped and rocked her hips.

I repeated the move, fucking over her sweet pussy, but not entering her. Teasing her clit, parting her with my cock.

"God, that feels good." She moaned.

Her nails bit into my shoulder blades, and I groaned at the pain.

Angling my cockhead, I used the piercing on Ella's clit. Bumping over it again and again. Picking up speed. Breathing hard.

Sitting back, I kept up the move but slid two fingers inside her. Then I dragged one through her wetness and over her ass, holding her down with my other hand at her hip.

Ella gripped me like her life depended on it. "Don't stop! Never stop."

I worked her hard, an onslaught of pleasure, as good for me as it looked to be for her.

"Oh God, oh God," she chanted. "Gonna come. Fuck, G."

I pushed at her rear hole, riding her relentlessly.

Her internal muscles clamped down on my hand, and she moaned out my name, grinding into me.

One hand shot out, and she took hold of my cock, holding it exactly where she needed. Rubbing it right into her clit.

Her sobs filled the room, her orgasm loud and proud.

Grasping both her hips now, I kept up the rhythm for a few strokes longer, teetering on the edge.

My movements staggered as my own orgasm hit, fast and unexpected.

"Ella!" I yelled.

She gripped me harder.

Shocks hit me in lightning strikes.

Then I came like a fucking flood. My cock jerked, come

spilling, covering Ella's belly and breasts, dripping onto her thighs. Making a mess of her as I saw out my pleasure.

I dropped my forehead to her shoulder, trying to centre my spinning head.

"Fuck," I mouthed against her skin.

A wave of pure satisfaction rolled over me. It weighed me down, and I cloaked Ella like a blanket. With reverence, I nuzzled her neck, and she became the centre of my world. I'd never felt this good, this content. Everything was perfect.

Then realisation dawned.

I jerked up. "Please tell me you're on the pill. That's gone everywhere."

The lass giggled, a beautiful sound. "Implant. I've got it covered."

"Thank God. I didn't think. I got carried away."

"Hey, it's okay, G. I don't want babies either."

I felt around for my t-shirt, then used it to mop up the mess I'd made.

My sudden panic lingered.

I had never, ever slacked in that area. Always using condoms. Always safe.

"You make me crazy. I never want to do anything stupid with you," I said, pulling my boxers on.

Ella rose. "That scared you," she said then climbed onto my lap and huddled in. "Pretty much everything about you scares me, so that makes us equal."

I watched her mouth. "I scare you?"

"What you do to me. How it makes me feel."

I wrapped my arms around her and tucked my head down. "That makes two of us."

We sat together in the cool darkness. Too close to a subject that could slice us open.

If I told Ella how I felt, and it wasn't the same as what

she was talking about...that shite would hurt. Even so, I had to trust her.

Before I could even think of a way to start, Ella spoke again. "I had hardly anyone for a long time. So making claims..."

"Touches on something deep down and broken. I know exactly how you feel."

Then she gave me a meaningful look and stretched to pull her hair into a ponytail. I followed her movements. Then I saw it. Ink on her perfect skin.

A tattoo?

I gaped, and craned my neck to see better. "It's a stag."

"Don't ask about it. Not yet. Just file it away with the conversation about making claims."

Ella's vulnerability was clear. She'd had a tattoo done, a beautiful wee design that suited her perfectly. It suited me. It looked like the McRae stag from our coat of arms but done in a delicate watercolour.

Fuck.

My heart thundered. All the ink I had, yet one elegant piece on a lass's neck, and I was floored. She'd had it done for me, claiming me. I fucking hoped so anyway.

She dropped the ponytail and continued, "James and I are closer now, but it's been hard going. We were separated for so long. The times I did see him as a child, he was further and further from the big brother I knew. Richard tried to make him in his image. Selfish and superior."

She shivered. Shifting, I moved us up the bed and dragged the quilt around us. With her back to my chest, I held her close, spooning her, then laid a kiss on the tattoo and nudged her to continue her story of all her broken pieces.

"I had Taylor, then I didn't. Then I had to build a relationship back up with James." She drew my arm tighter around her. "This is a really terrible thing to say, but I didn't trust him. Not for a long time. Beth bridged our conversations because neither of us knew what to say to each other."

"And now?"

"Something changed. Maybe Sebastian coming along. It proved to me that James is there for his family. Nothing of Richard remains."

"You have your family back."

She inclined her head against my arm. "It doesn't heal all the crap in our past, that scarred part, but it's more than I could've dreamed of a few years ago." She traced a finger through the hair on my forearm. "And then there's you."

"Then there's me. Who pushed you away, too." I was such a dick for walking away from her. My chest ached, and I buried my face in her hair, my fingertips on the tattoo. My new obsession.

"No, no. That isn't what I meant. I'm just... I want to give you space to talk."

I saw what she was doing. Exposing the dark place she'd come from. Some small understanding bloomed in me that this was how we made a real connection.

"What do you want to know about me?"

"Everything." She turned in my arms. "Your dad's violence. It makes me so fucking angry every time I think about it."

"It does? He's long dead." Not like her uncle, though they had things in common.

"Why, G? Why did he pick on you?"

My words came readily. "You know how your uncle's issues all stemmed from him being born outside of marriage?" James had told me that story, how Richard had been the older of two brothers but born before his parents had married, thus leaving him ineligible to inherit the vast Belvedere estate.

Ella nodded. "It twisted him. He's mentally ill because of his obsessing over it."

"Same problem in my family."

She paused. "Who, your dad?"

"No. Callum."

"Callum's illegitimate? I don't understand."

It was so strange, talking about this openly. But my brother didn't mind and had given permission. I had to do it if we were going to get anywhere. I pushed on. "Ma got pregnant with Callum before she and Da were married. She had Callum in secret. Da didn't meet his first son until he was a toddler."

Ella blew out a breath. "That's messed up."

"I know. Then they had me, and soon after, Ma died. I don't really remember a time when Da was happy because he was always drunk and bitter. A hazard. Someone we avoided. He remarried pretty quickly. Then the twins came along." I was back in the castle. A small boy, excited over meeting his baby brothers.

The first words they'd heard was how I was a waste of space. How I'd killed my mother by being born—not true, but that one still cut deep.

"What was his problem with you? I can't work it out."

"I'm the legitimate heir to Castle McRae. To the land, to being laird," I whispered, indulging in words I'd never said out loud. "If I wanted, I could press a claim over Callum. By rights, all he owns could be mine. That's what Da wanted to beat out of me."

21

DISTURBED

*E*lla

Of all the people in the world, I thought I hated Richard the most. But he had a challenger for the title. Gordain's father, though dead, was just as warped as my uncle.

Worse, in that he'd laid his fists into G.

"My stepmother explained the situation to me when I was about seven or eight," Gordain continued. "Da had been on one. Hitting the whisky and ranting about our family's legacy. Taunting me in his usual way. She'd hidden me until he passed out. Callum stayed with me, too, and I could tell it wasn't news to him. I guess he'd worked it out."

"But isn't there a legal issue?" My brother had had acres of paperwork to go through to receive his inheritance.

"There's no covenant on Castle McRae or the estate like there is on Belvedere, but there's tradition and old laws. If I wanted, I could have insisted on being recognised as the heir, and there was nothing Da could've done about it."

"But you didn't want that."

"No. I never wanted Castle McRae, and I'd never take a

thing from Callum, but it probably explains why I set my heart on Braithar. Remember I told you the estate was once one huge parcel of land? The chieftain at the time had twin boys, and he carved the estate down the middle, building Braithar to give them an equal inheritance. Braithar means 'brother'."

Oh. My heart hurt for the little boy who loved his older brother but dreamed up his own escape. Braithar was made for him.

"If I had the money, I'd buy Braithar for you," I said, holding him tight.

Gordain chuckled. "What would you want with a big old place like that?"

"Are you kidding? If I could, I'd set up a recording studio there. It's got the space I need, and the acoustics are amazing."

Gordain relaxed into the bed, his small smile just visible.

"Nope, no sleep yet. We need to take a shower." I jiggled him.

He made a sound of interest. Then he leapt up and scooped me into his arms. "Deal. But I'm just going to get you dirty again in there."

He kissed me as he marched into the en suite. Under the hot water and bright lights, we got even more acquainted, getting dirty before we got clean, just like he promised.

After, we dried off with white fluffy towels, and the black and blue lines tattooed on Gordain's back caught my eye in the steamed-up bathroom mirror.

He saw me looking. "Wasp copped a beating once. It was my fault. The first and last time Da went for either of the twins."

"How can it have been your fault?" I ran my fingers down the slashes.

"Ally's school report had come in. We'd all made a pact to hide any reports from Da. I slipped up and didn't hide the letter before he got home. Da read how his son was failing in everything, then grabbed the wrong boy and beat Wasp black and blue."

I knew Ally was dyslexic. He'd told me once when I'd found him using a text-to-speech function on his phone.

"It was the night Da died. We all had our own way of commemorating it. Callum has a sword tattooed down his back. Wasp took a nickname to reflect the marks on his back. Ally carries his guilt under a permanent jackass character."

I winced. Then pieces slotted together. "Where you separated yourself from your family by taking the rooms in the tower. You work in a job that took you away. That held danger. You set yourself aside."

He shook his head, but I was onto something.

"You save people, G. In the RAF and in the mountain rescue. I'm on that list, too."

"You're overthinking it."

"Your father was a terrible person, but you're the best person I know," I finished, staring at him and feeling all kinds of things I wasn't sure I knew how to name.

Gordain took my hand and led me back to bed. He found me a t-shirt, and we climbed under the covers, no more conversation to be had.

We kissed, settling to sleep entwined and so close his heart made its beat against mine.

And though he soon breathed deeply, sleep taking him under, I lay there awake. Disturbed, panicked, even.

When I was sure Gordain wouldn't wake, I climbed from his bed and left the room.

* * *

Cold air swirled around my naked legs, and I hurried through the night-darkened halls. Gordain's room was only two corridors from mine, but still, I trod quickly, my bare feet silent on the polished floor.

I'd never been creeped out at Belvedere, but then again, I hadn't been here enough to wander at night.

A spooky feeling dogged my heels, like I was about to be grabbed.

A creak sounded nearby, and I jumped around, my heart slamming.

Nothing.

Just paintings on the walls and the silhouettes of marble statues on side tables.

My pulse made a steady *thrum-thrum-thrum*, and I laughed under my breath at my edginess. Still, the mansion was a big place with countless entrances and exits.

Anyone could sneak in.

Hide out in one of the hundreds of rooms.

Tucking my head down, I scurried around the corner to my rooms.

"Who's there?" a voice demanded.

I shrieked, clamping my hand over my mouth.

A dark figure emerged from an alcove.

Mrs Hinchcliffe raised both her hands to her chest. "Gracious, child. You terrified me. What are you doing wandering the house in the early hours?" She peered at my clothing. "Don't tell me, I can guess."

I laughed in gasps and threw myself at her with a hug. "You nearly gave me a heart attack. I didn't expect anyone else to be up. What on earth are you doing?"

She patted me on the arm. "I got into the habit of

wandering since Sebastian was born. I wake, sometimes, worrying about Richard. He used to be so obsessed with your brother. Or his title, anyway. Once I'm awake, I can't drop off again until I've assured myself all is well by going on my little patrol."

"What would you do if you find him?" Fucking Richard, making her do this.

Hinchie winked at me. "Never you mind about that, but I have my resources. Now get yourself to bed. Your own bed!"

I complied and left her to her watch.

In my rooms, I closed my door and dropped onto my new couch, staring up at the dark ceiling, asking myself the question that had kept me awake.

Why had I left Gordain's bed? Why couldn't I stay? I was on a precipice and couldn't work out whether to cling on tight or let myself fall.

Gathering my phone from the table, I dialled the one person with whom I used to share my innermost thoughts.

Taylor answered on the first ring. "Babe!"

"Hey, can you talk?"

Chatter sounded on the line, then a door closed. "I can now. I'm at my dad's."

"What's that like?"

"Frantic. Full of phoneys. His election plans are underway, so it's go, go, go with the marketing machine."

Strain sounded in her voice, and I held the phone closer. We'd talked about this at school—her father's political aspirations and what it meant for Tay, her carefully controlled appearance and stage-managed lifestyle.

"That must be rough."

She made an off sound. "Yeah, well, nobody ever died from being over-pampered and smiling a fake-ass smile night and day. So tell me, how are you? What prompts a call in the middle of a deep, dark, Manchester night?"

I chewed my lip. "I'm at Belvedere."

"Uh-huh."

"With Gordain."

"Oh!" Tay elongated the word. "It's on?"

"I hope so." I jumped up from the couch and walked heel to toe along a line of the floorboards. "I've got a problem, though."

"What's that?"

Perhaps Taylor wasn't the right person to give advice on this subject, but my mind was still rushing, and who else could I choose? My university friends were becoming more like colleagues, and everyone else I knew also knew Gordain.

My head spun with all the thoughts that had risen tonight.

"I'm in love with him." My pulse pounded in my ears, and I forced myself to continue. "I think he has feelings for me, but what if they aren't the same? He said all this stuff about taking it slow, but tonight we were anything but. Then we shared all this intensely personal history, and now...now I can't sleep."

"You're scared," she said softly.

"One hundred percent correct," I whispered back.

"Virtual hug! I wish I had advice to give, but my dating life is messed up. My whole life is a fucking joke. It would be the blind leading the blind."

"I guess neither of us are going to be any good at this. What hope is there for girls who were raised like we were?"

Taylor sighed. "One thing is for sure, we're never going to love small. Or have tepid feelings."

Wasn't that the truth?

She continued, "I sometimes wonder if we'd be different people if we'd been brought up in stable, happy families."

I mused on the point. "I spent the last year thinking I needed to be different. That I didn't know my own mind because how the hell could I? I didn't trust myself. But do you know what? The plans I made then are the ones I'm working on now. I'm going to run my own company, date the guy I love, and make a life for myself."

"And you'll be massively successful." Then Taylor's voice came out forced. "I wish I could fall in love, too."

"Got anyone in mind?"

"Someone normal, like William. But I can't even date anyone my dad doesn't approve of now. It's fucked up."

William? Oh, Wasp! She meant Gordain's brother.

"Tay," I breathed. "I didn't even know you liked him that much."

"I won't let myself because it can't go anywhere."

I dropped onto a chair, and we sat in silence together for a moment. I didn't tell her how incredible it would be if we dated brothers. She didn't confirm the reasons why she couldn't. It was pointless.

She needed her dad on her side, and the only way was by going where he sent her. Dating someone he approved of. Presenting the all-American family, even if she was half English. She'd blown her one shot at choice on my brother.

A Scot would never do. One a year younger than her with no money? No chance.

"Love you," I told her.

"Love you, too. I better go. Go get back into Gordain's bed. When you're ready, tell him how you feel. It'll work out."

We hung up, and I gazed into the dark.

My phone screen lit with a notification.

An email. The sender: Richard.

Fool that I was, I opened it.

Elinor.

Further to my last message, I find I am in need of that favour. The birth of the heir has made me realise how fondly I miss family life. Your brother refused me access to his child, you recall.

Change his mind.

I will soon be permanently relocating back to England and expect this small interlude of distance in our lives to be forgotten.

In exchange, I will award you the monthly stipend that once came to me. I'm sure you can find a use for that money, considering the fees you'll need for the second year of university.

Alternatively, you could quit that waste of time and take up a real degree. I believe it is within my gift as your guardian to direct your education as best I see fit.

I will be in touch.

Yours, etc.

Richard Fitzroy

I stared at my phone screen, nausea rising.

He couldn't, in his wildest dreams, expect James to let him near his son. The man was toxic. Sebastian would never hear the evil words that came from his poisonous tongue.

Nor would I help him. In any way.

How did he get money again? He'd been broke, the lawyers had said. And did he really have the power to change my school? I was legally an adult, nobody could force me to do anything I didn't want to do.

I was just getting my life in order.

It was that last thought that broke the dam inside me. I picked up my phone, opened the email again, and so, so stupidly, hit reply.

Stay away from my family. Don't contact me again. There's nothing for you here but the hatred you earned.

I sent it, my hands trembling with my outrage.

When I calmed, I opened a new email and sent an urgent message to Howard Marks, our lawyer.

Then I sat and waited for dawn.

* * *

At five-thirty, a fresh email dinged. Howard Marks, asking if he could call.

I rang his mobile number, rubbing the lack of sleep from my eyes and pulling myself up from my slump on the couch.

The lawyer answered on the first ring. "My Lady Elinor."

In short sentences, I updated him on Richard's message.

"That's interesting timing. As soon as I read your message, I checked what little updates on your uncle I am able to monitor. I found out that this morning, the New York apartment he resides in is due to be put up for sale."

"He's selling up?"

"It's likely his only remaining asset. Your brother forced the closure of his business ventures." Howard's voice took on an urgency. "Which led me to a short but telling paper trail to the history of him purchasing that building."

He paused, and I leaned forward, clutching the phone.

"Mr Fitzroy bought the apartment almost immediately after your parents' death. When he took over your care."

"Where did he get the money?" I asked the question but already knew the answer.

"Your inheritance, I believe." Howard sped up. "My Lady, this is no insignificant sum. The sale is likely to be agreed quickly. It's being put up for cash only. In order to prevent your money being laundered directly into Richard Fitzroy's hands, you will need to make a claim."

My mind buzzed. "But he's still my legal guardian. Won't that stop me? Is there a way to change that?"

"None that we haven't already explored. It will take months, still, to change the order to your brother."

But months ago, Howard had given me an out. "What if I were married?" I uttered. "Does that option still apply?"

"But you're not," he spluttered.

"Work it through for me." I leapt to my feet.

"You'd have to obtain a marriage certificate, present it to legal counsel, be declared in your majority, and lodge a claim. All in a very short time."

"How long are we talking? Weeks?" It took three weeks to register to get married in the UK. I knew that from James's urgent wedding.

"No, Lady Elinor. Days. As soon as Richard signs a contract, you could lose your ability to challenge. If he hides that money, you may never see any of it."

Two options existed. The first, to let Richard sell the apartment and hope I could one day sue him to get the money back. Or the second, to propose to a man I loved, who'd turned me down once, and who desperately wanted to take things slow with me.

I needed to talk to Gordain.

22

THAT FUCKER STUNG

*G*ordain

In the most relaxed state I'd been in years, I woke, my limbs heavy, my body well-used, and a smile pulling my lips. Alongside the lingering sensations from the hot night Ella and I had shared, I'd dreamed about the RAF hearing in a couple of days, imagining being able to tell Ella the result. My family, too.

I stretched, reaching out.

Cold, empty sheets met my touch. Ella was gone?

The dawn light fell on an empty bed. Yeah, long gone, by the lack of warmth on her side. I sat up; the room was empty, the bathroom door ajar, and the space dark.

She'd left in the night.

That was...unexpected. Rejection rose its ugly head, the feeling uncomfortable and raw. The time she'd slept in my bed at Castle McRae she'd fled as our families returned.

Ella leaving hurt. No bones about it.

But there could be a hundred good reasons why she'd left.

I needed to rein that shite in until she was in the same place. Except that tattoo and her stories... I pushed away my stupid mood. I could respect her needing space. It wasn't her problem that I was emotionally messed up.

I'd keep my mouth shut.

I rolled off the bed and rubbed the heels of my hands into my eyes, banishing tiredness. I used the bathroom and dressed quickly.

Knowing James to be an early riser, Sebastian, too, I left my room and headed down the hall to find him. Most mornings this week, we'd gone for a run, taking the baby with us. Or worked out with the bairn in a Moses basket, looking on.

At his door, I stalled. I wanted to walk past. Go to Ella. Demand the closeness I'd missed by waking alone.

Fuck. Fuck, fuck, fuck.

I tapped on James's door instead.

"G?" Ella's voice sounded behind me.

At the same second, the door swung open.

I bounced my gaze between the Fitzroy siblings.

"Er, come in?" James said when no one spoke.

I watched Ella.

"Okay," she said, like this was somehow deciding something.

I held my ground as she walked past. Her shoulders were raised and her gait stiff.

Something was wrong.

I followed her in and closed the door, then took a seat at the table, half a room from where Ella perched on the edge of the sofa.

"How's Beth this morning?" I asked James after a beat.

"Tired." He tilted his head, looking between us with a furrow on his brow. "I'm a little worried, but she's promised to rest up. Sebastian is still asleep. I'll go get him if he wakes. Is... Did something happen?"

"No," I answered.

"Yes," Ella replied at the same time. "I had an email in the night."

I sat taller. "From whom?"

"Richard."

James took the seat next to her. "What did he say?"

"That he's planning to come back, and he wants me to persuade you to let him back into our lives. Into Sebastian's life."

James reared back. "How can he think he'd ever be welcome? He's delusional."

"He won't set foot near this family," I vowed, willing to throw myself in between any one of the Fitzroys and their enemies.

Ella took a breath. "There's more. He thinks he's calling in a favour after he approved my university fees last summer."

"He's contacted you before?" James asked, his voice flat.

Ella paled but didn't falter. "Yes. I was in my independence phase. I should have told you, but it was about me, not you and your family."

"You are my family," James ground out.

She held up a hand. "There's more. Save your outrage." Then she looked my way. "This could involve you, too, G."

I stood and moved to sit on the adjacent seat of the L-shaped couch, almost knee to knee with her.

Ella regarded me, pink flushing her cheeks. She dragged her gaze back to her brother. "Richard is about to sell his apartment in Manhattan. Howard Marks told me this morning. Howard also believes that the place was bought with my money."

James stilled.

Hot outrage pooled in my stomach.

Ella continued, "I need to challenge the sale. Within the next few days, if I'm to stop him walking away with the cash. Howard thinks that if I try after the fact, I'll have little chance of seeing a penny of the money."

"I'm there in any way you need," I said. "But what does this have to do with me specifically? Did he mention me?"

"I was about to ask the same question," James said.

A faint cry came from down the short hall at the end of the room. "Sebastian." James jumped to his feet. "Be right back."

He paced down the hall, leaving me and Ella alone.

"The problem is that Richard is still my guardian. There hasn't been time to transfer it or to cancel it. Which means..." Her words dried up, and she dropped her gaze. "Oh boy. This is too hard."

Then I got it.

Understanding cut into me, knife-deep and twisted. I knew exactly why Ella was cringing. Because she was about to ask me something she'd already tried once.

And I'd said no.

Fuck. That could give her her inheritance back.

She raised her gaze, and I winced at what I saw. *Regret.*

This was not happening.

"You need to get married for this plan to work," I helped her out.

"I don't have to. But it's an option."

"Then, Ella?" I sank to my knee, a sucker for punishment. She said I liked pain, and I guessed this proved her right. Because proposing to the woman I loved, who didn't love me but would accept me for the sake of money? That fucker stung.

"Marry me?" I finished.

"Yes," she whispered, her eyes wide and round and so utterly fucking beautiful.

Without another word, I climbed to my feet and stalked out of the room.

23

THE OH-SHIT MOMENT

Ella

With my stomach in knots and my heart in tatters, I finally found Gordain outside the front of the house. He hadn't been in his room, so I'd called his phone, but there had been no answer. He'd gone running. I might've guessed.

He slowed his steps, gravel crunching under his feet.

"Hey." I lifted my hand to shade my eyes.

"Did ye need me?"

"I'm booking the flights and I need your passport number."

His hands went to his hips. "We need to fly someplace?"

God, this was awkward. A wall had descended between us, and it was all my fault. "New York first to see the lawyers' partner firm and get them ready to go with all the paperwork, then," I swallowed, "Vegas."

"Las Vegas?"

"We can get a marriage certificate almost immediately. Then hold the ceremony the same day."

He looked at the sky, his big body tense and his workout

shirt straining over his muscular frame. "Maybe we could have Elvis conduct the service."

I forced a laugh, feeling anything but amused.

"When do we fly?" He brought his gaze back to me.

"This afternoon. If that's okay?"

"Aye. Whatever you need." Gordain passed me, heading back into the house. After a few steps, he paused, as if realising something. "What day will we get back?"

"Maybe Tuesday? It depends on how long it all takes once the lawyers are doing their thing. But you're off work, right? Is there somewhere else you need to be?"

Emotion flitted over his face. But whatever it was that had given him pause got quickly locked down. "I told you, I'm there for however long you need. I'll pack a bag."

He took another step then turned back. "Did you tell James the plan?"

"I would've, but he's taken Beth to see her doctor. She woke feverish. If they aren't back before we leave, I'll call them from the States."

Gordain gave me a salute. Then he left me standing there, knowing I'd caused this, knowing I'd broken us, but with no idea how to fix it.

* * *

We drove to Manchester in almost total silence. Gordain hid behind sunglasses, and I hid behind driving. At the airport, we checked in and went through security, still not talking. A weariness came over me, and I sank into a seat in the waiting area.

"Did ye sleep much last night?" Gordain asked.

"Not at all."

"We've got two hours until boarding. Close your eyes."

He didn't touch me, but his tenderness coupled with my tiredness sent a wave of emotion tumbling through me. He cared about me, and I'd messed everything up.

"I'm sorry," I uttered. "About all of this."

Gordain tipped his head back and, from my angle against my seat, I couldn't see his features. "Hush," he said, his voice tight.

So I did.

* * *

The flight had been almost fully booked, so we were in separate seats. I didn't see Gordain again until we landed. He arrived at my shoulder, silent, his sunglasses back in position.

A sentinel. A guard at my back. I trusted him with my life, despite the fact I had no clue what was going on in his head.

Our taxi took us from JFK into the city, heavy traffic surrounding the car. It being late afternoon in New York, the time difference worked to our advantage.

"What's the plan now?" Gordain asked, his first words in forever.

"We go to the lawyers' office. Then back to the airport for the flight to Vegas."

"Tonight?"

"Yep. Sorry." My heart ached, and all of a sudden, I needed to say more. Say everything. Tell him why this was both perfect and awful at the same time. "Listen, I know this is ridiculous. You and me—"

"Stop," he cut in, his tone kind but final. "We're doing this. We're both adults and we ken the consequences. Don't we?"

He'd be my husband. I'd be his wife. The consequences couldn't be more serious. I inclined my head. Cars blared horns, our driver swore in a thick accent.

"There's nothing more to be said."

I did as he'd asked and shut up. For now, at least.

* * *

The appointment with the Manhattan lawyers— three stony-faced, sharp-suited women—lasted for hours. They knew their business, and I signed my name on rapidly drafted paperwork.

They confirmed that the plan was sound. As well as being my only shot.

Gordain waited, his expression unreadable. He drank the proffered coffee and agreed to his part as my fiancé. Otherwise, he kept to his statue impression.

He stepped out for a short time, where, I didn't know. When he returned, he seemed…jittery. He paced, rather than sitting.

Then we were back on the road, to the airport, and in the air, flying to Las Vegas.

This time, we sat together. Just us on the row of three. Me at the window, Gordain in the centre. The engines roared, and the plane rumbled forward, angling as we soared into the New York night.

It was then that the oh-shit moment hit me.

This was happening. Not the inheritance, or the taking back of what my uncle had stolen, but I was getting *married*.

Not an event I could take lightly. No matter how it had come about or the initial purpose.

I wanted this.

Him, for life.

Soaring in a plane, high over the bright lights of a big city, I made a quiet little vow to my husband-to-be.

"What is it?" Gordain murmured.

"Hmm?"

"You were staring at me, and your lips moved but nothing came out."

They did? "I was thinking about the next step."

Gordain's steady gaze held mine. Since this morning, England time, he'd been near me, within touching distance for much of it, but barely making eye contact.

"You don't have to worry."

"I don't?"

His mouth curved at one side, but it was a short-lived expression. A fleeting movement of lips I loved kissing. "Aye, lass. I know my part and I'm good with that. When it's done, you send me the papers, and I'll sign."

"What papers?"

"Divorce. Annulment. Whatever works."

I stared. "End it?" Then words burst out of my mouth. "Married couples should know each other really well. We should fill in the gaps."

"You think someone will quiz us?

"No. I mean for us."

Two honey-dark eyebrows shot together. "I ken ye well enough."

"Enough to marry me?"

He tilted his head. "Your favourite colour is blue like the hoodie of mine you kept. You're afraid of spiders. You love your nephew above anyone else in the world and you should be running your own business by now but you delayed it in order to test the waters at university—a decision you regret. You prefer coffee to tea. You have a sensitive spot on your neck that makes you shiver when I kiss you there, and your greatest fear is…"

He stopped.

"My greatest fear is what?"

Gordain broke eye contact and dropped his head back on the seat. He gazed up as if seeking inspiration, then sighed, giving no answer.

"See," I said, "this is why we needed this chat. You're wrong about some of those things. My favourite colour?"

A pair of beautiful eyes found mine once more.

"Gordain's eyes—grey. There are multiple places on my body that quiver when you even look my way. And right now, my greatest fear is that my problems are going to break us apart."

My hands shook, but I reached over and took his nearest one.

Gordain faced me, his brow furrowed but his mouth a straight line. "I told you, I'll do whatever you need. It's just a piece of paper."

We both winced. Because that wasn't true at all. We'd been at the cusp of a huge change in our relationship, then bam, marriage had landed in our laps.

It altered everything.

"Can we not talk about ending it?" I pressed his hand, dropping my gaze. "We have all of this process to get through for the sake of money—"

"It's not just the money, is it? You're taking back your birthright. What that man stole."

"I'd give it up if I thought I'd lose you."

Gordain sat taller, palming the armrest. A look of frustration came over him. "How much is that place worth?"

"A lot." Tens of millions. A life-changing amount. "But I have a home. I've got the ability to make a career for myself and earn money. What I could never replace is a stubborn Scot who doesn't know his own value."

He shook his head, but the corner of his lips twisted, a smile trying to force its way out.

It wasn't much, but it was enough to thaw the ice between us. A few minutes later, Gordain lifted the armrest. His hand took mine, and he pulled me against him.

"Then we'll do this thing and stop talking about what comes after." His voice, so low, almost became lost in the rumble of the plane.

"Sounds good to me," I answered, just as quiet.

His chest heaved on an inhale, but nothing more was said.

The five-hour flight disappeared in a fog of dozing. Gordain held me against him, and the flight attendants dimmed the cabin's lights. All the travelling had exhausted me, but I'd cat-napped waiting for the first flight. I was pretty sure Gordain hadn't slept. He did now. The gentle movement of his chest told me so. I shifted to lay across his lap, and he curled around me.

When this was done, when the papers were signed and handed over to the lawyers, I'd find a way to make this up to him.

An idea came to me in a rush. My heart raced.

If all went to plan, I had an inkling of what that making-up might look like.

Yeah. I knew precisely what I was going to do.

24

VOW

*G*ordain

From the plane, Ella and I journeyed directly to East Clark Avenue in downtown Las Vegas to pick up our marriage licence. Despite the early hour, the heat rose from the road while we waited for the office to open. Ella swayed on her feet, the effect of going without solid sleep for so long apparent.

"Why is it I'm a dead woman and you look like your normal self?" She balled her long curls into a tie at the back of her head then stretched out her arms in a yawn.

"Practice from being in the RAF. Your body learns to catch sleep when you can and keep going when you can't." I eyed the tattoo on her neck, visible with her low t-shirt. "You're beautiful."

The office door opened, and a woman beamed at us— her first customers. Ella explained our need, and she ushered us inside. Ella had my ID so I zoned out, picturing the hearing that would be happening back in England tomorrow. Even if I wanted to, I couldn't make it back in time.

Maybe it didn't matter.

The RAF was in my past—I was increasingly sure. Not that working for Sky's the Limit was my future, but I couldn't go back to being a serviceman.

If Ella had meant what she'd implied, with us staying married, that meant putting work into our relationship. Not disappearing for months on end.

I needed a new start. Honesty in all things.

I had an idea where that new career might be.

Callum had mentioned that Mack's helicopter training school had finally gone onto the market. With a bank loan, I could maybe take over ownership. Steal a couple of good pilots to take with me and add a sideline of private hire. There were one or two pilots who I knew were qualified trainers, just treading water in our company, waiting for the right job to come along.

Where better than the Highlands? Flights over gorgeous, sprawling mountain ranges, practicing landing in glens.

Excitement had my stomach muscles taut. I'd be able to join the mountain rescue—at the controls of the heli this time.

I eyed Ella. It would mean I'd be a short flight from Belvedere.

Then again, married couples shouldn't live apart.

"There you go! All done. There are chapels all around, so take your pick. Happy wedding day!" the woman chirped.

Ella led me back outside.

"I just had a moment of realising how insane this is." She slipped her hand into mine, and we walked the short distance to Las Vegas Boulevard, taking in the too-bright day, the tourists with huge, trundling suitcases, the hustle of a city in the morning. "We're in a city in the desert about to get married. This afternoon, we'll be back in Manhattan. How crazy is that?"

"Insane." I grinned at her. We had no time here at all, needing to get back on a plane to New York City. But married. Married!

We hit the main strip. Enormous buildings with mismatched architecture rose around us, traffic roaring by.

"First one we find?" Ella asked.

"Aye. Let's do this thing."

We strode on until we found a sign advertising weddings inside.

"Guess this will do," Ella murmured.

It would, but I stopped her outside the door, moving us into the shade. "Just one thing. Can I ask something of you?"

"You haven't asked a single thing. Not this whole time." She gave a short laugh and shook her head. "You've got on and off planes, sat around while I've had meetings. Held me up. You're even carrying my bag." She pointed at my shoulder where I held our luggage. "So yes, G. You can ask anything and, if I can, I'll give it to you."

I lifted her chin and laid a soft kiss on the corner of her mouth. "Honesty. From this moment on. Honesty and complete openness. About everything."

Because wedding vows had specific words, and we couldn't say them if we didn't mean them. She wouldn't, I knew it. Despite sleep deprivation, we had to go into this with our eyes open. She'd spoken of it not ending, which had my heart squeeze with hope.

I was about to marry the woman I loved.

"Deal," Ella said. "I wouldn't want anything different."

We entered the chapel hand in hand and ordered one on-the-spot wedding.

25

DEVOTED

Ella

From the moment we'd landed in Vegas, Gordain had paid for everything. I'd booked the flights with my savings, but Gordain had insisted on managing everything else. The taxi, our marriage licence, the iced coffees we bought as we'd waited for the officiant to get our paperwork ready.

Our wedding itself.

He handed over his card and told me to let him handle it. It was a strange feeling, having someone I could share responsibilities with.

I was going to pay him back so big.

"Ella and Gordain?" Our names announced, we left our chairs and followed the man through a curtain and into a small hall.

"Ladies and gentlemen," the officiant announced, though it was just us plus another member of staff who was acting as our witness. "Welcome to this special event on this beautiful morning, the marriage of these two people. Ella and Gordain have been lucky enough to find one another in the sea of people in this big, big world. Their search is over. Today, we join them together and make them one."

Gordain's hand tightened around mine. He'd chosen the vows from the selection offered and the order of service.

"Both have travelled far to be with the other. Alone, life has thrown obstacles into their path, but together, they will overcome all their troubles. That is the meaning of marriage and the ultimate function of true love." The man beamed at us, and I wobbled on my feet. So tired. So...confused. It was moving too fast.

Under my skin itched a dawning sense that what I was doing wasn't right.

"Marriage is a commitment where our happy couple accept each other as a friend, companion, and lover for life. It is an honourable estate not to be entered into lightly but thoughtfully, reverently, and wholeheartedly. Ella and Gordain. Today, you bring two families together and make your own." He glanced at his paper. "The Fitzroy and McRae names will be forever united in your love. Marriage is not a casual event but one of great significance. The vows are binding and, with that in mind, Ella, repeat after me."

That was it.

I couldn't tell Gordain I loved him in my wedding vows.

Panicked, I held up a hand. "No. I mean yes. But wait."

The man stopped, his mouth open.

I took a breath. "I just... Can you give us a second?"

The officiant snapped his mouth closed. I pulled Gordain by the hand, dragging him after me to the thankfully empty reception outside the curtain.

"Did you hear all that? The commitment and how we can't take this lightly?" I said, my hand at my neck and with a glance back to the hall.

"Aye. I'm not."

I gawked at him.

"We promised each other our truths," he said. "This might have started for a specific reason, but ye told me on the plane not to talk about it ending. Which means we won't end it."

It wasn't the tiredness that had warmth rushing through my veins.

He took my face in his big hands and tilted up my chin. "Want me to go first?"

I opened and closed my mouth.

"I love ye, Ella Fitzroy. It started when I came for ye at Belvedere and it's grown stronger every day since."

"You love me?" I whispered.

"Aye."

"I love you, too." My voice broke, and my heart cracked wide open. "I couldn't say it for the first time in front of strangers."

Gordain smiled, wonder in his expression. He stroked my hair. "I didn't mind. Seems to me once ye start saying it, ye can't stop."

"How the hell can we get married now?"

He choked out a laugh. "Now we've decided we love each other?"

Did that make more sense or less? "You don't have to do this."

"I do."

We linked gazes.

This was scary. Or perfect. But mostly terrifying.

"I'm scared," I said.

"You're scared? I've never loved a lass before."

I melted against him. He crushed me to his chest.

"I'm so sorry, G. This is so messed up. There has to be a million things we need to say to each other, to do with each other, before we get anywhere close to marriage. Don't you want that?"

"On the flight out, I decided that this would go however you needed it to, but for me, it's the start of something wild and incredible. So we get married first and then work out the rest? I want to go wherever that takes me. But, Ella," he released me and pressed his lips to my cheek, "if you don't want this, that's okay, too. I meant what I said. End it, if you want. Or stay in it. Your call. Just give me your truths."

I took a deep breath. "This all feels upside down now. I want our families here."

"Aye. I want to be in my kilt, my family tartan, with my brothers and your brother at my back, their lasses and bairns with us. I want us to be in the Highlands with mountains at the door. I want to celebrate this with everyone we know looking on and witnessing the statement we're making. But most of all, Ella, I just want you."

He pressed my fingers as suddenly, I couldn't speak. "We need to go back in."

"But—" I started.

Gordain, so calm and in control against my reeling nonsense, kissed my other cheek, trailing his lips over mine to get there. Fire, ready and hot, blazed up my spine.

"Save those lips for your vows," he commanded and led me back into the room.

The officiant fixed his smile in place and steepled his fingertips. "Are we ready?"

"We are," Gordain and I said in unison.

"Super. Ella, repeat after me. I, Elinor Isla Moncrief Durant Fitzroy, take thee, Gordain Lennox McRae to be my lawful wedded husband." The man mock-wiped his forehead. "Fancy names, folks."

I said the words, taking in the increasing intensity in Gordain's looks

Then it was his turn, and he said my name like it was beautiful.

"And now for the vows." The officiant dipped his head at me. "Ladies first."

He gave me my line, and I repeated it.

"I promise you, Gordain, before these witnesses, that I, Elinor, will commit my life to you. I will love you, with my whole heart, I will nurture you, and cherish the bond that we have made. I will celebrate you and our love so long as we both shall live, and this is my solemn vow."

If we hadn't stepped outside to talk, I couldn't have said the words without adding an explanation, a caveat, to make sure he knew he had an out. Now, I meant every word. I loved him, and the vows gave me a path to follow. A way to work through the brand-new feelings.

Peace bloomed, immediate and soft.

"Gordain, please place the ring on Ella's finger."

"Oh!" I turned to the officiant. "There's been a mistake. We don't have a—"

Gordain pulled a box from his pocket. I stopped and gaped. Where on earth had that come from?

He opened the box, and I clasped my hands to my mouth.

The ring was platinum, fine and elegant, with a stone. A sapphire. Deep blue-green and stunning.

It must have cost a fortune.

"When did you...?"

"Manhattan."

"You stepped out and..."

"Lucked out in the first antique jewellery place I found. The stone matches your eyes. It was made for ye."

My eyes filled with water. "G…"

"You like it?"

"I love it. I love you."

I swear Gordain's eyes got wet. He inhaled hard, nostrils flaring and his lips pressed together.

A waving hand broke our eye contact. "Listen, kids, I'm sorry to rush you, but we have another couple waiting. Your conversation has put us behind. We have two little bits, then you can take this show on the road."

"Sorry. I'm good. That was just unexpected."

Gordain took my hand.

"Repeat after me," the man continued.

"I've got this." G shook his head then looked me squarely in the eye, his fingers poised to put the surprise ring on mine. "I promise ye, Elinor, my Ella, before these witnesses, that I, Gordain, will love ye my whole life. I will be there whenever ye have need of me. I'll support your plans and aid ye. Everything I have is yours. Anywhere you need to go, I'll fly ye there, and I'll fly ye home again, too. You are my world. My heart and my soul are devoted to yours. This is my vow."

He slid the ring onto my finger, and two tears streaked down my cheeks. Gordain swept them away with his thumb.

"Well, all right then! Now, with the power vested in me by the laws of the state of Nevada, I pronounce you husband and wife. Gordain? Kiss your lady."

G ducked his head, and his mouth met mine in a tender peck. It was nowhere near enough. With a small sound of need, I kissed him hard, happy to forget we had an audience. Gordain smiled against my mouth then took my lips in a plundering kiss.

Only the celebrant's polite cough had us separating.

It was done. We were married.

The creeping exhaustion took its toll, and I sat in the reception while Gordain got the paperwork in hand. I jolted when fingers touched my shoulder, and I opened my eyes to G's bright expression.

"Done. We can go to the airport now. Back to New York for round two with the lawyers."

Another flight was the last thing I needed. I wanted to hole away with Gordain and kiss him until my lips ached and then burn up all that lust with our bodies.

"It'll be over before you know it," he said, reading me correctly. "Then we'll check into a cosy hotel and sleep for two days straight."

"Sounds like bliss." I hauled myself to my feet, and we left the chapel, and Las Vegas, behind. "But don't expect much sleep."

* * *

*T*he return flight was pain in an aluminium tube—broad daylight and busy. It was all I could do to keep my buzzing head steady. Gordain held my hand, and we leaned against each other, senses jarring from the noise and every jolt.

Five hours had never seemed so long.

By the time we'd fought our way through the New York traffic to the lawyers' office, both of us were staggering.

I stopped Gordain outside the door. "I'll check if you're needed, then you go find a hotel. Get some sleep."

He made a face of sheer disbelief. "Like I'd leave ye."

That was that.

Inside, the lawyers were ready and waiting with a new round of paperwork. I signed legal declaration after legal declaration, Gordain having to add his signature too. Our promises to each other, and the initial paperwork we had, appeared good enough for the antiquated system we were working within. My head ached. My arms ached. My brain whirred.

Eventually, the head lawyer handed off the last stack of papers to a frazzled-looking assistant. Then she dusted her hands together and brought her attention to us.

"Is that it?" I asked, almost ready to beg.

"For now. We have to wait on clearance from the guardianship body in the UK, then we'll be able to file the injunction against the sale. At the earliest, this will be in the morning, but it could take longer."

Gordain hauled himself to his feet. "Ella needs rest. Can ye recommend a decent hotel?"

The woman gave a professional smile. "I've taken the liberty to have a room booked for you. My assistant will organise a taxi and give the directions."

I nearly fell over myself in gratitude, though I knew the bill would be included in the lawyers' fee—a debt I'd repay to James, then Gordain and I were out of there. Fifteen minutes later, we were checking into a busy reception, then another ten and we tumbled out of the lift and to the door to our room. A suite, apparently.

Gordain dropped our bags then took me in his arms. Lifting me with ease, he carried me over the threshold and to the bed. Then he retrieved the bags, dropped them on a chair, drew the blinds to block the floor-to-ceiling windows and their dizzying view, and commenced a regimented removal of his clothes.

Zombified, I could only watch.

When his fingers took his jeans button, I widened my eyes.

Gordain grinned and stripped entirely, standing there

gloriously naked. The silver ring bobbed on his half-hard cock.

I pushed up onto an elbow and tugged at my shirt.

"Let me." He knelt on the bed in the dim room and carefully helped me out of my clothes.

"You're so beautiful, wife." He kissed me then lifted me so he could pull down the covers.

Nude, we huddled together under the sheets, our legs entwined and no space between our bodies.

"I am so in love with you," I whispered, just audible over the dull roar of blood in my ears.

"Good," Gordain said, his mouth moving into a smile. "Sleep now, love."

Everything went black.

* * *

The warmth of solid flesh woke me an unknown number of hours later. Night held the room, and the city lights silvered Gordain's outline. Sixty floors up, the hum of traffic made the backdrop to our private space.

Under me, around me, Gordain slept on, his arms a steel band, holding me close.

I laid a gentle kiss on his neck.

He stirred.

One more kiss met his chin, rough where he hadn't shaved, the scratch sending tendrils of delight over my skin.

A hand roamed down to my backside. Squeezed.

I pushed up so I could reach his mouth, the sheets concealing us from the slightly parted curtains and the surrounding skyscrapers. My first soft press of lips elicited a rumble of approval. My second, open-mouthed reciprocation.

We kissed, half awake and half asleep, our bodies crushed together, my soft flesh giving way to his hard muscles. Languorous movements took our limbs, automatic, unhurried, and feverishly seductive. Not like newlyweds, full of energy and buoyed by a party in their honour. Instead, we were two souls taking refuge together. Handing over our hearts for the other to store. Our hands shaking and breath catching. Testing the edges of the new *us* and all the pleasure that would bring.

The kiss turned sloppy, and my pulse sped as I dug my fingers into his biceps, into his shoulder blades. Gordain's hand coasted between us and over my belly, skimming lower until he found the centre of me.

Two fingers slid into my wetness then slipped inside. He stretched me, and I moaned, my nipples pebbling and aching. *So good. So hot.*

Our mouths fused, the kiss never-ending. Drugging. Keeping us on the edge of wakefulness, our minds content that this was *right* and *good*, our bodies following the pull of sheer desire.

More, my mind told his.

I shifted back to put space between our bodies. He withdrew his hand and made slow circles over my clit. I gasped against his mouth.

Then I reached out and found his cock. A masculine growl surged from him. I stroked him, lightly, and ran my thumb over the ring. I was seconds away from straddling him and pushing him inside me. My virginity lost to his rock-hard body.

Gordain left my mouth bereft and kissed his way south. He tongued my nipple then sucked, using his thumb on the other. Stroking me. Teasing.

He dipped lower, laying his lips on my torso. My belly

fluttered and I held my breath, because this was it; all I'd dreamed about. The love. The man. The freedom to be happy.

Gripping my hips, Gordain buried his tongue in my folds, long licks followed by his full attention on my clit. His fingers resumed their action, hitting the spot over and over.

I arched into him, giving up a long moan, and wedged my fingers into his hair. A tremor began deep inside, his skilful mouth igniting parts of me I'd never reached by myself. It startled me how well he knew my body.

Then I ignited. The surge of a stunning orgasm hit me, and I cried out, breathless and spiralling. I pulsed around his hand. Gordain worked me through it, slowing, before moving back up my body.

His eyes, when I opened mine, gleamed with hunger.

Reaching down, I took his thick cock and aligned it exactly where it needed to go.

"We don't have to—"

Still trembling, I kissed him, silencing him. Then I rolled my hips so the blunt, pierced tip of him stretched my entrance.

He made a broken sound. "Ella…"

"I know," I whispered. No condom, but no risk of pregnancy, either. I knew if he had any doubts about his health, he wouldn't let me touch him. We were married. I didn't want him to be scared of this.

I wanted to be his first in the same way he was mine.

"Husband," I added.

Gordain's arm muscles locked, and he reared over me, his forehead on mine. "Say that again," he uttered, his voice thick.

"I love you, husband."

Surrender came with the surge of his hips. He plunged halfway inside me.

We both roared.

Grasping his neck, I brought our mouths together, my brain scrambling to handle the wealth of new sensations, the stretch of him, so alien and strange, my body adjusting. It didn't hurt, but it wasn't entirely what I expected.

"Are you okay?" Gordain asked, strain in his voice.

I nudged his face with mine, words failing me now.

"You have no idea how good this feels. You are perfect. Ah fuck, I need to move." He slid an inch deeper. Then another. But we weren't skin to skin yet. He held back.

"I want it all," I managed.

With a broken cry, he charged home.

I gasped, and he swallowed the sound. Then we were joined, and I was full of him, the completeness alarming.

I writhed, testing the new feeling.

Gordain jacked his heavy, hard cock in a stuttering rhythm. The discomfort changed to something different. Pleasure bloomed where he touched me inside.

"More. Everything."

Without breaking our connection, he sat back then lifted my knee, pushing it flush to my body. The dim light coming through the window cast a glow over the raw power, the beauty that was Gordain McRae. Holding my legs, he worked himself in and out, his gaze bouncing from mine to the place we joined, his movements speeding up. His breath came in halting shudders.

Mesmerising to watch.

Addictive, and we'd only just begun.

I palmed my breasts, pinching and teasing my nipples. Gordain took a sharp inhale, and his strokes changed. He pulled back and concentrated on just the end of his cock. On that ring, the smooth edge of it on my flesh.

Then he withdrew and ran his pierced cockhead over my sensitive, swollen clit.

I gasped then took hold of him, using him as a tool.

My hot-bodied Highlander threw his head back and hauled in a breath, stilling to let me work myself into a frenzy with him. My breathing got heavier, and the tension at my clit grew almost unbearable.

My second orgasm broke, splintering me. "G!" I yelled, the sensation overwhelming. Gordain seemed to know. He snapped his hips back then entered me in one deep slide.

I throbbed around his cock, helpless against the waves of pleasure.

He'd made me come a number of times, but this, with him inside me, heavy and hard and making me so full of him—nothing could compare.

"God," I muttered, blissed out and spinning.

But Gordain wasn't done. He withdrew then slammed home. And again.

We both groaned. Over and over, he fucked into me, setting an irresistible rhythm. Igniting my blood with his power and his devotion. If I hadn't already told him I loved him, there was no way I could hold it back now. I surrendered to him completely, and he did the same to me.

"I love you."

"Fuck, Ella!" he growled.

"Come, G," I said, sensing his precipice.

"Tell me this is okay." He threw his head back, chest heaving, breath coming hard. "Tell me I can come inside ye. I need to."

"Yes. Yes!"

Gordain roared and rocketed home. I yelped at how

thick he became, and he froze. Inside me, his cock pulsed, setting off all kinds of mini tremors. Then he collapsed on me, spent and glorious.

With my legs splayed wide under his, I swam in the sensation of what we'd done.

Lovemaking.

So powerful. So right.

I was in so deep.

26

THIS WAS GOING TO BE GOOD

*G*ordain

The next time I woke, Ella bounced on the edge of the bed, returning from somewhere. She swung her bare legs in and curled straight into my waiting arms.

Naked, warm, and mine.

"Bathroom," she explained. "I rushed. I didn't want you to wake alone."

I hugged her hard.

"I checked my phone," she added. "No messages."

"What time is it?"

"One in the morning." She giggled. "Our body clocks are so messed up. But I have an idea of how to tire us out to get back to sleep."

One of her hands wound around my neck, and the other dug into my hair. Her mouth took mine, and I let her own the kiss.

Until my blood surged. Then I had her on her back in a flash.

Ella crossed her ankles over my arse, her legs tight around me.

"Promise me again that you can't get pregnant," I said, gazing down at her. So pretty in the room's half-light.

"I can't." She blinked up at me. "You like not using condoms, aye?"

"It's freaking me out, but it feels amazing. You feel amazing."

She cocked her head to one side, affecting ignorance. "And why is that?"

"Because I'm in love with ye."

A slight movement, either from me or her, I wasn't sure, and we were nicely aligned for round two.

"You're not too sore?"

"No." Ella shifted her hips, and my cock slid inside her.

I gave a rough exhale. The sensation—how well we fit, how the ring pulled on sensitive flesh—was fucking everything.

Almost.

Nothing, ever, could beat the feeling of making her come. Earlier, the first time we'd had sex, after we'd woken from our deep, exhausted sleep, she'd come first, but not with me inside her. I'd made her come then slipped inside.

I could do better.

My new goal had my heart racing, and I worked my hips, watching her face.

She met every move, a wee frown of determination on her brow.

"Ride me," I told her.

We adjusted our position, and Ella landed astride me, her slight weight adding a new pressure.

This was going to be good.

With my gaze fixed on hers, I took her hands, and she rose, then sank into place, impaled on my steel pole.

"Fuck." My eyes rolled. Pleasure bloomed through my groin, my balls tightening. "This might be too good."

Ella chuckled and arched her back, pushing up on her knees before sinking down again. My cock thickened more. A few more strokes this way, and I was in danger.

Concentrate, man.

I bit my lip, thinking of mundane things. Helicopter gearbox failure. Lightning strikes. Leaking castle roofs.

Ella. Ella, Ella, Ella.

A groan escaped me.

She released my hands and placed her palms on my chest, gaining better purchase. Giving me freedom to up my game.

I cupped her breasts, supporting their weight, then swept over her nipples with my thumbs, dragging them into peaks.

"Clit," Ella breathed, and I jumped to my task, my fingertips glancing over her most sensitive parts.

We fell into an escalating rhythm, Ella running the show, me clamping down on my drive to fuck hard and slam into her.

Every time she lifted, the draw dragged on my piercing. When she sank, it hit a place deep inside her that had me seeing stars.

I wasn't the only one enjoying it. Ella's breathing grew faster along with her movements. Sweat ran down my forehead, but I kept up my work, her moans spiking my fever.

Then she arched up with a cry, clamping hard on my cock.

"God, fuck, Ella," I uttered and thrust hard into her.

She cried out again, coming, her muscles turning liquid.

She dropped down, and I was done. Grasping hold of her thighs, I bucked into her.

It was a celebration, being with Ella. That was how I felt, like I'd won a fucking gold medal.

Fever took me, and I let loose. One, two, three strokes, and I followed her into a head-spinning orgasm. A strangled yell burst from me, and my balls pulsed, emptying into her. Instantly making us sloppy. Dirty, in the best possible way.

I would never get used to that.

The utter delight of being all natural with her.

The fear that maybe in time would go away.

White lights sparked in my eyes, and I pulled Ella down onto my chest, dizzy and so fucking happy. "Love you," I said into her hair.

Ella melted onto me.

This. This was my life now. Ella. Us. Forever.

* * *

A couple of hours later and we were bouncing around the hotel room, energized from the sleep and keyed up on the drama the past few days had brought. Still dark— my phone showed me it was three AM—we showered, fucked again, then dressed and hit Manhattan, on the hunt for food.

The still-busy streets had us leaping into the first pizza place we found. We chose meat-feast toppings for energy and ate the slices around our smiles, Ella's leg between mine, under the table.

When we were done, we stood outside on the pavement, and Ella tilted her head.

"What now?"

Across the road, the neon sign for a tattoo parlour

blinked. I took my wife's hand and gestured at the place. "Mind waiting around for me?"

"Just try and get rid of me now."

I led the way into the parlour and explained to the artist what I wanted. Ella laughed as I produced a picture of the Fitzroy coat of arms—I'd snapped it on my phone a long time ago—then held my hand as I settled in the reclined chair.

The artist drew the outline then started work on the blank piece of skin right above my heart.

It wasn't the first tattoo I'd had done, and it might not be the last, but it meant the most. I asked for the black stencil-style of Ella's ink to be incorporated. We made a matching pair.

An hour later, and the artist finished.

"Do you like it?" I asked Ella. The artist taped a breathable cover over the design then took my card to make the payment.

"You're asking now? What if I said no?" She held my t-shirt in her hands, but her gaze remained on my new ink. "I love it," she added softly, maybe not wanting to hurt me with her joke. "Of course I love it. I love you."

Then she took out her phone and snapped a picture of me. I grinned at her coy expression.

"If you want to buy me a wedding ring, I'll wear it." I took the shirt and dragged it over my head. "But this way, you're always with me."

She took my face in her hands. I circled her waist with a tight grip.

"I'll get you a ring," she replied. "And I'll inscribe *Property of Ella* on the inside."

I grinned at her then kissed her hard. Who the fuck

thought I'd want that so badly? The world to see I was claimed and owned.

Commitment had made a man of me after all.

* * *

few hours later, we were in a cab, coffees in hand, heading to Central Park, killing time until it was reasonable for the lawyers to have news.

Ella peered out of the window. "That's Richard's building."

I followed her gaze to a large, brown skyscraper. "Not his for long, with any hope."

She only stared, quiet as she worked through whatever dark thought process held her captive.

The cab drew to a halt at the park entrance, and we paid up then, in a few minutes, had skirted the boating lake I'd seen in a dozen films and were on quieter paths. Spring sunshine filtered through the trees. We drank our coffees as we walked.

"Did you talk to your brother?" I asked. Yesterday, Ella had sent James a message to tell him our plans and to ask for news on Beth.

"Nope. I'll wait until I have something concrete to tell him."

"More concrete than the fact we got married?"

She threw me a sly grin. "I told him that."

I stared.

"Did you think I was ashamed of you? Marrying you is the best thing I've ever done. I'm not about to hide it from anyone."

I choked on a sip of my drink. "What did he say?"

"He just said to call him." She beamed now and danced a few steps ahead. "Have you told your family?"

"Not yet. I'd prefer to do it face to face."

"James won't tell them, I'm sure. Something like this, he'll wait and let us deliver the news ourselves."

A buzzing came from Ella's pocket. She leapt to grab her phone but then tutted at the screen. "False alarm. Just my reminder about something I needed to do at uni."

It was Monday. The trial would be underway today. I pushed back the thoughts. "Did you ask for time off?"

"No. I'll email later so they know I'm still alive."

"Will it cause you any problems?"

Ella shrugged, and I followed her to a sunny bench.

"Depending on how it goes with the lawyers... No, irrespective of that, I don't think I'm going back." Ella sat taller, her eyebrows two slashes. "Last year, I doubted every thought that went through my head. I second-guessed myself in all things. With you, with my plan for running my own business. You remember our lunch at Braithar with your relatives?"

"There isn't a second of our time together that I've forgotten."

That earned me a swift grin. "Marianne told me that she'd learned all she needed but ditched the exams. All I have left of my first year is exams. Then the course outline tells me exactly what I'll be learning in years two and three. That got me thinking. Why don't I kickstart my business now, buy in the skills I don't have, and learn the rest as I need to?"

"It's a great idea."

"You think so? Your opinion means the world to me." Her look turned bashful, and she peeked at me under her lashes. "I need to get into the mindset of thinking as part of a couple now. How does that work?"

I raised a shoulder. "Beats me. All I know is I want to be around you all the time. I think I'd go crazy if I couldn't see you."

"G?" Her gaze turned feral. "I won't be parted from you either. You'd better understand that."

My heart swelled, and I tucked her into my side.

We quieted. People passed by, the park getting busier.

"I hated my life until pretty much the moment you came into it," Ella said, low and sweet. "Until you swept me off my feet with your flying rescue. I was angry and scared all the time."

"If I ever see your uncle, he'll regret what he did to you."

The skyscraper Ella had pointed out from the cab loomed in the skyline, unmissable with its position overlooking the park. I blinked at it, a thought occurring. "Do you think that apartment is still on the market?"

Ella sipped her coffee. "Probably? Wait, we should be able to find it online."

She produced her phone and performed a search.

"Motherfucker," she swore. "Here it is."

She passed me the device, and I blinked at the screen.

Then I spotted the price guideline in the corner.

I wasn't naïve. I knew an apartment in Manhattan with views over Central Park would be expensive, but the figure against Richard's place was insane. Tens of millions.

"G?" Ella poked me.

I snapped my mouth closed.

"Bet you're even happier you married me now?" She laughed at my expression. Then her smile dropped. "Here's a crazy idea. Let's go and see the place."

She leapt to her feet and pressed something on her screen.

"What are you doing?" I asked.

"Hello?" she said into the phone, a wicked grin playing on her lips. "My name is Mrs Gordain McRae. I'd like to book the first appointment this morning to see the duplex in the Steinway building."

She answered a number of questions, but all I heard was *Mrs Gordain McRae* over and over in a loop.

Ella's smile soon dissolved, and she hung up the call and took a deep breath. "The realtor said they are organising a single block viewing for two hours and they expect to have a buyer by the end of it. Fuck!"

"Can we get in?"

"No. We need to be preapproved for the asking price. Which there's no way of us being. We don't have the money."

We both stared at her phone.

"Mathilda is one of the wealthiest people I know." I cast my mind to my sister-in-law. "But even she doesn't have that kind of money. The only person I know who does is—"

"My brother," Ella finished the sentence. "But with Beth ill, I don't want to bother him. Wait a minute. Maybe this will work."

She placed another call, talking rapidly to her lawyer. She gave me a worried look halfway through then muted the call.

"The lawyers are going to try to get us in. She suggests we call ourselves Laird and Lady McRae so we can pack a punch. If you're uncomfortable with that, I'll say no."

I pictured my da turning in his grave, outraged at me using the title he'd so adamantly denied was mine. Fuck him. I could borrow it for a morning. "I don't mind, so long as it works."

Ella finished the call. Now, in the dappled sunlight, she paled. "They're going to ring back to say if they've been successful. James has enough money for them to not lie about the backing, but it's all in the careful wording."

We stared at her phone, then I reached out and took her hand.

"Are you sure you want to do this?"

"I am. Richard won't be there, and it's not like it was ever my home, but I'm facing all kinds of demons. I need you to keep holding my hand to keep me steady."

"Always," I said, my throat thick.

I'd realised something crucial.

Ella's uncle had taken her inheritance and bought himself the fanciest pad around, all while he'd abandoned her to a boarding school. No love, no family.

No real home to go to.

When we got back to the UK, I was going to create Ella a home. How, I had no idea. I lived with pilots in a shared apartment. She had her space under her brother's roof.

Neither worked for both of us. Definitely not long-term.

If I broke my back to do it, I'd give her everything she'd missed.

27

FALTERED

*E**lla***

On shadow-strewn Fifty-Seventh Street, I stood outside Richard's building, my hands shaking and my stomach contorting itself in knots. The lawyers had been successful—we had a booking to view my uncle's apartment —but my age-old visceral response to all things Richard held my body taut.

A selling agent waited in the lobby, a glossy brochure in her hands. We closed in on her, but she looked past us.

"Laird and Lady McRae for the apartment viewing," Gordain said, his voice strong and his shoulders back.

The woman gave us a rapid glance, taking in our casual clothes—me in a pretty dress and Gordain in jeans and a t-shirt—but she welcomed us all the same then led us to the elevators.

The *ding* of the elevator halting thrust us into Richard's domain.

At the door, I faltered. Gordain gripped my hand, and I stepped through the hall and into the open doorway.

It was exactly as I recalled. Polished wood. Tall windows with insane views. The place was clear of any personal effects—Richard must had moved out already.

But that wasn't what hit me. The place smelled of Richard. Of the cigars he occasionally smoked. Of whisky and whatever old-man aftershave he splashed on. My lizard brain recoiled, disgusted. I forced my feet to move.

Couples milled around. The smiling realtor pointed out features and offered to let us explore. Gordain eyed the view —straight down the length of Central Park. I tried to unstick my muscles and remember why I'd thought this was a good idea.

"What do you need?" Gordain wrapped his arms around me from behind, my back to his broad chest.

"My head examined? Why am I here?"

"Because you are stronger than him. You're taking back what is yours by rights and showing him that he ultimately lost."

"But look!" I indicated to a couple who stood with what appeared to be the lead real estate agent.

They ducked their heads and whispered, the woman of the couple writing something on a piece of paper.

"They are talking numbers. This place is going to sell quickly. The lawyers aren't going to get their shit together in time. All I'm doing is showing myself what I never had. It's going to make it worse!"

Gordain spun me around. "Stop panicking."

"I'm not panicking!" My eye alighted on the enormous bookcase that divided the lounge from the hall. "Oh God!"

I stomped over and grabbed a heavy book from the shelf. "This is his."

Gordain angled his head to read the cracked spine. "*Debretts Peerage and Baronetage.*"

"It's an encyclopaedia of all the noble families in the UK. Yours will be in there. Ours is. I can even tell you the page number. Richard was obsessed."

I rested it against my chest and flipped to the right place.

The version of the book was an old one. My dad was listed as the heir. The print was smudged—evidence of my uncle's obsession over not being in line to inherit.

I dragged my fingers over it. The page ripped.

"Miss?" One of the agents appeared at my shoulder. "Please don't touch the privately owned objects. Any items included in the sale are listed in the information pack—"

"Is it listed in the information pack how the so-called owner was a liar and a narcissist?" The words fell helplessly from my mouth.

The woman took a step back and glanced over her shoulder.

"Fuck that." Gordain took the book from me and in one almighty heave, tore it in two, straight down the middle of the spine.

I gaped at him.

The woman gave a little shriek and tottered away.

"Oh my God," I said to my handsome Highlander, my eyes wide.

He threw the pieces onto the floor. "He has no power over you now. No matter what happens."

To my left, in front of the backdrop of the city, three of the realtors formed a line. Gordain stepped in front of me, his hands on his hips, ready to defend me.

My phone buzzed in my pocket.

I snatched it out and answered it, breathless and wired. "Hello?"

"Lady Elinor, this is Pamela Forde from Dawson, Forde,

and Lowell. I am pleased to tell you that your outstanding matter has been concluded this morning."

The lawyers. "My... It has?"

"Your guardianship order was concluded with immediate effect. We then served the injunction overnight, but it was deemed unnecessary."

Unnecessary? Had I lost already? "Why?"

"It was simpler than expected. The apartment in question was never in Mr Fitzroy's name. He held it in trust for you. Now he is no longer in the position of your guardian, ownership naturally falls to you. Therefore, he cannot sell it. My colleague is notifying the realtor now."

I sagged against the bookcase.

I'd won.

"We've won," I said to Gordain.

"If you don't leave, I am going to call the police," the lead agent snapped.

"Wait a minute—" I raised a weary hand, but the woman wasn't done.

"I had my doubts from the moment you walked into the room. These viewings are not a joke! This is someone's well-loved home. You destroyed our client's personal property. He is within every right to sue you."

She took a step closer, and I ducked under Gordain's arm to stand next to him.

"I'm sure he'll try," I almost cackled, high on the moment. "But he's lost."

"What are you talking about? Never mind. I don't have time for this. Leave now, or the police will remove you."

The lead agent held up her phone. It rang in her hand and the line of women jumped. She answered it and placed a manicured finger against her other ear, still glaring at me.

Gordain took my waist, turning me to him. "It's done?"

"Aye." I gave him a wobbly smile. "We did it. You made all this possible. Thank you."

His answering smirk had my knees weak. He twisted back to the realtors. "Ladies, as I'm sure your boss is just being told, you're addressing the real owner of this place. If she wants to cause mayhem, I recommend you dinna stand in her way."

* * *

Three hours, multiple explanations, and bundles of emailed paperwork later, and the real estate agents worked for me.

They'd had three offers on the duplex already.

With my hands now steady, I instructed the highly apologetic lead agent to accept the highest bid and wrap up the sale as fast as possible.

Then I booked first-class tickets on the next flight to the UK. Gordain and I were going home.

* * *

Side by side in ultra-comfortable, reclined seats, Gordain and I made the return trip across the Atlantic. We held hands in the cosy, dimly lit space and talked.

We drank a glass of champagne each and toasted my uncle's demise.

All was well, but still, a sense of foreboding hung over me. The depths of Richard's control and hatred couldn't be so easily overcome, and I knew he'd retaliate somehow.

But there was nothing I could do about that in midair. I sent texts to James, warning him that Richard would be angry, and to be vigilant, then I quietened my worries by giving my full attention to Gordain. I wanted to know everything about him, every bit of history, every like and dislike.

I wanted him to tell me, again, his closest-held dream.

Because his wife was about to make it come true.

In London, we checked onto an internal flight and made the short hop to Inverness. It hadn't been difficult to persuade Gordain to see his family first. My brother knew the highlights of what had happened and, after all, we'd be there tomorrow.

I thought I detected excitement in Gordain's voice when he called to tell his brother we were on our way.

At Inverness arrivals, the laird and lady waited at the barrier. Mathilda held a bouquet.

I leaned into Gordain. "They know?"

"Aye." He threw his arm around me and drew me in, our bags over his other shoulder. "I found it too hard to keep ye a secret, wife."

We rounded the barrier, and Gordain's brother marched over. He enveloped Gordain in a hard bear hug and thumped him on the back. I grinned at the reunion and faced Mathilda.

"Congratulations." She beamed and presented me with the flowers.

"I didn't expect this. I thought you'd all think we were mad." Or that I was using him.

Mathilda tilted her head at where Gordain and his brother were talking, their hands still clutching each other. "We knew Gordain was in love with you, so once he told us the plan for your uncle, we knew it would end in one of two ways. Either this would injure him, and he'd go straight back to work to lick his wounds and then no one would hear from him for months"—she took my hand and brushed over my wedding ring—"or this. He'd bring you back with him. Proud, and grinning, and with his spark returned."

"I love him so much," I half whispered.

"That is obvious." She hugged me.

I returned it, then angled us so Gordain couldn't see my face. I eyed Mathilda. "I need your help with something. It's important but needs to be a secret. For now, anyway."

Mathilda raised a perfect fair eyebrow. "Luckily for you, I'm excellent at getting things done. Let's get moving. We'll find time to talk, perhaps when the twins are yelling questions at the two of you." She linked her arm through mine. "Welcome to the family."

* * *

The twins, who'd been babysitting the two new and super-cute mini-McRaes, were in raptures at our return. The evening meal became a party, and I had to postpone my chat with Mathilda.

I tried to call my brother, but there was no answer. He replied with a text an hour later saying Beth was having a bad night, but he really wanted to talk to me. He made a point of stating how secure their apartment was in Belvedere—there was even a fire escape newly added—and I relaxed, knowing they were safe.

In Gordain's bed, in the tower, after he'd carried me up the stone flight and made love to me at the top on the hard stone floor, I gave him a gentle kiss. "Can we leave early to drive to Belvedere tomorrow? I'm worried about Beth and I want to see them."

Gordain stretched out, gloriously naked and confident in

his inked skin. "Actually, I have a better idea. How do you fancy a helicopter ride there?"

I grinned and laid another kiss on him. "Are you kidding? That will be perfect."

"I'll go to the old school and pick one up first thing."

Which would give me just enough time to pay a little local visit myself.

* * *

Mathilda reversed the four-by-four in a neat circle then took off down the road leading away from the castle. In the back, the baby twins gurgled in their car seats.

"It's not that Ally and Wasp are bad at babysitting," she murmured, checking her mirrors, though there was no other traffic on the remote Highland road. "It's just a little early to expect them to be awake and sensible. Besides, if I can have my babies with me, I prefer it. It's like I'm missing a limb when I can't see them."

"Beth is the same about Sebastian." I slid my phone from my pocket. "Do you mind if I try my brother as we drive? I can't shake this feeling of worry."

Mathilda waved me to go ahead, and I made the call.

James answered, despite it being barely seven AM. "Elinor."

"Uh-oh, you full first-named me. Is everything okay there?"

"Beth is still unwell, an infection, I think, but wait, I was going to ask you the same thing. I've been trying to get hold of you for days. What on earth happened?"

I bit my bottom lip. "Well, you know the highlights. I beat Richard—"

"You got married," my brother interrupted. "To my best friend, who—"

"Who I love," I interrupted right back.

Silence held the line. Then James chuckled. "Last time you were here, I worried that you two had argued. Now you're husband and wife?"

"Very happily."

"I might need a second to get my head around this."

"You're happy for us?"

"I am." He drew a hefty breath. "I'd love to have had that wedding here, but I know why that couldn't happen."

"Maybe we'll have a blessing at Belvedere," I said, clutching the phone, suddenly emotional. "Or maybe we'll have it at our own place."

Ahead, the destination of our short trip loomed.

"Your own place? What are you talking about?" James asked.

In all the months I'd been at university, planning my career and coming into my own, I had one place in mind when I'd envisaged running my business.

Castle Braithar.

The size was perfect, the appearance breathtaking, from the babbling river that splashed through its front garden, to the snowy mountain backdrop. The quiet surroundings, nature, and towering forests could inspire even the most reticent mind.

I could write here. Piece after piece.

Gordain would own the place that had given him sanctuary as a broken child.

With the sale of Richard's apartment, I was certain I could afford it.

At the front of the castle entrance, Lachlan and Marianne waited, curious expressions on their faces. My heart raced, preparing me for what I was about to do.

"This might sound a little crazy," I said to my brother, "but I'm going to buy a home."

28

LONG-HELD FEAR

Gordain

Callum and I exited the hangar at the helicopter school, and I jangled a set of keys in my hand. It had taken far longer than expected to carry out my task. For one, Mack loved to talk, and he proudly showed us every heli and explained the facts about the business.

He wanted me to buy the school. I wanted to buy the school. Callum wanted me home.

But would Ella want to live in Scotland?

"You've always been one for saving your pennies." My brother eyed the view across a heavily wooded glen. You could see Mhic Raith, our mountain, from here. "Can ye afford it?"

I'd done the calculations. There was enough saved in my bank account for the down-payment, and I'd be able to raise the rest with a business loan.

"Aye." I kicked a stone and waved off Mack as he drove away. "It means sacrifices, ye ken."

Callum grunted, understanding my meaning. Buying

this place meant forever giving up my dream of owning Braithar.

That was a bitter pill to swallow, and it pulled at a thread of security I'd always carried, but with Lachlan wanting to go, and me needing to do the responsible thing, running a business made greater sense.

No matter how wealthy Ella might one day be, I had a duty to her. Who knew if her uncle had another trick up his sleeve? Or some other reason why things could go wrong with her inheritance.

"Ye never know what life will bring." My brother clapped me on the shoulder, and we strolled to his car. Something in his tone gave me pause, but he continued before I could land the vague idea.

"In the meantime, you'll live with us. We'll take out the gym from the tower and make more space. Anything ye need."

"I really appreciate it. But I'm jumping the gun. I need to discuss it with Ella."

First, Ella had to want to live with me. We'd talk about it —I wouldn't make any decision alone. Hopefully ever again.

"Aye, I get it. I'll see you back at the house." Callum raised a hand and clambered his huge frame into his car. "Fly carefully."

"Always do." I saluted back, a painful reminder that I hadn't made the RAF hearing, then boarded the heli.

One thing was for sure, I wanted to impress my wife like never before.

* * *

I landed on the beach at the side of the loch, just down the slope from Castle McRae. Mathilda's car drew to a halt at the same second I jogged into the car park.

Ella sat in the passenger seat.

Opening her door, I lifted her out and brought her legs around my waist, carrying her back a couple of steps. "Hello, wife. Missed you."

An amused smile took her mouth. "Hey, husband."

I nuzzled her neck, taking in a deep breath of her unique scent. "Did you go for a drive with the bairns?"

Ella raised my chin with her finger. Her gaze held mine captive. Heat, thrilling and fierce, shot through me, lust dancing in my veins. I would never get enough of this woman. One look from her, and I was a goner.

"Later," she said, "I have something to talk to you about. But I want to do it when we're alone, in bed, with the door locked. Just you and me and all the time to make plans. Is that okay?"

Plans. Good. I managed a nod, and she snickered at my hazy expression.

A small wail came from the car's back seat. A second joined it.

Mathilda opened the door her side. "They'll be hungry. Can one of you please grab Lennox? I'll get Skye. We better hustle. By the look of those black clouds, it's about to rain."

Ella slipped down my body, and we jumped to help, darting back into the castle.

One round of goodbyes, including a selfie with the twins, Ally immediately uploading his congratulations post online, and we were ready to go again.

We ran through the downpour to the heli and threw

ourselves in, laughing. A quick report to air traffic control on our route and a check on the increasingly bad weather—still safe enough, I'd never risk Ella's wellbeing—and we lifted off.

Silence claimed the first part of our journey, down country and over the Lowlands.

I concentrated on steady flying. Ella's attention flitted, something clearly on her mind. Rain and wind buffeted the heli, the storm chasing us south, but as soon as we crossed over the border to England, we outran it, clearer skies giving me a breather.

"I'm sorry if that got intense." I glanced at Ella who stared through the glass at the rolling green hills below. "We were safe, though. Out at sea, it can get horrible. Particularly at night."

She shivered and reached out to take my hand. "I wasn't afraid. But I really don't like the thought of you flying those oversea trips."

Yeah, maybe I wouldn't be doing much more of that. I opened my mouth. "Can I ask you a question? An us-type question. Maybe something about how much time we spend in Scotland."

Ella blinked and seemed to hold her breath. I took a quick look at the view then back to her.

"Not now," she said, her voice crackling in the head-phones. "All the stuff on where we live is a tonight-in-bed conversation. Deal?"

My lips twitched, sheer joy trying to beam out of my face. I loved it, the fact we were talking about us. That there was an us.

"Deal. But only if you tell me how much you love me."

Ella gave a happy laugh. "You have no idea. A life-changing amount. The sort of big love that makes me want to give you everything."

I held her gaze for a moment. "Yeah? I can't wait for this chat. But I have to warn you, there's going to be a whole lot of naked time before that."

Her eyes widened, like the idea wasn't a bad one.

My cock grew heavy, an ache starting in my balls.

Fuck.

"Change the subject, sweetheart, or I'm going to touch-down in a field and take you right there in the seat."

Her lips curled at my gruff voice and my coarse words, but an intensity remained in her gaze. We were closing in on Belvedere. Minutes to go. "I have a question, but it isn't a nice one."

"If it stops me getting overexcited, go for it." I had to drop her hand to flip a switch, but I grabbed it right back up again.

"In the hotel, our wedding night…"

"Ella! You're meant to be cooling me down."

"No condoms. We went bare." Her cheeks flushed red. "I get that you'd never done it before."

I winked. "You took my virginity."

"But there was something else there. You panicked. About me getting pregnant." She broke our contact and pressed her hands to her cheeks. "I don't want a baby, but you seemed terrified of it."

Ah, that.

I wanted honesty with Ella, in all things. I'd told her about the incident that had lost me my job, but I hadn't told her the thoughts I'd had that left me cold. All linking back to a crappy childhood.

"You remember the reason I left the RAF? I had these panics for months after. That I had no idea if—" I broke off and shook my head. "I knew there was little chance that anything had happened between me and the woman. I was almost certain of it. So I worked back to what I was really worried about. What my mind had fixated on."

Ella's eyebrows drew in. "You were worried about her being pregnant?"

I nodded, my throat suddenly thick. "I'd been an unwanted child. To be so irresponsible traumatised me."

"Oh, G." She drew a deep breath. "I met her, I think. Autumn, right? She asked me about you when we were at the base."

"That's her."

"She certainly wasn't pregnant."

I swallowed, the long-held fear dissolving. "Good to know. You didn't say at the time."

"I know. I wish I had. Things were a little tense between us. I'm sorry."

Ahead, the craggy edges of the Peak District marked our path. A pretty wilderness.

"Can we agree to always share information? Big deal or small. We include each other in the important shite." I couldn't look at her now, as I had to watch my controls and the ground.

"After tonight, I agree one hundred percent," Ella said carefully.

Her tone niggled at my attention. Belvedere came into sight, and I angled the heli to take us around the front. Making small nudges at the stick, keeping us even as we coasted in to land.

"Why do I get the idea I'm not going to like this discussion?" I said.

"I made a decision without you and now I'm worried," she blurted. "It was meant to be a surprise. A wedding gift."

Shutting off the urge to question her, I set us down on the lawn, then powered down the craft. We undid our restraints.

"G, if you want to know, I'll tell you now. I hate the idea of you not trusting me. But this is a big subject, and we need time to discuss it. My brother and Beth are going to want to talk, and this is huge."

I stared at her, all manner of thoughts intruding.

She said she wanted to talk to me tonight about where we stayed.

Christ. What was it she had to say?

Behind Ella, figures appeared in the entrance to the house.

I opened my mouth. "Don't leave me," I said, right as Ella almost yelled, "I bought Braithar!"

We gaped each other.

"You did what?"

"Why would I leave you? I love you!"

One of the figures closed in on the aircraft. James.

"Ella, Gordain!" he shouted over the racket of the slowing rotor blades. "I need help! It's Beth."

Ella dragged in a shocked breath and leapt from her seat.

Cracking open the doors, we jumped down to the grass, ducking as we ran to James. He carried Sebastian in his arms, the bairn crying.

"Beth's ill. She has some sort of infection, and it's getting worse. I need to take her to hospital."

I reached out for Ella's hand, and we jogged to the house. Fat raindrops hit the ground, the edge of the storm catching up with us.

In the vast marble hall, Beth waited on a chair, a woman next to her, a small child over her shoulder. I barely spared the second woman a glance, but Ella gasped.

James handed Sebastian to his sister. "Can you take care of him? I'm not sure how long we'll be. Mrs Hinchcliffe will be home in an hour if you need help."

"Of course." Ella collected her nephew and hugged him close, her features pinched in worry.

I was all action, ready to help James. He stooped to pick up his pale, faint-looking wife. Beth gave us a wave, but it was weak, and she dropped her hand quickly.

I picked it up and took her pulse, my training kicking in. "I'm not second-guessing you," I said to James. "I just want to make a couple of checks. Beth?"

She cracked open an eye.

"Talk to me. How are you feeling?"

"Like I've been hit by a truck. Multiple times." Her head bobbed against James's chest, and her eyes closed again.

"She's on antibiotics for a postpartum infection. They said to bring her in if she got worse. This has happened in the last thirty minutes. She nearly fainted, and her fever is back. I was about to carry her to the car when we heard the helicopter."

Her pulse raced; she was tachycardic. Maybe a response to the medication. I jerked my head up, my rapid assessment enough. "We'll take her in the heli. It's nae distance by air to Manchester Royal Infirmary. I've landed there a number of times, taking doctors for surgery. We'll get her to A&E in no time."

"I was hoping you'd say that. Let's go." James held his wife close, then we started to move.

Then another voice rang out. "This is a really bad time. I'm so sorry I intruded. I'll leave."

I paused, recognition dawning.

From the military base. From polite conversations held before *that* day.

Autumn Phillips.

I twisted and glanced at her. What the...?

She was here with a baby.

A *baby.*

James continued to the door, and I took a half step after him, torn down the middle and confusion reigning.

"I've got this, G. Go, help Beth." Ella's words centred me.

I closed my jaw. "But—"

"G, go!" Ella prompted.

"I'll be back as soon as I can." Then I sprinted across the lawn, pushing everything from my mind so I could fly safe and get back to my wife.

And whatever the hell else was going on.

29

OVER MY DEAD BODY

Ella

The helicopter rose, Gordain taking my brother and Beth to hospital, and I closed the tall door at Belvedere's central entrance, taking a breath. I turned to face Autumn and her baby.

"Hello again." I gave her a ghost of a smile.

"I'm so sorry," she started. "I was in the area anyway and I saw that you and Gordain were going to be here this afternoon. He was tagged on a photo of the two of you, and a few of his RAF friends commented on it, which is how I saw it." She waved a hand, her face flushed. "I had no other way of contacting him, and there's something important he needs to know. But my timing is terrible. I do hope your sister-in-law will be okay. I'd only just got here when you landed."

I stared.

"Whose child is that?" I unhinged my jaw and asked the one question that must be haunting Gordain now.

"Oh! This is Benjamin. My nephew. My sister is having some troubles, so I'm looking after him for a while. He's a little older than yours there." She smiled at Sebastian, asleep in my arms.

Not Gordain's. A funny sort of laugh, relieved and border-line hysterical, came from my lips, and I shook my head, getting myself under control. "I apologise. Where are my manners? Let's go upstairs and get a drink. You've come all this way. We can put the babies down and talk."

I led the way, my mind reeling.

With the children settled and snoozing in Sebastian's cushioned playpen, I made tea and sat across from Autumn on the couches.

"I believe congratulations are in order." She indicated to my wedding ring.

"Thank you." I twisted my cup in my hands, wondering how I could politely demand she get on and tell me why she'd come.

Autumn took a sip of tea before putting the cup down. "I see now why Gordain didn't turn up to the hearing on Monday. Getting married is a much better way to spend your time. But when I found out he'd cancelled his slot, I couldn't let it lie."

"Hearing?"

"Against Dad." The pink splotches on her cheeks paled. "There are so many charges now, I can't remember half of them, but I stood up in Gordain's place and told them what happened with your husband."

He'd missed a hearing with the RAF? Despair and pure love mangled in my gut. He'd given up his chance at redemption to come with me.

Autumn continued, "Do you know what happened? Why Gordain got in trouble with my dad?"

"Your father found you and G...together." I winced and stopped.

"I never meant anything bad to happen to Gordain. But I did take advantage of him. I knew Dad would walk through that room and I knew if I was found in a compromising position, he'd be angry and send me away."

"You did that? You lost Gordain his job?"

"I didn't mean to!" She fluttered her hands then clamped them in her lap. "I thought Gordain was interested in me and I followed him out of the bar. But he was stumbling around, and I figured he was drunk. Then he passed out on the couch. I had no idea that Dad would throw the book at him. But Dad was already drawing attention over the under-hand deals he'd done, and he took his frustration out on Gordain."

I sat back, aghast. "That was his career. He'd been in the RAF since he was sixteen and worked so hard. He wanted to be a search and rescue pilot. You took that away."

Autumn recoiled, her eyes welling. "I know! It wasn't what I intended. He's a good man. At the time, my father was controlling my every move, and I needed to get out from under his thumb. It's different now because he's in trouble, but even if it had worked, I couldn't justify the cost. That's why I stood up on Gordain's behalf on Monday."

From the playpen, her baby nephew squawked. She collected him and balanced him on her hip, her expression chagrined and her gaze on the floor. "They'll offer him his job back. I made a bargain in exchange for giving them paperwork I found of Dad's."

I rose and picked up Sebastian. "Do me a favour. Call Gordain and leave him a voicemail summarising that. Then if he has any questions, he has your number to call him back."

I rattled off his number. She programmed it into her phone.

"I'll do it now. Thank you for listening. I've hated the past year. I gained freedom but had a cloud hanging over me the whole time, and now everything is awful again. Dad will go to military jail, and there are all these awful people trying to get to him."

After everything Gordain had been though, it was hard to feel sorry for this woman. But the parallels between her life and mine tipped the balance.

I would have done anything to get away from Richard. Begged, borrowed, lied, and stolen. Certain evils justified extreme actions.

Strapping Sebastian to my chest with a carrier Beth used, I walked Autumn back downstairs. "I'll make sure Gordain knows you were in a bad place. He isn't one to hold a grudge, and I know he'll be grateful for what you did."

"Thank you."

"What will you do now?"

She paused at the door. "Dad's friends and allies have deserted him. That includes most of my old friendship group. There are rumours that he's done much worse than has so far been revealed, and I've had threats to watch my back. His enemies want revenge. I'm leaving the country. I just need to persuade my sister to come, too. We're not exactly close. She's more like Dad. But she and Benjamin are all I've got."

Shit. Well, now I felt bad for her. "Good luck with everything. I hope you find a better place."

Autumn gave a little wave and walked away.

But as I closed the door, the overtones came of a brief conversation before her engine revved and her car trundled away. Was Mrs Hinchcliffe home already? James had said an hour.

I halted my actions and peered outside.

Then the door flew open, knocking me.

I fell, banding my arms around Sebastian. We jolted, hitting the cold, marble floor. The baby awoke with a wail, though I'd protected him from harm.

A man appeared, standing over me.

"Well, well, Elinor. Don't you look the part of nursery maid."

Richard.

And his gaze clung to Sebastian.

"Give him here. Let me meet my new heir. I've been waiting for this moment for so long." He reached out to pluck my nephew from the baby carrier.

My heart sped, and I let out a cry, scrambling back. "No!

Then energy flooded my limbs, and I sprang to my haunches, holding my nephew close.

"How dare you," Richard said with a curled lip. "You forget yourself."

"No," I said again, quieter, my mouth drying from fear.

He was here. In front of me. Looming large and evil in every move.

"Don't think I'm ignorant of what you've just done. Why won't the realtors talk to me about my home? Or the fucking lawyers? Why won't they return my calls about you? I'm your guardian." He took a step. "What have you done? Speak, Elinor. You owe me answers."

I slid on the marble, inching away. In the distance, a car engine roared, becoming distant. Autumn leaving.

Which meant I was alone with him. Just me and the baby he wanted.

"You think you're clever, don't you? Like your stupid bitch of a Scottish mother. I own this family. I raised you. Who knows what would have happened to you if I hadn't taken an interest in your care? That child needs me, just as you and your brother did. Let me see him. Undo those straps. Hand him over."

"Over my dead body," I snarled. "How can you even—"

Then I remembered myself. There was no reasoning with this man. There never had been. He was made of malice and spite, his mind twisted.

I wasn't afraid of him anymore.

But I'd never put Sebastian at risk. I needed to get away.

Outside, my car waited, the keys inside and the doors unlocked.

I had to be fast.

Even so, I couldn't leave without a parting shot.

"You seem confused." I stood, cautiously, one hand out to ward him off. "You lost, Richard. You're a jerk. A vile, disgruntled, piece of shit who is now homeless and hopefully penniless. If I never see you again, it'll be too soon."

At his dropped jaw, I fled. Passing him, I shoulder-barged the ajar door, clutching a sobbing Sebastian tight to my chest. As I half stumbled down the steps, Richard made a grab for me, only just missing.

Then I was on the gravel and sprinting. Richard was right behind me.

Only at the last second did I heard the screech of tyres. Saw the whites of our housekeeper's eyes above the steering wheel.

Over my dead body, I'd told Richard.

The car hit with a sickening crunch.

30

MY BONES

*G*ordain

My older brother, after his wedding, had confided in me a secret. He said he felt such a strong connection to Mathilda that he found himself distracted when she wasn't around. Worrying about her. Even fearful for her safety. Like his heart was walking around outside of his body, at risk and needing constant care.

Falling in love with Ella was having the same effect on me.

Something was wrong. I sensed it in my bones.

The farther I flew from Belvedere, the stronger I had the urge to turn around.

By the time I touched down on the helipad at the hospital, I was almost frantic. James and Beth disappeared inside the hospital, supported by hospital staff in scrubs, hurrying to escape the now-driving rain.

I checked my phone, anxiety having me twitching.

No messages from Ella. But there was a missed call and voicemail from an unknown number. I played the message, turning up the sound to counteract the drumming rain on the heli's glass.

Autumn Phillips's voice came out of the speaker. "So sorry for the confusion, and for showing up with my nephew at such a bad time. Ella said…"

I stopped listening, my head in a spin. I knew the baby couldn't be mine, but we'd just had that conversation, and I'd tried to work through my trauma. Autumn being there had rattled my cage.

Even so, *thank fuck* was the order of the day.

I tuned back in as she wrapped up her message. "Anyway, call me back if you want to discuss any part of the case. I hope I did a good job representing you. You'll be able to join your old team in the RAF, if you choose. Your wife mentioned you had a new career now, but I wanted to fix the mess I'd made. She's a really lovely woman. Congratulations. I just saw her uncle and said the same thing. He seemed surprised, so I hope I didn't let the cat out of the bag. Goodbye."

Uncle?

I replayed the last few seconds, my throat seizing.

Richard? He'd gone to Belvedere?

My throat constricted, fear gripping my muscles.

I shot a text to James then fired up the heli, setting a flight plan to the Peaks, circumnavigating the multiple weather warnings. I had to fly.

Ella needed me.

* * *

The storm ripped open the sky, lightning tearing holes in the thick cloud. Below, the craggy Peak District hills jutted, menacing in their starkness. A world away from the pleasant land Ella and I had surveyed not long before.

I hauled on the stick, all my energy going into keeping flying straight.

Strong wind buffeted, worse than I'd ever flown in. But even so, I had total control. My weeks on the oil rigs had served me well.

Then a flash of light and a bang rocked the craft.

The engine stuttered, and I jerked, the harness dragging over my new tattoo.

The heli had been struck?

Holy fuck.

I knew the drill. This happened all the time in the North Sea—heli's acted as lightning conductors—but the damage was usually minimal.

A warning alarm gonged.

What the hell?

Oh no. No! My navigation system had blown. My Terrain Awareness and Warning System knocked out.

Smoke billowed from a large hole in the tail.

The heli plummeted from the sky.

31

HERO

*E*lla

Sebastian's loud wail pierced my stunned state, and I blinked at the body at my feet.

A *body*. Not a living person anymore. Nobody could've survived that.

In his attempt to catch me, Richard had fallen under Mrs Hinchcliffe's wheels.

On the side, his skull was crushed, his body crumpled by the opposite wheel. It made a gruesome sight, and I clutched my nephew closer, blocking his eyes from the scene.

"Oh, Ella!" Hinchie keened from the driver's seat. "I didn't see him in time!"

I took two steps away from the mess that had been my uncle and spun around. At Hinchie's door, I helped her out of the car. She shook, peering around me.

"Is he...? Did I...?"

"Hush now. Don't look." Pushing her lightly towards the rear of the car, I clamped down on rising nausea. Then I guided her into the house and paused on the steps, taking out my phone to call for help.

Richard was dead, his feet visible under the front of our housekeeper's car. For years, I'd despised the man, wishing for something just like this to happen. I'd imagined it over and over: his bloodied remains, the sneer wiped from his evil face.

Well, I had my wish.

"You're through to nine-nine-nine. Which service do you require?" came the voice in my ear.

"There's been a terrible accident," I uttered. But there hadn't. It was just desserts.

And it couldn't have happened to a more deserving man.

* * *

"Tell me again." I tried to impress my will on the paramedic.

Her face remained sympathetic but firm. She folded her arms. "Only a doctor can pronounce a person dead. I can only tell you what I've already said."

"But he is dead, right?" I gestured at the ambulance where the second paramedic closed the doors. Richard's body lay on a gurney.

"His injuries are not conducive with life. I'm sorry for your loss. Would you like to follow us to the hospital?"

Not conducive with life.

Good enough. I already knew it, but the confirmation was everything. I'd sat on Belvedere's front steps and waited for this—for a professional to release me from the years of abuse at this man's hands. My shock settled into a cool kind of realisation.

He'd never hurt us again.

Behind the ambulance, a police car drew to a halt, two officers exiting the vehicle.

"No, thanks. I need to talk to the police."

"That's fine. If you call later, we'll be able to discuss the next steps." The paramedic left, and I hurried back to where the police officers made a beeline for Mrs Hinchcliffe. She'd slipped past me and stood, staring at the ambulance, tears streaming down her face.

In my arms, Sebastian slept. Unaffected by the drama, or by our narrow escape.

I took a breath and greeted the two men, then began the story.

* * *

Nearly two hours later, thick clouds had me turning on the lights, despite it being the afternoon. The police were concluding their questions and readying to leave.

A car crunched on the gravel outside. I peered out of the window to see my brother exit a taxi. He was alone.

Where was Gordain? Where was Beth?

I skittered out of the room and into the hall.

"Did you see my messages?" I demanded. I'd sent him several, telling him what had happened.

"I just got them. I had to turn my phone off in the hospital and only turned it back on in the cab. The battery had gone, but the driver let me charge it. Beth's staying overnight, but they think she'll be fine."

James threw out his arms, and I embraced him.

"Is he really dead?" he asked, his voice tight.

"He is."

"Are you all okay?"

"Sebastian and I are fine. We should worry about Hinchie. She's shaken by it. She's lying down with Sebastian in your rooms. Mr Hinchcliffe is on his way home. The police breathalysed her and asked a hundred questions, but it seemed routine. They are just about to go." I cocked my head to one side. "Why didn't Gordain come back with you? Or did he?" I craned my neck to look over my brother's shoulder, but there was no movement in the dark afternoon outside the front.

My brother didn't answer. When I brought my gaze back to him, he'd gone deadly still.

"Ella, Gordain took off not long after he delivered us to the hospital. He was coming here to see you."

Cold spread through my veins, heading for my heart. "He didn't show," I almost whispered. "I've sent him messages, like I did you. He hasn't answered."

James's face creased in worry. "He flew out into the storm..." He snapped his mouth closed.

"Oh God." Gordain had been gone so long. That could only mean...

I was going to be sick.

"He would've let us know if he'd been diverted elsewhere," I uttered, misery rising.

Snatching up my phone, I called his number. No answer came.

My boots slapped the marble floor as I raced back to find the police.

* * *

L ast known position. He has a last known position.

In a flurry, I threw myself into my car. A search party was being convened, but I knew this area.

Knew where air traffic control had tracked Gordain's borrowed helicopter. When we were kids, our parents would take us hiking all over the Peaks. Last summer, before I'd returned to Castle McRae, I'd driven the remote lanes and traversed the valleys.

My brother swung open the passenger side door.

"Don't ask me to stay. Or wait. I'm going," I said.

"I wasn't about to. I'm coming with you."

I shot a look at him. The flashing lights of a fresh set of police cars reflected on his face, damp from the relentless rain. "Are you sure?" He must be exhausted.

"Gordain is my best friend. My brother now. Like I could stay home and rest with him missing. We can cover more ground together. Besides, I'd never let you go alone. Not ever again."

Emotion swamped my throat. "We'll find him," I managed.

"Hit the gas," James instructed.

* * *

"*H*ere."

At James's exclamation, I braked, stopping the car on a barely there track in the middle of wild countryside.

My brother held an OS walking map, unfolded to a huge sheet. "Northcote Ridge is the highest point closest to his last known location. If he had to bring the helicopter down fast," he pressed his lips together, stifling emotion, then continued, "it's more likely that he'd aim for higher ground. Don't you think? So it wouldn't pick up so much speed."

Unless it fell from the sky.

Neither of us said it, but the thought couldn't be avoided.

James cleared his throat and pointed at a ridge that dominated the skyline ahead. "Drive up the hill as high as you can. From there we'll make sweeps."

The light was dying. The storm had finally lifted, leaving a blustery cold and wet dusk. We had maybe forty minutes before I'd need to put on my headlights.

It would leave us blind to anything outside of the beam.

My eyes filled and overspilled once more, and I batted away the tears, pushing the car on to reach the ridge. Crying was no good. Crying meant I couldn't see as well.

I'd cry when there was something to cry about.

"You know the last thing I said to him? I told him I'd bought Castle Braithar," I said to James, not taking my attention off my scanning the moorland. "I saw Lachlan McRae this morning and made him an offer. He accepted. I should have consulted Gordain, I really should have, but I so badly wanted to make him happy, and if for some reason it couldn't work out, if maybe Lachlan had already sold the place, I didn't want G to be hurt by raising his hopes."

James's warm hand landed on my shoulder. "The two of you will be very happy there."

I let the tears fall this time.

At Northcote Ridge, I drove to the highest point, and we jumped from the car, yelling Gordain's name across the hillside. The wind whipped our voices away.

I strained to hear a response. Squinted to see the silver-and-blue helicopter.

Nothing.

James pointed to the edge of the ridge. "Let's climb to the top. We'll be able to see better from there."

Silent, I jammed my hands into my armpits and marched behind him, my feet catching in divots on the uneven ground, my legs soaked from wet foliage.

We reached the top and stood on the stacks of smooth, rounded boulders.

"Gordain!" I screamed, twisting to scan the hill below.

The faintest of sounds filtered over the wind.

A voice? A trick of my desperate imagination?

The police had been way behind us, forming an official search party. It couldn't be them.

"Did you hear something?" I asked James.

"I don't know. I think so." My brother sprinted across the plateau and clambered onto another stack. He hollered Gordain's name once again.

I chased him, my heart hammering. My fear couldn't let me believe we'd found him. I needed to see him. To hold him and to take him home.

The faint sound came again, carried by the wind, working in our favour now.

My brother's face lost its muted anguish and formed of steely determination. "I can't see anyone, but that's definitely a shout. It's coming from this way."

He pointed west. In that direction, the sky still held the faintest glimmer of light.

"There's no way we can get the car around this side of the hill." I scanned the ground. Nothing beyond animal tracks, piles of loose rock, and thick undergrowth.

"Then when we find him, I'll carry him."

A sob broke from my lips, but I stifled it and nodded. James grabbed my hand, and together, we descended the rough terrain of the hillside.

Then my brother stopped abruptly.

"What?" I demanded.

He blinked then dove forwards, picking something up.

A blue painted piece of metal.

I touched it. *Cold.*

"Wreckage?"

James swallowed. "Part of the helicopter."

He'd gone deathly white, and I suddenly realised why. A decade ago, James had been in the car crash that had killed our parents. He'd been badly injured. They'd been crushed to death. No, this was not happening again. Not with Gordain.

A sob broke from me. "He'll be okay. He's here somewhere. Keep going."

James palmed my shoulder and shook me once in solidarity. Then my brother ducked his head, and we pressed on, sliding down the slope.

Night was almost upon us. The ridgeline behind us made for easy navigation to get back—so long as we could see it.

I led the way, screaming Gordain's name.

We rounded a rocky outcrop. Across the ground, a long drag mark marred the hillside.

"Ella!" The answering shout—Gordain's voice—nearly made me lose my footing.

It was him. He was alive. Oh God, oh God.

"G!" I screamed.

James and I ran, passing scattered pieces of debris.

"Gordain!" I screamed again.

"Here! Ella! Thank God you're okay!" he called from the gloom. "I've been so worried."

He'd been worried? About me? Oh my life. "Where are you?"

"Stuck. Follow my voice," he called back, clear as day. The next thing he said was lost to the wind.

"Just keep talking. Say anything." I strode on, my brother at my back.

"Take it steady," James said to me, his voice tight. "Don't twist an ankle. We've got him."

"I'm so sorry," Gordain yelled. "I love you. You're my life. I acted like a jerk. I didn't even tell you how glad I am that you bought Braithar. You're fucking amazing, do you know that?"

A silver limned object appeared ahead, half-concealed by trees and undergrowth.

The helicopter.

"You didn't thank her?" my brother called back. "Shame, brother."

"James!" Gordain's laugh resounded, so close, so vibrant. "You have no idea how happy I am to hear your voice."

We picked our way over the ground. Then a light shone ahead, illuminating Gordain sitting in the wreckage of his helicopter.

"G!" I dashed the tears from my cheeks and stumbled the rest of the distance.

When I reached him, he dropped the arm holding his phone and pulled me into a hug. He was damp and cold. But alive.

"Fuck, I thought I'd lost you." He hissed as I crushed him to me.

"Are you injured?" I drew back and examined his face. Dark, sticky blood decorated one cheek, leaking from a gash at his temple.

"Broken leg's the worst of it. I had dislocated my shoulder but I fixed it. Couple of scratches. Other than that, I'm good." He gazed at me, a beautiful smile on his bashed-up face.

I laid a soft kiss on his lips, my pulse slowly coming down from the high-speed race I'd been in for hours. "You crashed. I can't believe we found you."

Gordain cupped my cheek and examined my features. "A freak accident. I was flying back to help you. Your uncle... Are you okay?"

"He crashes and asks after everyone else." James appeared at my shoulder.

Gordain reached out and hauled my brother in for a hug. "Get me the fuck out of here, aye?"

James gave a short laugh. "I'll retrace my steps and call for help. You sit tight with that broken leg."

"Ha ha," Gordain uttered, but stark relief held in his gaze.

My brother left us, and I carefully scrutinised my husband. He pulled me into a hug, grunting slightly, no doubt hurting.

"Richard's dead." I ran my fingers over his hair and gave him the short version of what had happened. I hadn't processed any of it. In hours, my life had been turned upside down over and over.

"Autumn left with her nephew," I said carefully. "She stood up for you at the RAF hearing. Why didn't you tell me you'd miss it by helping me?"

"Because, my lass, none of it mattered compared with being with you and fixing the wrongs your uncle made. Your life is more important than mine to me. Ye ken?"

"Yours is more important to me," I whispered back.

We held each other in the dark afternoon.

A distant chopping tore the air. A helicopter.

Rescue.

Gordain relaxed onto me, his breathing heavier. "You saved me. You're my hero," he said, his voice quieting, probably in exhaustion.

"You're mine," I replied. "Did you know that once, ages

ago, when I was at university and missing you so badly it hurt, I Googled your name? It means *hero*."

How apt.

Gordain chuckled again but didn't reply.

After a short wait, action hit us. The helicopter lowered a man with a stretcher.

"You're fucking kidding me." Gordain threw back his head and laughed. "Jordie! I didn't know you volunteered. For how long?"

"Long enough so I could save your arse. How's the leg?" The rescuer beamed at Gordain then got to work checking him over.

"My buddy from the RAF," Gordain explained to me. "Jordie, meet my wife. My Ella."

"Pleased to meet you." Jordie raised his eyebrows at me but didn't slow in his task.

Gordain winced when his friend pressed his shoulder muscle then gave a strangled yell at his examination of his leg.

"I know you missed me," he said through gritted teeth, "but you don't have to beat me up to show it."

With care, Jordie manoeuvred Gordain onto the stretcher and got him onto the helicopter. Then he fastened me into a harness, got me aboard, and we flew. James had returned to the car and, far below on the moor, headlights flooded the tracks, the search party guiding him home.

Finally, finally, I permitted my muscles to relax.

Gordain was alive.

We'd found each other.

I'd never let him go again.

IF YE SAVE A MAN'S LIFE, HE'S YOURS

*E*lla

At the hospital Gordain had flown to earlier in the day, he was now admitted as a patient.

Not a very *patient* patient—other than getting his broken leg bone set, he laughed off his other injuries. I made him get fully checked over.

He listened, those gorgeous grey eyes rolling as he finally admitted he was tired.

They operated on his leg that night.

I clung to my seat in the waiting area, so afraid that something else would go wrong. Jordie, his friend, joined me in waiting. James did, too.

In the early hours of the morning, the surgeon came out and gave his update. The bad break had been fixed. He'd need to stay in for a couple of days before they put him in plaster and let him go. Then it was strict bed rest for a week and no weight to be put on the bone for longer.

The doctor left, assuring us that G would make a full recovery, a statement that left me stifling a surge of emotion.

"Can we live at Belvedere for a while?" I asked my brother, shuffling to my feet. There was a canteen downstairs. I'd grab a coffee then wait on the ward until they brought him out of recovery. "Unless G wants to go back to Castle McRae, in which case, I'll move there with him."

Nothing would part us again.

"He won't get up the tower's spiral staircase." Jordie gave his opinion from my other side. "Don't give him the option —just tell him what he's going to do."

James tilted his head, his lip curling in a small smile. "Belvedere is as much your home as it is mine. You don't even need to ask. Live with us until you take ownership of Braithar."

I leaned on his shoulder, and he put an arm around me.

Then we said our goodbyes, and he went to find Beth in a different part of the hospital.

"When he's ready to leave, I'll arrange for you both to be flown home." Jordie gave me a salute.

"That's kind of you." I offered up a weary smile. "Unless he's scarred for life by the crash and doesn't want to see a helicopter again."

Jordie waved me off. "Nah. He's been downed before. Ask him about being shot out of the sky, that's way more exciting than crashing on a moor. He'll jump right back into the saddle."

But what saddle? Would he take up his old job in the RAF?

I shivered and made my goodbyes, Jordie leaving for home.

Then I waited for the love of my life to wake up.

* * *

"Marry me."

"We're already married."

"Marry me again. Marry me always," Gordain babbled, blindly reaching for me, the drugs they'd pumped into him making him high.

"Loved you from the minute I saw you," he mumbled. "Seventeen and fucking gorgeous. Delicate as a flower. I was a goner."

The nurse at the end of the bed chuckled, recording something on a chart.

"Sleep, G. If you're feeling better, we can go home tomorrow."

"Don't leave me."

"Never."

He slept, and I dozed against his bed.

The next day, Gordain's x-rays came back good, and they set him up in plaster. To his horror, he wasn't allowed to walk to the landing pad, and he almost howled when Jordie collected him in his arms to get him into the helicopter.

"I am never going to live this down," he grumbled.

"Just like a wikkle baby. Poor walking wounded." His friend grinned brightly.

Gordain punched him in the arm, groaning after and clutching at his injured shoulder.

Jordie flew us home to Belvedere. We set Gordain up in my bed—our bed now—and I took a shower then crawled in next to him. He'd decorated this room for me. Pale walls and a dark floor. Love in every paint stroke.

He'd risked his life to fly through a storm for me.

"I love you," I whispered to his sleeping form, then unconsciousness took me under.

He woke the following afternoon, ravenous. In more ways than one.

"How do you feel?" I pulled back the sheets to check his leg.

Gordain adjusted himself through his boxers—the only clothes on his body. "Perfect. Help me get these off then hop on."

His cock bobbed under the material.

I laughed and took in his features. Clear eyes, determination on his brow.

"Are you sure?" I wanted him. Needed him. That closeness when we joined.

"God yes." He took my arms and dragged me onto his chest, then laid his lips on mine. "Don't ye ken if ye save a man's life, he's yours?"

We kissed with a hunger made of survival and adoration.

Taking care not to jostle his injured leg, I made quick work of undressing us both, urgency driving me. Then I threw my leg over him, bracing myself on the headboard.

Gordain took both my breasts in his hands, groaning as he played with me. One hand skimmed my waist until he gripped my backside. "Hard and fast. Please."

I lined us up and sank onto him, ready and raring to go.

Then I made love to him, riding him like our lives depended on it.

They did, in a way. My life was his and his mine.

We came together, loud and long, celebrating love and grateful we had this chance.

The moment was perfect. I had everything I needed.

* * *

*J*ames prepared a feast for our recovering partners. Beth had been allowed home before Gordain, nearing a full recovery. She waited at the table, pale, but beaming at us as we entered the room, Gordain swinging his leg and stabbing the floor with his crutch.

At Beth's shoulder, Sebastian flapped his arms. He made a squawk. "La!"

"My name!" I crowed. "His first word and he said my name!"

Beth jiggled him then handed him to me. I sat, gathering the baby onto my lap, snuggling him and putting my cheek to his silky black hair. The last time I'd held him was with Richard chasing us. I clutched my precious nephew close.

"Thank you for protecting him," Beth said. "I'll never forgive myself for not being there when Richard threatened him. Threatened both of you."

"Same here." My brother placed a bowl on the table— spaghetti Bolognese, heaped high.

The scent of basil and garlic had my mouth watering.

James served up a portion for his wife, then one for Gordain before making up my plate and his.

"God, I'm starving." Gordain made big eyes at his dinner. "And ye can't all feel as guilty as I do. How do ye think it feels that my wife needed me and I wasn't here?"

"Can we stop with the guilt?" I waved my hand. "Look at where we are. We're all alive. He's dead. We won, all of us. We're free now. Finally."

Murmurs of agreement sounded around the table.

"I spoke to the authorities this afternoon. They said we can arrange Richard's funeral, if we want." James paused in eating. "In his will, he demands to be laid to rest in the family mausoleum. But there are other options."

"He doesn't deserve it," Beth said, a flash of fire in her eyes. "That man was nothing but evil. Why should he get his last wish? He did everything he could to destroy this family."

I glanced between them.

James had a gentle heart. The damage done to him by years of manipulation made him reflective. Still, I didn't expect the answering blaze in his gaze at his wife.

"He'll be cremated and his ashes scattered in some far-flung corner of the grounds. Father loved him, so anything else would be a disservice, but I will not honour him more than that."

We all stared at James.

He shook his head then continued with his news. "The police cleared Mrs Hinchcliffe of any charges. I'm going to gift her and her husband their cottage by way of thanks."

"For running over Richard?" Gordain lifted his head, bewilderment in his gaze.

That was it. My brother and I burst out laughing. The seriousness of the conversation coupled with the events of the previous days had us hysterical.

It took a minute until we calmed.

"For services to our family, but maybe I'll add that in when I tell her." James wiped his eyes.

We ate as a family. Happy and together.

Later in the evening, Gordain and I made our way outside and sat on the steps. The setting sun warmed the stone, and I huddled in close to my husband.

"I emailed my professor to tell her I'm quitting school." I took his hand and interlaced our fingers. "After we move into Braithar, I'd like to run a production company from there. If you don't mind the yowling of musical instruments in the great hall."

Gordain stiffened. "Ye still want to live there with me?"

"Always."

He rolled his shoulders, his relief palpable. "I should tell ye something about my own career plans. I want to run the helicopter school. Maybe even move it onto the estate. I made enquiries before we left Scotland. I can afford to buy it and—"

"You're not going back into the RAF?" I interrupted and slipped in front of him to fit between his legs, kneeling on the step, my face before his. I'd wanted so badly to ask him this, but without pressure. It was his choice, and I didn't want to influence it.

"And leave you for months at a time? Risk one day not coming home at all? Ye ken I spoke to Jordie about that day again—he thought it was heatstroke that affected me. I don't need that risk. It's grand to have my name cleared, and I can face my colleagues without shame now, but I want to make my own way. Be my own boss."

"You won't miss it?" A tight knot in my stomach disappeared.

"I don't need the safety net of the RAF. I have you, our families, and life is good."

"We'll both be running our own businesses. How about that?"

Gordain slid an arm around me, removing the distance between us. He kissed me. "One thing is for sure, when we take ownership of Braithar, we're going to throw one massive party."

I laughed joyfully with him, and we planned out the details.

Life had truly begun, for both of us, and we were going to make it perfect.

EPILOGUE

*G*ordain

With excitement holding me tight in its grip, I trundled our car along the road, going slow to drag out the suspense, breathless with anticipation of what was to come.

We eased around the corner.

Castle Braithar shone ahead, beautiful and lit by sunlight.

Ella gave a yip of happiness. In the past year of waiting for legal work and for Lachlan to finally move out, we'd visited often, but this was different.

Today, the place was ours.

I sped the remaining distance, and we almost fell from the car, rounding the bonnet to clutch hold of each other.

"We did it! We're home!" Ella cried.

I lifted her in my arms, bride-style. Just like I'd done at the hotel room after our wedding. Just like I'd done the day my leg cast came off and we'd returned from the hospital to Belvedere.

We'd stayed at Castle McRae periodically, when needing

to be in the Highlands, but the last couple of months we'd been at the Peak District. I'd miss living there and seeing James, Beth, and Sebastian every day, but nothing could beat being back in the mountains.

Owning the place I'd dreamed about as a boy.

"You made my wish come true." I kissed Ella's cheek and carried her over the threshold. My kilt flapped against my legs—it had been a symbolic choice, wearing McRae tartan the day I took ownership of a McRae castle, but I liked the freedom.

And how my wife eyed me when I put it on.

I'd wear it often.

"You *are* my dream come true," she returned. "I guess that makes us even."

Inside the airy and bright great hall, I clung on to her for a moment longer. "This is it for me. My life is complete." Then I kissed her. "Happy birthday, love."

Ella turned twenty today. In a few days, we were throwing a big moving in and birthday party. Then we'd start on changing the place to suit us. Adding a recording studio. Putting up housing for a heli I'd keep on site.

The commute to work had never looked better.

"Hello!" Ella called out, her voice echoing to the rafters. "Is anyone here?"

We knew Lachlan and Marianne had already left and, though they kept a housekeeper and several groundskeepers who we'd employ, all had the week off.

No returning shouts came.

Ella slid out of my arms and walked backwards, her gaze claiming mine. "When we first came here, I sat at the dining table and watched you. I admired your strong forearms, your easy manner in this home."

I stalked her. "Aye."

"Do you know what I wanted to do?" She entered the dining room then hopped up onto the table.

"Likely something tamer than what I'm about to do to ye now."

Kicking the door closed behind me, I stepped between her legs, pushing them wide around me.

Ella hooked her finger in my waistband. "I didn't even have the imagination for it. But now I do."

In easy movements, she lifted the kilt, freeing my already hard cock.

I slid my hands up her thighs, pushing her summer dress out of the way. "Fuck. No underwear?"

She lay back, baring herself. "What was the point? I'd only have lost them now."

"True." I dropped to my knees and buried my face in the apex of her thighs, having her shouting in minutes before I reared up and plunged deep inside her.

"Gonna fuck you in every room," I managed, tipping my head back, the sensation so great. It always was between us.

Except here, at home, this was something new.

"Plan." Ella pushed up on her elbows and exhaled hard. "Pick me up."

"Huh?"

"Up!"

I complied, and she giggled as she adjusted herself, her legs tight around my waist and my cock hard inside her.

She blew a lock of hair from her eyes. "Where next? The great hall? Let's go."

"Do you know how many rooms this place has?"

Carrying her, I left the dining room but walked down a private hallway to a study, my need to fuck impeding my ability to move fast. There, I placed her on a leather couch and climbed on top, working myself in a nice slide. "We'll get through them, but right now? Hold on tight."

Ella's laughs soon turned to moans, and I joined her, shouting my happiness to our new castle home.

* * *

A few bliss-filled days later, Callum paid us a visit, Wasp at his side. In the last year, the twins had taken different paths, their adult lives separating them more and more. Wasp had gone to university in Edinburgh, while Ally stayed at the castle, working for Callum.

Both men hugged me.

"How are you settling in? We've gave ye some time, but you know the hordes are about to descend." Callum planted his hands on his hips and gazed around the great hall, his typical stern expression in place.

We'd created a stir, Ella and I, and our party on the weekend was now an open invite, the villagers and estate folk for miles around notified.

Lachlan had often thrown large parties here. Ella and I planned to do the same.

Wasp spied my wife across the hall. "Gotta chat with Els. See ye later." He darted over, and they disappeared out of the hall.

"Life is grand." I raised my eyebrows at my brother. "It's good to be home."

"Aye, I imagine. This place always was more of a home to you." He paused and stared at me. "Ye should have been laird. I've been thinking about it more and more over the last year. Now Lachlan is gone and I'm chief, I'm going to hand the title of Laird of McRae to ye."

My jaw dropped. "Don't joke."

"When have ye ever known me to joke?" He reared back, outraged. "We'll announce it at your party, unless you'd prefer not to."

Laird. I'd be Laird Gordain McRae. The title Da used to taunt me with.

"I don't know how to feel about it."

Callum palmed my shoulder. "I know, but I'm fixing a wrong. It's in my gift to name you my heir and pass it on. Ye can use it or not. It's your choice."

Our bearhug followed naturally.

Emotion swallowed me whole. "I can almost hear Da's horror from here."

"Aye, so stick it to him. Let the fucker see how happy ye are." Callum thumped my shoulders and released me.

Not even I could see the extent of that. It was all encompassing.

* * *

*E*lla

Wasp leaned a solid shoulder against the doorframe of my makeshift recording studio. Always the quieter of the twins, it was strange seeing him without Ally. His twin spoke first, always. Wasp saw life through his camera. He seemed to pace himself, taking the measure of an idea before he acted on it.

It had served him well at university, and he'd won awards for his landscape shots of the Highlands. But it didn't work quite so well when he had something specific to say.

Like now.

He'd made a couple of enquiries about the party, and I knew he was leading up to something.

"Would it be easier if I guess your next question, or are you going to tell me yourself?" I cocked an eyebrow at him.

He pursed his lips but didn't speak. Carrying muscle tone like Gordain's, and the same height now at six-three, he wore a stubborn set to his jaw that was all Callum.

"Is it about the catering?"

He shook his head, a little smile blossoming.

I swiped imaginary dust off my violin stand. "Maybe you'd care to check out the guest list?"

Wasp exhaled, losing his humour. "Aye, I'll take a peek."

"I'll save you the trouble. Taylor's coming. She'll be late, though. She'll miss the ceremony." The secret ceremony that Gordain didn't know about.

Wasp's eyes flared, but he didn't say anything more.

Whatever had happened between Taylor and Wasp, I'd never forgotten the despair in her voice as she'd told me how she wished she could fall in love with someone like him. But that was impossible. My gorgeous, quiet brother-in-law was a year younger than her and had nothing to his name. Taylor's father was advancing his bid for the political seat he coveted. After the debacle with my brother, he'd told her outright that she had to stay single and professional, or marry a high-profile American citizen. One of his choosing.

They had no chance.

"Dinna think too much about it, Els. I'm only asking." Wasp shook off his serious look and summoned a smirk. "Now, everything is planned and underway. All ye need to do is make sure Gordain leaves for Castle McRae at the right time. We'll do the rest."

Before the party, with just our closest friends and family attending, I had a certain gift to give Gordain. I hadn't forgotten my promise to get him his own ring, and I'd had one made out of a piece of gold mined in Scotland.

We'd missed out on having a wedding like our brothers had had, with promises made before our loved ones, so it was time we did it right.

And if the McRae brothers had plans for Gordain ahead of that, that was nothing to do with me.

* * *

*A*n hour before the secret ceremony, Gordain lay on our bed in his now-familiar kilt. Skye sat on his chest, and Lennox and Sebastian jumped around him. Babies no more, the three toddlers were a little gang, as cute as they were devious. At eighteen months old, Sebastian could run. The moment Lennox had seen him do it, he'd needed to keep up, an infant rivalry in the making.

"Gee Gee. Fly!" Skye commanded her uncle, and he picked her up and flew her over his head, making helicopter noises while she squealed in delight.

I loved this. I loved our life, our families, and our happiness. "I love you," I said softly to him.

"Love you," Skye repeated.

"You you!" the boys crowed and descended into fits of laughter.

Gordain's phone buzzed on the bedside table. "I'm not getting that." He kept up his game with the babies.

I feigned worry. "What if it's important? I don't want anything to go wrong today. Please check it."

Kissing Skye on the nose, Gordain swung his legs off the bed and collected his phone. He frowned at the screen, reading.

"Oh, for fu— I mean, for heck's sake."

"Problem?"

"Aye. I need to head over to see Callum. The new boiler

exploded, and he needs another pair of hands to help fix it. I swear I won't be long."

"There's plenty of time. I hope everything is okay." I offered my cheek, earning a kiss as he passed, then my husband was gone.

And I had a ceremony to prepare.

* * *

*G*ordain

Castle McRae was still standing when I halted my motorbike outside, and I strode into the great hall, expecting a flood.

The flagstone floor was bone dry, and silence reigned. No hammering or clanking of old pipes.

"Hello?" I called, marching into the kitchens.

"Grab him!" came a howl.

I whipped around but too late—Callum got an arm around my shoulders. Then, in a coordinated attack, the twins swept my legs from the floor, holding one each.

"What are ye doing!" I yelped, wrestling at their grips.

"We've got rapid-fire bridegroom trials to put ye through. Did ye think you'd get away with it by eloping?" Ally cackled.

"How could ye think we'd let it lie?" Wasp added, tutting for good measure.

Callum only smirked at me, and I swore a blue streak back which only made them laugh.

Despite my struggles, and I was a big man, they carried me through the great hall and out into the fresh air.

"Where are you taking me? My wife knows you've got me. She willnae let ye get away with this," I threatened, but a grin split my face.

The only thing I'd regretted about marrying Ella in Las Vegas was this—not having my family there to celebrate with me. In every other way, I couldn't care less. I only wanted her.

My brothers carried me past the cars and out onto the track that led to the loch.

"Wait!" a sudden panic hit me. I'd assumed they were going to put me into a car, but no. There was nothing this way but the water.

They reached the beach, manhandling me all the way.

"Ah ha. You caught him. Nice work." James's voice had me lifting my gaze. He appeared at my head, a bucket in his hands.

"What the hell? Help me!" I made pleading eyes.

"When I married Beth, you made me run, climb, and covered me in mud. My friend, it's your turn." Delight lit James's eyes, and he upended the bucket, slopping freezing cold muddy water over me. It soaked my hair, my shirt, and ran under my kilt.

"Argh!" I yelled. "You arseholes. That's freezing! And you've ruined my clothes. I was going to wear this tonight!"

"Tough luck, groom. Stage two, lads!" James crowed.

My brothers bayed agreement and hauled me down the boat launch, their boots clattering on the wooden planks.

"No. Don't you even think about it," I threatened, eyeing the grey loch.

"Ready? Three," Ally counted. "Two. One. Throw him!"

They swung me wide then released me into the water. I had just enough time to hold my breath before hitting the choppy surface. It rushed over me, soaking me through.

Oh FUCK, that was cold.

I pawed the water, surfacing and coughing, glaring at the laughing swines.

"You wait." I carved my hand through the water, swiping a wave at them.

Ally danced back a step from the spray. Still, he was close enough.

I launched up and grabbed his leg. "Got ye!"

My youngest brother yelped, and I dragged him back with me, sinking down. Underwater, we shoved at each other, then kicked up.

"Who's the one getting married?" Ally grinned, loch water running down his face.

I huffed a breath, splashed him again, and swam for shore, stripping off my ruined shirt as I reached dry land. Realisation hit me. I was the one getting married. I *was* married, but clearly my wife had set this up. That lass... Whenever I thought I understood her, she surprised me again and again.

My brothers escorted me back to the castle and up to Callum's solar. Sodden and bare-chested, I dripped on every step.

"What next?" I asked. "I'm not going to be able to dry my clothes in time."

Callum made a ta-da gesture and opened his bedroom. I peered in. Suit bags hung from the wardrobes. The first was open, a smart dark-grey jacket, waistcoat, and a kilt in McRae tartan on display. I gaped.

"Fit for a groom, aye? We'll all be matching as we stand up beside ye."

"Stand beside me?"

My older brother punched my shoulder then shoved me towards his en suite. "Aye. Now stop dripping on my floor and get ready. We've got a ceremony to attend."

I choked on a laugh then followed orders, getting myself into a hot shower and scrubbing the mud from my hair. A groom at last, I'd have my wife in my arms soon. I needed to look the part.

* * *

*I*n Braithar's great hall, Ella waited, dressed in white. Angelic, gorgeous, and beaming at me. The most breathtaking lass that ever lived.

Candles lit the corners of the space, white flowers decorated a makeshift altar, and our family and friends waited.

I gaped at my wife then spared a glance at our audience. The three bairns wore little tartan outfits. Behind them, Mathilda dabbed her eyes, and Beth sobbed loudly. Earlier, we'd found out that she was pregnant again and we'd already hugged over that. Jordie gave me a thumbs-up, his wife cuddled into his side.

At my back, my smartly dressed brothers made rumbles of encouragement, and I shook myself out of my stupor and marched forwards.

"I know you weren't expecting this," my wife said, "but you gave everything to me with your proposal, and I wanted to give a little back."

"You give me the world just by being in it," I replied, taking her hands and holding tight.

Ella drew a deep breath. "You made beautiful vows on our wedding day, but I stumbled, overwhelmed. I have a couple more things to say. Gordain, when I met you, I made a huge mistake. I didn't snap you up right away. It took me a year to correct that error, and today is all about showing you how I'll never let you go."

"As if I'd let you," I replied and squeezed her hands.

"Good, because I have something for you." She reached

out, and Beth handed her a box. Ella opened it and removed the contents, holding it up for me to see.

A solid gold ring. Flat-edged, thick and masculine.

"It's inscribed with our initials and our wedding date," she pointed out, then placed it on my finger.

I stared at it for a wee moment. I'd wanted this, and she'd remembered. I'd wear it with pride.

"Take yours off," I replied, my voice coming out rough.

She did, and I held her fingers, the ring poised to go back on.

"You're my life," I said simply. "My whole life. You're beautiful and you're mine."

"We're each other's," she agreed.

To rapturous applause, we kissed, cementing our commitment to the other.

Then the party started.

Wine flowed and music played. With half the people in the area attending, we celebrated all we'd gained.

Midway through the evening, my brother took to the makeshift stage. "If I can have your attention." Callum's big voice boomed, and the music and chatter ceased in an instant.

I took Ella's hand and crossed the floor, going to stand next to him. My wife gave me a questioning look but followed. If she'd had a surprise up her sleeve, so did I.

"As many of ye ken, I have recently been made chief of Clan McRae," Callum announced.

"Aye, good for ye," called one of his tenants.

"What you might not ken is that my brother here is the rightful heir to the title of laird."

"Aye, that we did," the same man said loudly. "Young Gordain should've been heir, but yer da had it his own way, God rest his soul."

Callum blinked. "Well, today, I'm passing the title of laird to my brother. We'll lead the clan together, just like in old times."

At my side, Ella's lips parted. "You're going to be laird?"

I grinned at her, blocking out the rest of the conversation. "I am."

Applause echoed in the room.

"You're my lady officially now," I told Ella.

She beamed. "We're Laird and Lady McRae?"

"We are." We dropped from the stage, and the music started again.

Ella melted into my arms, and we slow danced, holding on tight.

A short while later, Ally caught my eye and grinned, tilting his head at the rear corner of the hall. Wasp and Taylor disappeared down a passageway, and I rolled my eyes at my brother. His twin never did anything without careful thought, but I hoped he knew what he was doing.

Ella snuggled closer, and I forgot everything but her.

It was everything I'd dreamed about—being here with my wife and my family. Having a position of pride, a job I loved with a thriving business and, at the end of every day, I got to come home to Ella in Braithar. What man could want for more?

Not this one.

"I love you," I spoke in Ella's ear. "My lass, my life, my hero."

The End.

Thank you so much for reading Gordain and Ella's story!

The next in the series, Wasp's emotional romance, Picture This (Marry the Scot, #4), is available to buy here: mybook.to/PictureThisMtS

Read on for a sneak peek at the opening chapters.

To be first to hear my publishing news, access giveaways, and receive bonus content, sign up to my newsletter here: https://www.jolievines.com/newsletter

ACKNOWLEDGMENTS

Dear reader,

Ella and Gordain's story had been calling me for such a long time, and I'm so relieved to have it down on paper, published, and in your hands. Gordain, the braw military hero, had such a sensitive side hidden under his tattooed skin. With Callum and James settling down, he could see the life he wanted and was ready to change.

Ella, on the other hand, was champing at the bit to realise her freedom. Her resilience and maturity helped her survive boarding school, but it took longer for her to trust herself. She needed time to be ready for the secure commitment her Scot needed.

I have a question for you. Did you think the hero of the title was Gordain? Do you still think so now? I'd love to know jolie@jolievines.com

Now, three books into the series on the men of Castle McRae, we have a greater understanding of the damage the McRae father did but we're also seeing that family heal. For those of you who read The Rival, my series prequel, you'll see that Hamish's words to Lachlan came true with this story. I'll say no more as I don't want to spoil it.

As always, thank you for buying my books and supporting my writing. I read every review and appreciate the time taken to share the love for my mountain men and their adored lasses.

Next, I want to shout out to Team Rabbit (my critique partners, Zoe and Elle, plus me. Don't ask about the name choice. It's ridiculous, we know.) A year ago, we were all unpublished and had writing ideas coming out of our ears. Now, we have at least thirteen books out there in the world and many more to come. If ever I was to give advice to a new writer, it's to find your tribe. I love these ladies for their unwavering support but also for providing a hive mind with which to bounce off my ideas. We're a powerhouse, and it shows.

Hugs to my excellent editor Emmy Ellis, cover designer Natasha Snow, formatter Elle Thorpe, and proofreader Zoe Ashwood.

Tara and Katie, thank you for your comments, reactions, and for making this book stronger. You rock at beta reading.

Love to every blogger, ARC reader, and my wonderful fan art producers (Linda and Ella, in particular, I'm eyeing you). I adore your posts and reviews.

My final thanks go to N and M, my little family. I've gotten so used to writing with my boy playing cars at my feet and my other half cooking dinner and indulging my book chatter. I wouldn't have it any other way.

Jolie x

ALSO BY JOLIE VINES

Marry the Scot series

1) Storm the Castle

2) Love Most, Say Least

3) Hero

4) Picture This

5) Oh Baby

Wild Scots series

1) Hard Nox

2) Perfect Storm

3) Lion Heart

4) Fallen Snow

5) Stubborn Spark

Wild Mountain Scots series

1) Obsessed

2) Hunted

3) Stolen

4) Betrayed

5) Tormented

Dark Island Scots series

1) Ruin

Standalones

Cocky Kilt: a Cocky Hero Club Novel

Race You: An Office-Based Enemies-to-Lovers Romance

Fight For Us: a Second-Chance Military Romantic Suspense

Visit and follow my Amazon page for all new releases amazon.com/author/jolievines

Add yourself to my insider list to make sure you don't miss my publishing news https://www.jolievines.com/newsletter

Chapter One – The Quiet One

asp

The security team swarmed, ushering us through a side door into the Metropolitan Museum of Art. Away from the red-carpeted celebrity entrance at the front of the building.

Josie, my mentor, and the thorn in my side, heaved a sigh. "When this job is done, I'm drowning myself in a Cosmopolitan then going to bed for a week."

I was with her on that—the going home part. Tonight was my last assignment in the US, and tomorrow, I flew to Scotland. As great an opportunity as the past couple of months had been, my heart hurt every time I thought of seeing my family again.

Yet there was one specific draw that this final job had on me. A name I'd spotted on the guest list of actors and politicians. A lass I hadn't seen in years.

One who made me catch my breath at the memories alone.

A uniformed man, bigger than most but an inch shy of my height, pointed to my camera bag. "Sir, I need you to open that for inspection."

"Aye, but watch what you poke with that stick," I grouched, exposing the lenses and camera bodies, frowning deeper when the guard jostled my kit. Decent photographic equipment cost a fortune, and most of mine was borrowed.

Cleared, we entered a corridor that led to a cavernous, pillar-lined hall—the staging ground for tonight's glittering charity gala. Artwork adorned the walls, interspersed with elaborate floral decorations and a blue lighting scheme.

Automatically, I scanned the faces, searching for *her*.

For Taylor. The woman who'd taken my virginity five years ago, when I'd been a lad, and who I kept seeming to sleep with every time we saw each other.

Even thinking her name had my groin tightening.

"I'm going to mingle." Josie brought her camera back to rest on her shoulder. "Work through your list then shoot what you like, but be bold. Particularly when Senator Miller arrives. If you believe the polls, he's going to be our next president. If you can, get his son and his date. The kid's meant to have a new girlfriend. His running mate's daughter. Do you know who I mean? Irene someone..." She paused, tapping her lip.

A sense of unease had me shifting my weight. I knew an Irene. That was Taylor's first name. Irene Taylor Vandenberg.

Like she'd read my mind, Josie clicked her fingers. "Vandenberg. That's it. Fucking nepotism. My little bird tells me they'll be onstage together later. Maybe they'll even make the big engagement announcement here. Be front and centre for that."

My stomach dropped. "Engagement?"

"Wasp, seriously? If you don't keep up with this kind of news you won't make it as a celebrity photog. Look them up. Then go do your job."

"Got it." I offered Josie a ghost of a smile and peeled away into the crowded room.

Waiters circled with trays of champagne, dodging me as I stomped off to a corner by myself. Then I paged through my phone, searching as commanded.

I didn't read celebrity gossip—that wasn't the field I wanted to work in—but multiple sites spewed the news that the son of the hugely popular presidential candidate might soon be settling down. There were no pictures of Taylor, just of the guy with his famous father, but her name was there in black and white.

Christ on a bike.

The lass I'd held in my arms and fallen asleep on when I'd been seventeen, who I'd fucked against a wall in my brother's castle after a party at nineteen, and who I inexplicably missed, though we'd barely been in each other's lives, was going to make headlines in American politics, marrying into the first family.

I palmed my bearded cheek and sighed. I might be all man now compared with the boy she knew, but the idea of her marriage punched me in the gut. Yet I hadn't seen her in two years. The disappointment had no merit.

I buried my shock and threw myself into my work. Over the next hour, I racked up shots of socialites in incredible outfits, wealthy old guys in suits a thousand times nicer than my hired one, film stars I recognised and ones I guessed were important from their entourage, and members of the political scene. Josie's contacts landed her—and me—the insider scoop, numbering us among the few photographers permitted inside the building to document the night.

The opportunity to expand my portfolio and make money was immense, and I uploaded the shots as I went, operating on autopilot where my concentration was fucked.

"Lads." I raised my camera to three men standing together. Dressed in edgy, distressed suits and with punky hair, they were familiar. A band, probably. "Can I take a shot?"

The first man, about my age, so early twenties, and with a strip of blue hair, broke into a smile. He threw his arms around the other two. "Nice to hear a familiar accent. You're a Scot. Highlands?"

"Aye." I ducked, lining up the photo to get the charity banner in the background. Blue Hair nudged the other two to grin.

"Where are you from? South?" I asked.

Though Scots, too, their accents were smarter than my soft brogue.

"You don't recognise us?"

I pulled a face. "Sorry. I'm new at this."

"Kick in the teeth, man. We're Viking Blue. From Edinburgh."

"Viking?" I couldn't help my smirk at the name.

"Aye. Women love it. Wait a sec, Highlander. We'll give you a good shot."

The first guy broke his hold on his bandmates then leapt, forcing the two men to catch him. He lay in their arms and stuck his hands behind his head. "I'm Rex, singer and songwriter."

"Wasp," I introduced myself, snapping the ridiculous pose. People often did daft stuff when the camera was on them. Rex's behaviour reminded me of Ally, my twin. A painful pang of missing him rose.

Rex's bandmates dropped him, and he clambered to his feet, taking a bow for the people watching. He lifted his chin at me. "Got a card? I'll hit you up if we're ever in need of a cameraman. We're new to this, too."

I produced one and handed it over, and the guy slipped it into his pocket. Then his gaze found a target over my shoulder.

"Whoa," Rex said. "The evening just got more interesting. Check out Miss USA."

I twisted, following his gaze.

Oh boy.

Like a vision, Taylor stepped into the room. She shimmered, her sheet of blonde hair pinned up in a fancy style, and her floor-length blue dress accentuating her hourglass form. My camera would never pick up that detail.

Besides, I'd frozen solid.

Ingrid Bergman. Lauren Bacall. They could eat their hearts out. Hollywood's Golden Age had nothing on Taylor.

Alone, she paused for a moment then raised a hand, presumably spotting a friend. Another lass swept over, and they embraced without touching, gesturing at each other's dresses.

Taylor glanced again over the crowd. Her eyes found mine. Locked on.

Christ.

A surge of fierce emotion hit me, and I opened my mouth. *Engaged. Almost.* I ought to congratulate her.

But we both just stared.

"You know her?" Rex asked.

"Who's that?" Taylor's friend asked simultaneously, her words just audible from my position across the hall.

Taylor's eyes widened for a moment, but then she looked away. "No one I know. Let's get a drink, I have a feeling I'm going to need it tonight."

No one?

I was no one. Ouch.

That punch in the gut I'd felt? It had barely been a tap. I'd grown up with three brothers and an abusive da—I could take a hit. But the lass's dismissal knocked the wind out of me. I pressed a hand to my chest, stifling the ache.

She'd recognised me. She'd chosen to blank me. Aye, it stung and then some.

"I guess not," I told the band, suddenly needing to get away. "Thanks for the photos."

The men bid me farewell, and I strode off.

"Wasp?" Near the back of the hall, Josie found me, her short, stylish grey hair damp with sweat. "In twenty minutes, Senator Miller arrives. I'll cover the front, so back me up then take stage left and remain there through the speeches. After, you can go. Our contract is covered, and I'll only be staying to drum up more business. Your flight is in the morning?"

"Aye. Four AM."

"Get the best shots uploaded before. Drop me a line if you need a reference or if you're in town and need to borrow a spare body."

She meant a camera body, but in the six weeks I'd been on assignment at her New York studio, this was the kindest the surly photographer to the stars had ever been.

"Thank ye."

I wanted to say more, about how I'd learned a lot from her, and how I appreciated her advice and guidance, but Josie already had her viewfinder to her eye, and she strolled away, snapping new arrivals.

If I'd wanted to leave before, I was dying to now. But I had an hour of speeches to capture. I spun on my heel and marched down the corridor, heading away from the throng, needing a minute alone.

Security guards dotted every corner. They eyed me as I passed. I guessed with my height and brawn, I could be considered a threat. Maybe I should be the worried one—the sheer number of them was alarming—but I kept going until I was in a quieter part of the museum.

For a moment, I just stood there in the cool, darkened corridor. Artwork watched me.

I was homesick. That was all. Seeing Taylor's name on the list had made me think of Scotland. With her being friends with my brother's wife, it was where I'd seen her most.

In a couple of days, this would pass.

This fucking ache would dissipate.

I'd be back at the castle, throwing myself into the hard, physical work of restoring the crofthouse with my brothers. No moments to wallow in the meaningless rejection of a lass I barely knew anymore.

A door closed inside my head. A violent *slam* that cut off the what-ifs and maybes that came with long blonde hair and a bonnie smile.

"William?" a voice rang out, breaking the silence.

Holy fuck.

Even if I didn't know Taylor's clear tones, no one else here used my real name.

I rotated slowly, flinching at the sight of her gorgeous face close up. "Taylor. You did recognise me, then."

She wrinkled her nose and took a step closer, clutching a glass of wine and a small purse that matched her outfit. "Sorry about that. You took me by surprise. I didn't expect to see you here, especially tonight..." Her gaze flitted over my features, lingering on my beard. Then she cleared her throat. "I mean, how are you?"

"Grand."

"Are you working here?"

I raised my camera by way of answer, my tongue thick in my mouth. God, this was awkward. If only I had the natural chatter of my twin. But no, I was always the quiet one.

"Dumb question." With a rough laugh, she raised her drink, downed the wine, then placed the glass on the floor.

"How are ye?" I repeated her question, wincing at how I sounded. Then I continued, because it was good to see her, even if she'd originally cut me. Whether she had on a bombshell dress or a t-shirt, I could never resist her draw. "I'm glad you found me."

"You are? Even if I acted like a bitch?"

I tilted my head, inviting elaboration. She wasn't a bitch. Not her.

Taylor took a deep inhale. "Let me explain. I guess you heard—"

A *boom* interrupted us. An explosion, with the tinkle of broken glass, reverberated down the hall, coming from the direction of the party.

On instinct, I grabbed Taylor's arm and pulled her against my body, spinning her away from the sound.

"Shit!" she squeaked, huddling into my chest. "What was that?"

"I have no idea." I snapped a look down the corridor.

An alarm blared, a rising din that sped up my heart.

Cries echoed. Footsteps drummed. People emerged into the dark corridor. Two security guards ran towards the main hall.

Taylor gaped. "Was it a bomb? Is that a bomb alarm? Oh God. We need to get out of here!"

"Aye, we do." The entrance Josie and I had used was close. "Come on."

With practiced ease, I manhandled my camera into its space in the bag then grabbed Taylor's hand and jogged.

Taylor flew alongside me, agile in her heels.

We joined a group heading for the same exit. One man yelled into his phone a frantic message about terrorists. Another stumbled, pinwheeling. I thrust out an arm to right him, losing no pace.

At the closed door, a security guard waited, pressing his earpiece into his ear.

"Open up!" I roared.

The man gaped but flung open the exit, positioning himself outside. "Keep moving. Leave the building immediately and convene on the sidewalk."

"What's happening?" Taylor demanded as we passed.

"That is not yet clear, ma'am. Move on."

Outside, rain splattered us, instantly soaking and plastering my hair to my forehead. Sirens from emergency services vehicles filled the night, the approaching lights reflecting in the puddles at our feet.

Traffic stopped where attendees in evening wear spilled into the wet street. Scared people huddled behind a hastily erected police cordon while passersby got caught in the drama, drawing closer to gawp.

Panic built in the air. We couldn't wait around here.

Shite. Josie. The guys in the band. Already moving Taylor away, I peered over the heads of the crowd and spotted the small woman, her camera in action, ignoring the police officer trying to move her on. At least she was safe.

Behind her, the three band members spilled down the steps, an older man ushering them on.

"This is chaos," Taylor said. "They'll start grabbing people to search and interview any second. What should we do?"

"It isn't safe to hang around. My digs are close." For weeks, I'd bunked on Josie's photography studio's sofa. The place was empty at night and affordable, unlike anywhere else in Manhattan.

A loudspeaker whined with feedback before a stark voice ordered us to move into the police cordon.

The crowd shifted. People jostled.

"Keep close," I uttered, and we fled, diving into the crowd and the rain.

A river of people flooded in the opposite direction. Taylor blindly let me lead, and we kept on track. As we moved, I slipped off my jacket, placing it over her shoulders then put a protective arm around her.

At the junction of East 82nd Street and Park Avenue, I produced a set of keys from my bag and opened the door at the top of the steps, under a covered porch.

We climbed four flights of stairs and entered the studio. In the darkened space, Taylor headed straight for the window, peering out at the city and the route we'd just come. More flashing lights streamed towards the museum.

No more explosions had followed, but still my heart pounded.

If I'd stayed, I could've taken the pictures of my career—a first-hand account of a terrorist attack. But no, keeping Taylor safe had been the only thought in my head.

I deposited my camera equipment on the small table that acted as the reception desk then stooped and unzipped my sports bag that was stashed on the floor. From amid my packed possessions, I pulled a soft fluffy towel to offer my poor cold, wet lass.

Then I gazed at her for a second, silhouetted in the window, her hands grasping her elbows.

Every time we'd found ourselves like this before—alone, a dimly lit room, limited time—we'd torn each other's clothes off. Clawed at flesh to burn up our passion on the other's body.

I could never explain it, the sheer thirst I had for this woman. I'd had girlfriends, a few one-night stands. Nothing came close to what I felt around Taylor.

What was worse? It hadn't gone away.

Despite her news. Despite the man in her life.

The man she's about to marry.

That last thought had me clamping down on the inappropriate lust, and I crossed to stand next to her and held out the towel. Being the good guy, not a dick. "Here, bundle up. You must be freezing."

But to my horror, as Taylor peeked up at me, tears filled her eyes. Then the lass, the happy, joyful, force of personality I had always been drawn towards, drew a shaking breath, flung her arms around me, and crushed her lips onto mine.

Chapter Two – Heat Flared

Taylor

Kissing William McRae was a bad move, guaranteed to hurt more than just seeing him and walking away. But I never claimed to be smart. Only desperate.

And this man never failed to make me feel...everything.

Shock from the kiss zinged through my body, and my mind instantly went to my happy place. Somewhere dark.

Hot. With this huge Scotsman using his powerful body on mine.

I hugged William like my life depended on it. Our lips moved together, his new scruff scratching my skin, and I gave a moan of pleasure.

This. Home.

William dropped the towel he'd brought, bracketed me with his strong arms, and returned my kiss. I melted onto him. No one else could do this—hold me up. Keep me safe. He couldn't either, no matter what my body told me.

Then his tongue touched mine, and we both gasped.

"Wait. Fuck." William reared back. He breathed in through his nose, and his muscles flexed under my grip. Then he closed his eyes and rested his forehead on mine. "I shouldnae have done that. This is wrong."

Ever the gentleman—taking the blame for my lips on his.

"Probably. But I needed it." Embarrassingly, my eyes were wet, and I wiped them, not wanting him to see. The pressure from the evening had already been immense, pre-explosion, but I'd owned it. I'd been in control. Seeing William had knocked my resolve.

"Your boyfriend..." William started.

"Don't have one." We were still hugging. My heavy, soggy dress pasted to his suit. I'd barely noticed the room we were in, save for the fact it was a workplace. A studio with rigging for lights.

No bed.

William's shoulders lowered an inch, shadows deepening the furrow of his brow. He studied my face. "I read that ye were engaged. That it would be announced tonight."

"Oh, that." He was right. Didn't that throw the mother of

all wrenches into the works. "It might have happened. If someone hadn't tried to blow up the Met."

"Right." He released me from his warm hold and moved away. "I'll... Fuck."

I gripped my fingers together, suddenly compelled to explain what I'd told no one.

My bag buzzed—a phone call.

William's gaze shot to the clutch. "Go ahead, take it. Someone needs to know you're safe. I'll make coffee, then we'll check out the news."

He disappeared through a doorway, and I sagged gracelessly to the floor to collect my phone. Dad's name screamed from the screen. I had him by his job title: *Governor to the State of New York.*

"Irene? Where the fuck are you?" he barked.

I winced, pulling the device from my ear. "I'm at a friend's place. There was an explosion. We ran. Did you hear about it?"

"I heard. I've not been told what happened yet, but I'll find out. Luckily I've only just landed so I wasn't in the building." The line went muffled, and he barked at someone. Probably his driver.

It didn't bother me that he hadn't worried for my safety. I knew my father's priorities.

He came back. "Tonight's plans obviously have to change. We'll meet Linc and Theo at their hotel instead. I'll be there in twenty, then I'll send my car for you. Give me the address."

I paused. For months now, Dad had been constructing this plan. A match between me and Theo Miller, twenty-six-year-old beloved son of the next president. Tonight would have put our name on the front pages. No wonder my father was pissed.

Through the doorway, soft light glowed, and a coffee machine whirred into life. William moved, collecting mugs, and I got caught up, staring at the broadness of his shoulders under his clinging, damp white shirt.

"Address," Dad ordered.

"I'm soaked through," I spluttered. I didn't want to go. I'd never wanted this. Any of it. I needed to stall. "The road is closed off. Even if I could dry off, I'm only going to get drenched again."

Dad paused. "You mean you look like shit?" He wasn't wrong, but the insult stung. "Tomorrow, then. Brunch at the Four Seasons at eleven. Don't be late." Then he hung up.

William returned, placing a steaming mug in front of me. I clambered to my feet and landed on the couch, tracking him as he collected a laptop from what looked like luggage.

"Going somewhere?" I tipped my head at his bag.

William sat beside me and opened the machine. "Home. I fly in a few hours."

He brought up a news site and, side by side, we gazed at the silent pictures. A scrolling banner told us what we already knew. The explosion. The mass panic. No reports of serious injuries, though. No arrests.

"I heard ye say on the phone that the street was locked down." William pushed the laptop away and interlaced his hands, watching me. "Fifth Avenue might be, but this road isn't."

"That was my dad. We've been lying to each other since I could talk." I picked up my coffee and took a swig. William had sweetened it, just like I preferred. Had he ever made me coffee? My brain fixated on the question, just as much as my skin fixated on the inches of distance between us.

Then I shivered. Hard. The hot drink sank into my chilled flesh.

"Christ, woman," William said, his voice low. "You must be freezing."

My teeth chattered. "For such flimsy material, this dress holds a lot of water. Do you have anything I can change into?"

"Aye. Hang on." He leapt up and returned with his bag, pulling out a neat stack of clothes. "Long-sleeved t-shirt." He handed me the item. "I don't have any drawstring trousers. My jeans would dwarf you. Maybe keep your underwear then use the towel as a blanket for now."

My mouth twitched. "I'm not wearing underwear." At his outraged look, a shaky laugh burst from my chest. "What? You don't with dresses like this." I plucked at the ruined gown.

"Don't tell me any more. Christ, lass. You'll give me a heart attack."

I grinned then unclipped the buckles from my heels and let them drop to the floor. Then I stood in front of William, bundling the borrowed shirt and the towel in my arms. He'd always towered over me but he was bigger still; the last few years had added muscle weight to his height.

I liked it, the brawn. The sheer masculinity of this mountain man.

William McRae, all grown up. How about that.

"When we met, there wasn't such a height difference between us," I murmured, stifling a full body shiver.

William's green-eyed gaze held mine. "There's a lot that's different between then and now."

Wasn't that the truth? I left him and padded on bare feet to the room where he'd made the coffee. I closed myself in and commenced the wrestling match that was removing my dress. Couture was not meant to be soaked. It clung like it had been glued on, and I wanted to call for help, but William would blow a fuse at the sight of my boobs popping free.

I had nice boobs, but I didn't want to inflict an injury on the man.

A *rip* came as I tugged the frock over one shoulder. I blew a damp tendril of hair from my eyes and tried not to think about the cost.

Finally, I was free. In William's soft t-shirt, which fell to my mid-thigh, I returned to the studio floor.

"I have a small problem. The dress is dead. I don't think I'll be wearing it home."

William had changed clothes himself, out of his suit and into jeans and a dry shirt, instantly appearing younger and sweeter.

"I'm sorry about the dress. It looked incredible on you."

What a nice way of putting it—not that I had been enhanced by the dress, but the other way around. What was strange was that, when I'd chosen the dress, William had popped into my mind. He had a thing for old movies, and it had reminded me of him. Once, we'd been on the same flight together, and the airline had been showing *Casablanca*. I'd watched it with him. And, alone, I'd watched other movies from the thirties and forties since.

"We'll work something out," he continued. "Where are you staying?"

"A hotel downtown. Later, when we're sure nothing else is going to blow up, I'll get a cab. There's nothing unusual about a woman skipping around New York City dressed in oversized clothes and a towel."

He pursed his lips but made no further comment.

Taking care not to flash him, I lowered myself to the

couch and wrapped my legs with the towel. Nothing new had popped up on the news report. If the all clear was announced, I'd have no reason to stay.

A not-so-small part of me wanted the police to delay as long as they could.

"I just sent a message to my family to let them know I'm safe. Is there anyone else ye need to call?"

"No." Mom wouldn't have a clue where I was supposed to be. "The acquaintance you saw me with left with her date. They were outside."

"Maybe we should report ourselves as safe to the organiser. Our names would be listed as attending." He took up the laptop and typed something into a new search.

Idly, I raised my hands to my hair, sorting through for the pins that were tangled in the mess. "I must look like a drowned rat. I'm glad you got to see me at the beginning of the night."

William frowned, his face illuminated by the screen. "Don't be daft. If anything, I like you better now."

"You're kidding?"

"I'm not. You look more like the lass I remember."

I giggled—God, when had I last laughed?—and extracted the last of the pins, freeing my hair.

William stared now.

"You always had a thing about my hair," I said without thinking.

He rumbled a laugh. "Aye. And every other part of you."

Another guy, and that would've come off as creepy. Not him. William was good. Good in bed, sure, but a good man, too. He loved his brothers, cared for his friends. I trusted him more than most people I knew, and I barely knew him.

"How long have you been in the States?" I asked, pushing past the unnerving thought.

He finished his message then sat back. "Six weeks. This was the final placement in my degree. I've been doing all the grunt work for Josie Addlestein but I've learned a ton."

"I've heard of her. Is this her place?"

"Aye. I've slept on this couch every night."

I scrunched my nose. It was a plush couch, but nowhere near long enough for William's big body. "You must be killing it to get a job here."

"Mathilda name-dropped a few times and got me the gig. I'm hoping it has given me enough of a profile for an agency to take me on."

Mathilda was his oldest brother's wife. His second brother, Gordain, had married my best friend, Ella. I visited her whenever I could, but I'd made a point of avoiding William on the past few trips to Scotland. I knew where my path in life was taking me, and getting hooked more on him wasn't going to do me any favours.

"And the beard, is that mandatory wear for a photographer?" I smiled, but it was weak.

His gaze took me to pieces. "If we're doing question and answer, want to tell me how a single lass is expecting a proposal?"

"Do you really want to know?"

"Aye. I really do."

"It's an arrangement my father is making."

William froze. "Arrangement?"

I sighed, switching my gaze to the rain-splattered window. The first time I'd met William had been after my original attempt at an arranged marriage. One I'd organised to get away from my dad and obtain something else I badly wanted. I'd been eighteen then and reeling from news I'd had. That plan had fallen through, and since then, the situation had only gotten worse. It made this second attempt even more important. "I know what you're thinking—"

He gave a short bark of a laugh. "I'm not thinking anything. Other than how different my world is to yours."

I felt it, then. The chasm between this good, kind man, who came from a happy, boisterous family of brothers, who had nieces and nephews to spoil, a wild Scottish estate to roam. Who had love pouring at him from every side.

Utterly unlike being raised in a boarding school because my parents' acrimonious divorce meant they couldn't share me. Not that they'd wanted to.

I curled in on myself, suddenly unable to speak.

"Hey." William lightly jostled me. "Come back. I'm not passing judgment. It's none of my business."

It wasn't. It wasn't anyone's.

My gaze landed on the laptop again. New words appeared. "There's an update."

We both leaned in to view the screen.

The catering company's use of pressurised gas canisters had not been sanctioned by the museum, and an investigation will look at the process that led to this chain of events. To recap, the explosion that caused the panicked evacuation of a red-carpet event, moments before the arrival of Senator Miller and Governor Vanderbilt, caused no injuries but damaged a number of works of art...

I stopped reading and blinked at William. "It wasn't a bomb, then."

"Christ." He palmed his neck. Amusement danced in his eyes when he brought his attention back to me. "I'm not sorry, though. Seeing you has been the highlight of my trip."

My laugh came unbidden. "You're joking, aren't you? All the people you must have photographed. All the places you must have been."

His lips quirked, but he just watched me.

I knew he was being sweet, but I'd store those words away and keep them as comfort for the hard times to come.

Pressure ate at me. I stood and looked out at the flashing lights that still lit the night in the distance. There were fewer now.

It was time for me to leave.

"Wait," William said. Like he knew I was about to bolt. "Sit down again, will ye?"

I hesitated. If I did, I'd probably do something stupid like throw myself at him again.

"In a few hours, I need to get a taxi to the airport. Stay here until then. I can drop you at your hotel on the way."

"You don't need to do that."

His gaze caressed me. "I want to. That way I'll know you got back safe."

"What shall we do until then?" Heat flared, blazing along my nerves.

Everything was about to change. As soon as the announcement was made, my low profile as the little-photographed daughter of a politician would be obliterated. The press would expose every secret that hadn't already been buried, and my private life wouldn't exist anymore.

I had one chance left to do something for me alone.

William rested back on the couch, his arms behind his head making his biceps pop. "Get your thoughts out of the gutter. We can chat. Catch up."

"Or," I dropped the towel and advanced, straddling him with one bold swing, "we can do something more fun instead. Just like old times."

Chapter Three – Hunger

Wasp

Ah fuck. This was wrong. I told myself to stop, yet my lips moved with hunger, and I gripped two handfuls of Taylor's bare backside.

Our tongues met in a battle, warring for dominance, sliding in and out with slick heat. Taylor tasted of wine and heaven, and I couldn't get enough.

On my lap, she pressed into me, the shirt I'd given her riding up around her middle.

In the dark of the room, I was right back in a place I'd dreamed about far too often. The lass was a year older than me. When we'd met, she'd been the experienced one. Every time since then, I'd wanted to show her what I'd learned. To prove to her that I could match her.

Please her.

Best her.

She moaned and broke our lips apart. We both breathed heavily, staring at each other.

Then, she grabbed the hem of her shirt and started to lift it.

I hated myself. I hated the values I had instilled in my blood.

I fucking hated being the good guy.

"Stop," I ground out. Gently, I took her fingers and held them, forcing myself not to look down at the soft skin revealed.

"Why?" Taylor's blonde eyebrows pinched in.

"Ask me again in a minute when my cock isn't battling for ownership of my thoughts."

She gave a sparkling laugh. "I've missed your cock. Let me say hi."

"Ah, stop." I closed my eyes and rested my head back on the couch, my lips pulling in a grin.

"You want me."

"I always have," I murmured to the ceiling.

"Are you seriously turning me down?"

"Aye."

"Did you get hit on the head since the last time I saw you?"

I burst out laughing now and grabbed her, swinging us around so she was on her back on the couch and I was on top of her. Then I rubbed the tip of my nose against hers, because if I didn't make this cute, I'd lose my willpower. "You make me crazy. You always had the knack." I kissed her softly then reached for the towel she'd dropped, covering her up. "But this will only make things harder next time we see each other."

"Huh?"

"You'll visit Ella. Bring your new husband. Arranged or not, you'll be part of a couple." One that didn't involve me. My chest ached again, and I shifted away. "We can't keep doing this. If we stop now, we can learn to be friends instead."

Taylor made a noise of frustration. "This might be my last chance of good sex. I might be a bitch but I'd never cheat. Even stuck in a marriage I hated."

Argh. "Sorry." Then my brain caught up. "You're not a bitch."

"I am. I've never been that nice a person."

"I disagree. I like ye." I spared her a look.

She gazed back, wide-eyed and fucking gorgeous. Blonde hair spilling over the midnight-blue couch. "Including if we're not sleeping together anymore?"

"Is that the only reason you think I like you?"

She blinked, appearing to consider the answer. "Yes. No. I don't know."

Granted, we hadn't spent much time together just talking, but her visits had usually been short and time with me limited. I gave her an outraged glare, and she giggled.

"So..." She put her feet on my lap. I took them in my hands, resisting massaging her. This was already hard enough. Quite literally. "We're friends?" she continued. "What does that mean?"

"We see each other without wanting to have sex."

Taylor blew out a breath. "I don't think that's ever going to happen. But if you want it, I'll give it a go. What do we do now?"

"Fill me in on the past couple of years?"

"You start. Your Highlands life has always been more interesting than mine."

For the next couple of hours, we talked. While my photos uploaded for Josie to sell, I told Taylor about my family and home, about university, my last girlfriend who'd suggested for my career I move to the city permanently—something I wasn't prepared to do—and Taylor gave me a few, small details of her life. Her dad's political aspirations, her strained relationship with her mother. The university degree she'd taken and aced but wasn't using.

Then she fell silent, and I glanced over to find her head dropped to the side, and her breathing gentle in sleep. We had to leave in forty minutes, but I didn't move. The chest pain I had worsened. I'd never told her, but years ago, when sex had been a mystery to which she'd given me the answers, I'd thought myself in love with her. It had been puppy love, but powerful all the same.

I'd never felt anything like it since. I doubted I ever would again.

But Taylor wasn't for me. Until the last possible moment, I just sat with her, letting her rest. Then I gently shook her awake, collected my bags, and straightened up the studio, leaving my hired suit and lenses for Josie's assistant to return. Then I took Taylor to her hotel. Red-eyed, she didn't speak, but before she got out of the cab, she leaned over and kissed me. Soft, now. None of the urgency of earlier.

She walked away in my shirt and bundled in my towel.

"It's hard saying goodbye," the cabbie told me, idling the car and letting me have my moment, staring across the grey pavement.

Strange. It felt like a sort of heartbreak, though that couldn't be right. I needed to board a plane and go home. Get back to my life and put Taylor behind me.

"You have no idea," I replied, and the cabbie drove me away.

uy Picture This (Marry the Scot, #4) now!

ABOUT THE AUTHOR

JOLIE VINES is a romance novelist who lives in the South West of England with her husband and toddler son.

From an early age, Jolie lived in a fantasy world and is never happier than when plot dreaming. Jolie loves her heroes to be one-woman guys. Whether they are a huge Highlander, a touch starved earl, or a brooding pilot, they will adore their loved one until the end of time.

Her favourite pastime is wrecking emotions then making up for it by giving her characters deep and meaningful happy ever afters.

Want to contact Jolie? She loves hearing from her readers. Drop her a line at jolie@jolievines.com, find her on Instagram, and join her Fall Hard Facebook group